Honorable Intentions

by

Margo Hoornstra

Honorable Intentions

Cover Art by *Nicola Martinez*

The Wild Rose Press
PO Box 708
Adams Basin, NY 14410-0706
Visit us at www.thewildrosepress.com

Publishing History
First Last Rose Of Summer Edition, 2009
Print ISBN 1-60154-576-2

Published in the United States of America

"I don't know what you think of me and, quite honestly, don't care." *Liar!* She pushed the protest away and swallowed quickly. "I might have been a little blatant in...my response to you earlier. It's uncomfortable to admit this," she went on in a voice hushed more by her unexpected embarrassment than his obvious antagonism. "You were a convenient diversion and my coming on to you was...just me...fooling around. A way to blow off some steam."

"Congratulations."

"Congratulations?" she repeated. "I don't..."

"You had me fooled."

His gaze roamed down her neck to her breasts and lower. "I didn't think anyone could come on as strong as you did without having something..." His gaze paused, then held just below her waist. "...to back it up."

Though her mind chose to ignore his comment, her body refused to obey the message as a flutter deep inside responded to the touch of his eyes.

"I'm sorry if I misled you." She placed intellect back in control over hormones. "The entire encounter really meant nothing." When she glanced up, he had looked away as well.

"Meant nothing," he repeated before his eyes caught hers again. "I can accept that."

"I do apologize, but this really should have no effect on either one of us any longer. Make no mistake, Mr. Canfield, I am quite capable of taking very good care of your daughter."

Praise for Margo Hoornstra

"Great" Reader Rating.
~Fictionwise e-books

"...I would definitely look into more work by this author."
~Night Owl Romance

"I look forward to more of her stories."
~The Long and Short of It

Dedication

To Ron Hoornstra,
who taught me all about unselfish love
and unbelievable possibilities

Chapter One

Sunshine in a clear summer sky was rare in downtown Detroit. Samantha Wells usually took time to acknowledge such gifts from Mother Nature, but this morning hardly noticed. Dressed in a nondescript beige suit, she blended with others who hurried along the sidewalk to waiting jobs. Most, like her, navigated familiar routes on auto pilot.

In four more blocks, she'd be at her office, Professional Security and Investigations. Could she slip back easily into PSI routines after being gone for three weeks? She wouldn't know for sure until she got there. No. Three weeks wasn't excessive for recovery from a gun shot wound. Tentative fingers touched the spot on her right side where a bullet took out a sizable chunk of flesh, and, by sheer luck, missed all vital organs.

Bob Anderson, her friend and boss, had urged her to take more time. She'd balked at that. *I'm fine,* she'd insisted. She *was* fine, she told herself, one hundred percent. Well, okay, maybe ninety something. The site was still a lot bruised and a little sore, but no one was perfect. She was a definite high end ninety, and would be at the top of her game soon, very soon.

Before she took that train of thought any further, the distinctive chords of her cell phone interrupted and she paused in the alcove of a building to take the call. Seeing a familiar number flash on the ID screen, she debated whether or not to answer. David Franks was one of the investigators who came with the agency when Bob bought it out the year before. The man had never impressed her. With limited people skills, his abilities in the field were worse. He'd been with her the day she was shot, with his gun.

She flipped the phone open and placed a necessary edge in her voice. "Samantha Wells."

"You okay?"

"Yeah, fine. Why?"

"I don't know. You sound a little..."

"Just keyed up to come back to work." No way would she allow this man the leeway to decide anything about her. "What's up?"

"You know you have a meeting this morning?"

"What meeting?"

"The one set for this morning." He had the gall to keep his words slow and distinct, as if she didn't understand him.

"Did Bob tell you to call me?"

"The Chief?"

She bristled at that. How dare he refer Bob as *Chief*. The term was reserved for subordinates when referring to commanding officers. He'd never worked with Bob at a police department the way she had. In fact, she doubted Franks ever hooked on at any police agency, a testament to his incompetence. And, if he insisted on using former titles, he should call her Lieutenant.

"You sure you're okay?"

That question didn't deserve an answer. "Are you in the office?"

"On my way in."

Of all people, she really didn't want to deal with him her first day back. "Then how do you know...anything?"

"I know your next assignment is chaperone duty." Another of his personality flaws was his preference for making statements as opposed to

2

asking questions.

"Bodyguard." She could make statements, too. If his intention was to goad her into self-doubt, he needed to try harder. And for the record, she was a security agent, not a babysitter.

"No. I'm sure I heard chaperone." The smug tone only added to her growing disgust. Not about the assignment—she trusted Bob and would take anything he asked her to—the disgust was for Franks.

"I called Jan at the front desk to check my messages." In perpetual suck-up mode, he always tried to give the impression of being a through and through company man. "Chief came up while I was on the phone with her. Seemed pretty excited. Told her to set up the conference room by ten o'clock and make sure you knew about it. Said he was sending you to Alaska."

Samantha moved the phone to her other ear as a city bus wheezed to a stop a few feet away.

"I wanted to warn you. Hate to see you blindsided on top of everything else."

Yeah, like he cared. The man bordered on delusional.

"On another note," he said, "some of us might go out for drinks tonight after work. Wanta come? I'll buy."

"I'll pass, thanks."

"Suit yourself."

She closed her eyes before tightening her grip on the phone. This conversation was going nowhere. The confines of the doorway where she stood blocked what little fresh breeze was left drifting around the city. She needed to move on. So did David Franks.

"I never mix business with pleasure." She winced at her poor choice of words.

"You know what they say about all work. No play."

By now, if she'd been unfortunate enough to be talking to the jerk face to face, she'd have decked him. "That's me," she countered. "One extremely dull girl. Is there anything else?"

"Nope. Except you might want to consider getting a life. Loosen up. Maybe learn to flirt."

"Are you included in this meeting?"

"No, but, I thought..."

"Thanks for the heads up." She snapped her phone shut, then shoved it into her pocket.

Teeth clenched, body tight, she didn't move for one full minute. All around her, the stop and go sounds of urban traffic—tires on pavement, brake squeals and skids—went on. Her forehead throbbed from a tension headache that snuck in while she was tied up talking to an idiot. Not even at the office and already her nerves were on edge.

True to form, Franks had moved beyond annoying and succeeded in pissing her off. Plus, his comment about her lack of social prowess hurt a little. So what if the mainstay of her current social life was the intramural high-school volleyball league where she refereed on Thursday nights? She managed to hold her own at an occasional girls' night out, thank you very much. Being reasonably attractive, she could go home with any number of barflies if she chose to. Which she didn't since she wanted more than the one night stands they offered. She'd had a fair share of more serious relationships in her forty-two years, just none lately.

Raising her wrist, she eyed her watch. Not quite eight-fifteen. She wasn't expected at the office until after nine-thirty. That was today. After that, her schedule could go all over the board. She touched her pounding forehead again and decided meeting or no meeting she'd take her time getting there.

Up ahead on the next corner, her favorite coffee shop, Café and Crumbs, provided a welcome diversion. Pausing in the entrance space between the door to the street and the one leading into the place, she almost changed her mind when she saw the length of the take-out line. The line to get into the restaurant section was even longer. Then, the inside door opened, releasing enough tempting aroma of coffee mixed with cinnamon and chocolate to hook her attention. For her favorite latte, she'd put up with the wait.

A rhythmic murmur and bustle drowned out further thought as she stepped into the muted frenzy of low-key conversations wrangling with shout-outs of orders ready for pick-up. She let her mind go blank listening to cappuccino machines hiss steam, dishes clatter into bus pans, then took her place in line. Up at the front end, a tall woman pulled a list out of her purse and began to recite an involved order to the waiting clerk.

Shifting her weight to the other foot, she reached up to massage away a persistent stiffness at the back of her neck.

Where does he come off saying I don't know how to flirt? The thought jumped out to fuel her growing irritation. *I can flirt with the best of them if I want. I just don't.*

It *had* been awhile since she'd experienced any real romance in her life—meaningful or otherwise—and she missed that. Not that she was foolish enough to expect anything long lasting. Love and family, she knew from first-hand experience, were grossly overrated.

When the neck massage failed to ease the ache between her shoulder blades, she arched her back to release unspent tension.

"Can't we move a little faster?" The grating male voice made a direct hit on her third nerve. *Bam!* the tension snapped back in place.

She closed her eyes and blew out an impatient

breath. *Were all men naturally born pond scum or was it a talent acquired with age?*

Primed for a fight, she jerked her head around with no way to ID the offender. *Just punch out the first available male.* She had to smile at the thought, then her gaze settled on the man who stood directly behind her. Fury gave way to wide-eyed surprise; the angry retort died in her throat.

She hadn't counted on this.

The guy was absolutely gorgeous. And, every one of her all men are pond scum convictions vanished.

Here's your chance. Prove Franks wrong and have a little harmless fun in the process. The idea came out of nowhere, but she liked it. This was way too good to pass up.

While he looked the other way, she grabbed the opportunity to check him out. Handsome by anyone's standards—she completed a quick one-two inspection down his frame—the rest of the package wasn't bad either. Tall, a good head above her five foot seven inches, and neatly dressed in a charcoal gray suit, red pin stripe shirt and matching tie. Hunk wise, he had a lot going for him. The clothes fit well over broad shoulders and a sleek torso. His waist was trim, with sufficient bulk where the shirt came up to his chest to suggest he took care of himself. Nice shaped hips gave way to long legs; and thighs large enough to keep the slacks from hanging too loose. The suit was impeccably tailored, but he appeared uncomfortable in it. Or maybe he was just tired of standing in line. He seemed intent on studying the lunch menu written on an easel to his right.

From a side view, his features fit perfectly between an angled forehead and strong jaw. His hair was dark brown with the barest hint of silver. The distinctive coloring would be noticed only if someone was seriously looking at the man—like her—with unabashed interest.

A surge of heat sprinted from the tips of her toes to the top of her head, hitting all the important female spots in between.

Who said men are the only ones allowed to have sexual fantasies? She was in the middle of one right now with this guy as the main attraction. They'd just moved into a sexy, if not ambitious, position when he caught her staring. To her delight, he returned her blatant stare with one revealing considerable interest. His eyes, dark brown like his hair with their own silver flecks, glowed with something she couldn't quite discern. Approval? No, something more like appreciation. Definite appreciation of her.

"Nice," she said, then immediately clamped her mouth shut.

"Thank you, I think." His voice was deep as she'd expected. Deep and sexy. "Or did you mean the suit?"

"That, too."

His eyes held an air of surprised amusement. "Well then thank you for that, too. I like your suit as well." He made the quiet comment with a measure of respect.

If she were smart, she'd take advantage of the graceful out he'd just given her. *Nice suit,* she could say, then walk away. A mutual exchange of innocent compliments would be the extent of their association, nothing more.

But, where's the fun in that?

She wanted to enjoy another visual pass down his body. And would have, if his eyes hadn't held hers in such a way she was almost afraid to blink. This time though, her latent cop mind surfaced, reminding her to check for a wedding ring or evidence of one recently removed. She broke free of his stare, did just that, and discovered neither.

"You're single," she announced. "I like that in a man."

"Do you now?" The tone carried a hint of teasing, and maybe a little innuendo. He edged forward. "I'm glad."

The physical advance and subtle invitation pushed her bold actions to just this side of reckless. Her gaze remained on the spot below his belt buckle long enough to tease before taking a daring cruise up the length of his torso, across his broad shoulders and along his clean shaven neck to his face. Where an unmistakable awareness filled deep brown eyes. Full frontal, they were heavy lidded and deep. Some would consider his mouth sensuous, and his chin had just enough of a cleft to make him all the more appealing. Then he smiled. His teeth were as perfect as the rest of him.

Her disdain at the entire male population evaporated beneath the warmth of that smile. Soon, she'd counter with a killer smile of her own. But not just yet. She'd schmoozed enough suspects and reluctant witnesses in her day, still did, and knew when and how to turn on the charm.

The idea such a dazzling guy would show interest in her did great things for a self esteem which had been slightly abused of late. Best of all, he didn't have so much as a remote connection to her job. That alone came as a breath of fresh air.

"Hurry up, will ya, lady?" The same rude male sounded again. "Some of us have to get to work, ya know."

Her coffee shop hunk sidled closer. "Some people can be pretty ignorant."

"They can be, can't they?"

She had to tilt her head back to look up at him and found herself momentarily intimidated. Something she didn't suffer often and liked even less. This close, she caught the scent of fresh soap and pleasant after-shave. The small razor nick on his chin gave a hint of vulnerability to make her relax.

"May I take your order?"

He indicated the clerk behind her with a slight nod of his head. "I think you're next."

"Oh. Am I?"

She wasn't quite ready to relinquish her attention from such a handsome face and just-wouldn't-quit body. Slightly flustered, she turned around.

****

Now that her back was to him again, Chase Canfield continued his previous appraisal of the woman in front of him. A severe beige suit couldn't hide the lush body within. Her hips curved just enough to catch a man's attention—they'd certainly caught his—and make him look for more. The skirt, while in his opinion too long, followed those curves, tapering above well-shaped legs.

Her fitted jacket gently hugged a slim waist. As she lifted an arm to pay for her order, the jacket rose, giving him a chance to enjoy the full swell of her backside.

For the first time, what he had done on impulse that morning hit him square between the eyes. When he saw her on the street, his attraction had been immediate, and strong enough to make him follow her into this coffee shop. He shook his head in self deprecation. *You spent way too much time undercover, my friend.*

He'd considered approaching right away, to introduce himself, get her name or number, and maybe ask her out. Then didn't. Now was not the best time to act on personal feelings. Not with Monica and her latest husband breathing down his neck for yet another, and totally unnecessary, custody hearing. No way in hell would he let another man adopt his only child.

Which husband was this for Monica? Five—or was it six? Whatever the number, Chase was glad he'd never fallen into her trap. Especially when he reminded himself how Monica's motives were wholly self-serving, even where their daughter was concerned. Case in point, she claimed to be too busy to accompany Lisa on the upcoming class trip to Alaska. When Chase offered, because he loved spending time with his only child, Monica and her damned primary custody arrangement dictated otherwise. As usual.

He was always so wrapped up in doing what was right for Lisa, while trying to counter the things Monica was doing wrong, their father-daughter visitations had become almost tedious. He hated the cold legal term *visitation* with all its impersonal connotations, hated the way it dehumanized his relationship with his daughter and, in the most devious yet efficient way, robbed him of his rights as a parent.

Convincing Monica to allow *his* aunt to accompany Lisa on this trip had been a major victory. One he wasn't about to relinquish, even after Aunt Francine called to say a slight problem had come up. She hadn't said what, but quickly added that she had a solution. Best of all, through some miracle of persuasion, she'd cleared the new plan with Monica. Which meant he would accept it no questions asked. He wasn't about to put this particular parenting decision back into Monica's court. A smile caught him as he thought of his favorite aunt. The lady, who epitomized the words prim and proper, would be a perfect influence for Lisa.

Unlike the woman standing before him now. Women like her were made for fun. His single-guy kind of fun.

Except you're not really single, in the strictest sense, his rational side cut in. *If I were, she'd be the first one on my list,* he countered back.

List of what?

He paused at the unexpected question, then let his purely macho side respond. *Willing ladies labeled For Pleasure Only.*

Which you know isn't enough. More than most, he understood the importance of love and family, and it had been a long time since he'd had a taste of either in his life. He took another half-step forward, being careful not to crowd her.

Lord she smelled good. Wavy chestnut hair tossed around her shoulders when she moved her head, taunting him to run his fingers through its fullness. He wanted to know how it would feel caught up in his hands, and suddenly felt like a gawking teenager driven by too many hormones and too little adult restraint.

She came on to you, man. The mild reminder did away with the need for such restraint; and he went on to imagine her warmth as he cushioned fistfuls of chestnut locks to slowly draw her face toward his to accept his kiss.

"It's your turn."

She'd turned around to look directly at him, eyes twinkling in a way to make him wonder if she'd read his thoughts.

"Double mocha." His voice sounded raspy and rough, he cleared his throat. "Save the whipped cream." He finished giving the order in a strong voice, pleased with the success at bringing himself under control.

Until he found he held his breath as the woman he'd been studying from behind continued to look at him, into him, right through him. Those bright green eyes ran so deep, he could easily be swallowed up.

Not able to breathe and not caring whether he did or not.

"It's usually not this busy." Her voice was light, almost musical.

So she was a regular. He made a mental note to visit this coffee shop again soon. If only he didn't have the ten o'clock appointment, he'd have more time to pursue what could develop into a very gratifying time.

He paid for his order, then joined her at the other end of the counter under the *Pick-Up Here* sign. His smile acknowledged the irony. There were at least three people ahead of them, including the lady with a very large order. Good. He could stick around awhile longer.

"What is it you do?" she wanted to know.

"I'm here to visit family." He dodged the question on purpose. Telling people he was a conservation officer turned environmentalist usually garnered odd looks, like he was some kind of save the whales, tree hugging fanatic. Most women lost interest the minute the words were out of his mouth. He wanted to keep this woman interested. "And you?"

She extended her hand. "I'm Samantha."

"Samantha," he repeated. The syllables felt good on his tongue. "I'm Chase."

Her hand was soft, her fingers delicate, yet her grip was surprisingly firm. He resisted the urge to step closer.

"You didn't answer my question." She said it without accusation, to let him to know she noticed but, at the same time respected his privacy.

"You didn't answer mine either."

****

She half smiled at the mild reproof. "I'm in public relations."

It wasn't a total lie. Usually blurting out she

12

was a former police officer who now worked for a private detective agency put a lot of guys on the defensive. The term *lady cop* tended to turn most men off. She didn't want to turn this particular man off, yet.

The barista with spiked hair passed her drink across the counter. "One skinny vanilla latte."

"Can I have a jacket?" she asked, knowing the paper cup alone would scald her fingers.

Darkly painted nails pushed a corrugated cardboard ring forward. From where she stood, Samantha was forced to reach across the man she now knew as Chase to collect her order.

Girl, you've gone completely over the edge. Senses on red-alert, the softness of her breast brushed lightly across his chest just above his abdomen. She felt him suck in a quick breath as her fingers closed around the cup.

Party's over, she insisted, retracing her movements until she stood beside him again. *Wrap it up. Bat your pretty little eyes at him. Put your hand on his arm and say good-bye.*

She placed her fingertips on top of his arm. "It was nice talking to you, Chase."

"You, too, Samantha."

When he reached to capture her hand, their fingers intertwined expertly, as if they'd been together a lifetime. With some effort, she pulled free then stepped back, thinking it didn't matter how much distance she placed between them. Because the heat of him stayed with her, and probably would for the rest of the day.

Or the rest of my life.

She had rarely seen such longing in a man's eyes when looking at her. The entire effect caused her lips to part, though she couldn't think of anything to say.

What in the world have I gotten myself into?

13

Inside her head, caution flags lifted and warning bells clanged—big time. When exactly had she lost control of what was supposed to be a harmless flirtation? Started as a spiteful joke, a way to burn off unwanted anger, the situation had turned on her in a very frustrating way. She had to tell the man this wasn't the real her. She had to tell him the truth.

And sound like what? Um, excuse me. The little episode back there, where I practically undressed you with my eyes and assaulted you with my breast? That wasn't really me. You were a convenient distraction. See, I'm really the pretty tame, stay at home type. All business. No play.

Say it, she told herself with an intensity bordering on desperation. *Tell him!*

She took another step of retreat. *Forget it. You'll never see him again.*

That thought was the most devastating of all.

"The mocha machine is jammed, sir." The clerk's voice brought her back to the here and now. "Your order will be a few minutes yet."

"No problem," Chase replied. His eyes shifted to Samantha. "I'll walk you out."

She couldn't prevent him from following her. They stopped in the empty area between the two doors and, for a moment neither moved, until he did. Toward her.

She offered no resistance when he lifted the cup from her hand to set on the ledge. Nor did she stir when his fingers settled beneath her chin or while his thumb stroked her cheek. She wasn't at all sure what happened next. Did he pull her mouth to his or did she eagerly meet him half-way? One second, their lips were touching, and the next, the ground beneath her feet began to shake. Then, a mind-blowing, heart-stopping free fall stole her breath, making her wrap hasty arms around his neck to remain upright.

When he released her, the free fall stopped. The ground beneath her feet may have been solid, but the legs supporting her had gone weak.

He handed back her cup with a slow, satisfied smile. "It was nice meeting you, Samantha."

Over a roaring heart, she kept her voice strong and even. "Nice meeting you, too, Chase."

She made sure her expression remained impassive until she made her way through the outer door and started down the street.

****

Watching Samantha walk away, hips swaying ever so slightly, Chase was convinced he was the only man on the planet attuned to her subtle message. He wanted to follow her again, but reality kicked in and he knew that wasn't a good idea. Right now his focus had to be on what little family he had. Anything else would have to wait for another time. Taking one last look at her retreating form, he felt as if a small piece of him walked away with her.

By the time he'd collected the mocha and made his way back out to the sidewalk, she was nowhere in sight. He juggled the Styrofoam cup when the heat of its scalding contents bled through to his fingers, and wished he'd waited long enough to acquire a jacket as she'd called it. But, he hadn't expected the damned mocha to be so hot.

A lot of things this morning he hadn't expected to be so hot. Like her.

Lost in the tangled mass of conflicting thoughts, he veered toward a trash can on the corner where he stopped only long enough to toss out the untouched mocha. That was when he saw her again.

Chapter Two

Samantha hurried down East Jefferson toward her office, determined to make sense of what just happened. Her hands were actually trembling! The coffee cup needed to be held at arms' length to prevent its contents from sloshing down the front of her suit.

Had it been that long since she'd experienced such an all out attraction to the opposite sex? Who was she kidding? She'd *never* been so much out of control. Her reaction to a simple kiss was so—primal!

During the short time she'd spent inside the coffee shop, she would swear the day had grown hotter. The oppressive morning heat was nothing compared to the heat simmering inside of her.

What did you expect? You played with fire, fire played back. A distinct little hissing noise like a red hot poker plunged into cold water, sounded inside her brain. Fueled by nervous energy, she picked up her pace, waiting just long enough at the corner for the light to turn green before she stepped off the curb.

"Hey!"

A deep voice bellowed from behind as an arm clenched around her waist. A hand locked onto her hip and the latte went flying as one yank propelled her backward. She slammed against a muscled form and, on instinct, lurched forward. As the arm tightened, she clamped down on the alarm flaring in her.

Keep your head. You can fight him off.

"Don't!" The tense voice resonated against her ear. Her elbow jab to his solar plexus was automatic; the next words rushed out of him on a startled gasp. "Fight me..." He bent forward, taking her with him, but his grip didn't let up.

Her body registered the solid frame holding her as her mind registered the roar of an engine; the ear splitting blast of a horn. She felt a gust of displaced air, smelled the rank exhaust as one car, then two, raced through a now empty intersection.

Kept snug along his length, she steadied herself until both their bodies relaxed.

The grip slackened, the voice calmed. "You okay?"

"Yes." She pushed out of his arms. "Fine. Thanks."

"Good."

She stepped away before looking directly into deep brown eyes with silver flecks. "It's you!"

"Yeah?" It was his turn to step back, his response containing the slowness of disbelief.

"I guess I should thank you." She fought to keep her voice under control. "I mean. Thank you. I should have been more careful."

"You're all right then?" Concern clouded a gaze now studying her face.

"I'm all right." No, she wasn't, but she couldn't tell him.

She looked away to keep him from seeing the utter confusion gathered in her eyes. Being pulled from the path of an oncoming car didn't bother her half as much as not being able to fight him off when she thought she was being assaulted. Granted, she was a little weak, but not that much out of shape. In the past, she would have had the perp on the ground in seconds, her on top cuffing him.

The waiting crowd surged forward. "Let's go," a

female voice called out.

"Come on," someone else demanded.

Stung by embarrassment, she started to follow other pedestrians into the street. "Thank you again. Good bye," she mumbled over her shoulder. If he said good bye as well, she didn't hear it.

The quick shot of adrenaline had zinged through her veins and now hummed in her ears.

She reached the opposite curb and sidewalk on legs she forced to keep moving.

Thankfully, the rest of the trip to work was uneventful. Soon, familiar green walls and golden oak trim in the PSI lobby welcomed her into its calm presence. A tall counter, covered in ivory leather, dominated one side, its black marble top reflecting the muted glow of overhead lighting. Plush beige carpet silenced her footsteps as she approached.

"Well, good morning!" a female voice exclaimed from its midst. "Welcome back."

She recognized the friendly greeting of Jan, PSI's office manager/receptionist, and, as Bob described her, its major anchor. She grabbed on to that metaphorical anchor now.

"Good morning!" Returning a beaming smile, she absorbed the sincere feelings that went with it. "And, thanks. It's good to be back."

"You're *looking* pretty fit." The remark was punctuated by a critical eye. "How are you doing?"

"Fine." Her quick response was designed to leave no room for discussion.

"No, really? How's the patient?"

"No longer a patient." As proof she bent forward then stretched side to side, ignoring the tiny ripples of pain. "Good as new, see?"

The move garnered her a skeptical glance. "Bob wants to see you in the conference room at ten. Can you handle that?"

"Of course. Actually, I already knew about it."

"You did? How?"

"Franks called to tell me."

Jan blew out a breath of disgust. "The office busy body strikes again; how does he seem to know everything."

"You give him way too much credit."

"No. He spends all his time concentrating on other people's cases, and not enough on his own." She leaned forward. "I've suggested to Bob he get rid of the guy." Her voice was so low, Samantha leaned forward too. "But, he apparently promised the former owners he'd give the man a chance." She sat back up. "For the life of me, I don't know why."

"Because he's Bob."

Jan smiled at that. "I suppose. And that's why we love him, right?"

"Right." She decided not to share Frank's supposed insight with Jan. "So what is this meeting about?"

"It's more unofficial. I'll let Bob fill you in on the details, but I think you'll be pleased. And..."

A bell tone chimed from the console on her desk. Giving a quick *talk to you later* wave, she pressed the blinking red button. "Professional Security and Investigations."

Leaning on the counter a moment longer, Samantha reached toward a maze of built-in cubbyholes to her right and collected a few messages and mail from the box above her name. After tapping the envelope edges a few times on cool marble, she started down the hallway, breathing a sigh of relief when she stepped through the door to her office.

Four water color prints, wrapped in thin gold frames, were the only adornment on the walls, painted in her favorite shade of blue. This space, like her life, adhered to the concept of less as more and contained only necessary furniture. A desk, credenza style file cabinet and bookcase all in rich oak. The only touch of luxury was two Queen Anne chairs, dressed in pink velvet, flanking her desk.

Seeing a tissue paper wrapped flower arrangement on one corner of her desk, she separated its covering. A dark green urn held a sprawling ivy plant infused with delicate white baby's breath and ten or so blush pink roses. The attached card read simply: *Welcome back. We missed you. Love, Bob and Jan.*

"How nice."

She smiled as she set the card on the desk. It was good to see their names together, and made her think maybe more than the usual business decorum was growing between the two. A recent widower, Bob deserved happiness in his life. Still single at fifty, Jan was able and willing to bring him that happiness.

Her attention turned to a larger arrangement resting on the floor. Already unwrapped, this one featured gaudy colored flowers mixed with extravagant greenery. She bent down to pull the card from its center. *To the future.* Underneath it said, *To OUR future. Love, David.*

"We have no future, Mr. Franks," she vowed, and stuck the card back into its plastic holder.

After depositing the tissue paper wrappings into the trash, she settled into her high-backed chair and swiveled to look out at the twin skylines of Detroit, Michigan and Windsor, Ontario, Canada. Tapered skyscrapers and low, squatter buildings lined the busy Detroit River. Among some smaller watercraft, two freighters of identical rusty orange sailed on opposite sides of the shipping lane, leaving drab green water, left in their wake, to wink and sparkle in the brilliant sunshine.

As she watched, wishing she still had her latte, brown eyes with silver flecks took shape on the iridescent surface. Her mind jumped to images of a man and memories of his embrace so vivid, she still felt his warm, hard body pressing against hers.

Hands on the chair arms, feet to the floor, she propelled herself upward and, in three quick strides stood at the bookcase. In an effort to dispel the unwanted recollections, she stared down at an assortment of books lining the bottom two shelves. Ones she intended to read someday, those she'd finished but couldn't bear to part with. Much of her recent history resided on the top shelf. The trophy earned after her college volleyball team won a national title, a photo with her parents, the angel figurine she'd bought herself last Christmas for no other reason than she liked it.

The framed photograph taken the day she'd graduated from the police academy caught her attention. Her memories about that special event remained clear, from a monumental sense of accomplishment, to eager anticipation of her future in law enforcement. How she'd yearned to fulfill the promise to serve and protect. With Bob as her mentor, she'd stepped onto the fast track from day one, earning Sergeant by her third year; Lieutenant four years later. She'd seen plenty of human misery in that time, maybe more than anyone should have. By the time she hit her twenty-year anniversary on the force, a newly retired Bob recognized the tell-tale signs of burn out in her and offered the sanity saving job at PSI.

She ran one finger along the top edge of the smooth wooden frame as she considered the faces of her parents in the photo. Her mother's perpetual smile hid so much discontent. With solemn regard, she turned to the image of her father, beaming with unbridled pride. Too bad the show of satisfaction hadn't been for her accomplishment, but his own. Moments before the picture was snapped, Attorney

Edwin Wells was congratulated on his recent win of a high profile court case. Still riding a wave of self importance, he reluctantly slipped into the family picture at the urging of his wife. The academy had been nice enough to hire a photographer to preserve the day, and other families were waiting their turn while the Wells family held up the line.

Fast forward two hours, and she and her father were locked in the same battle they'd fought many times before. *Be like me. Follow my footsteps. I did it for my father. You can do it for me.*

Never *what do you want to do with your life?* Never, *do what matters to you.* That would be too easy. He'd be giving her too much credit. Every time Edwin Wells looked at his daughter, his eyes didn't shine with pride, but were always shadowed in disapproval.

****

The door to the conference room was open when she arrived for the ten o'clock meeting. Bob Anderson sat at one end of the long, mahogany table, his back to the entrance door. A petite older woman perched on the edge of a chair to his right. Dressed in a smart navy suit with white piping trim, she couldn't have been more than seventy. Her hair was short, almost boy like, yet the neatly styled cut only accented its silvery tint

Heads together in the familiar comfort of good friends, they spoke in low tones. Samantha paused in the doorway, unsure whether to interrupt.

"That's why I'm determined to find a solution." The woman patted Bob's hand. "With your help."

A curious gaze shifted up to Samantha and his friend smiled easily as their eyes connected. The friendliness of that connection drew her into the room.

Bob turned at the exchange. "Samantha, come in." He rose quickly to walk toward her. The gesture was odd for him; he usually stayed seated while inviting her in with a smile and wave of his arm.

"I need you on this." He whispered so only she could hear as he made a pretense of shaking her hand. "It's personal."

Another oddity. Not one to take asking for favors lightly, this had to be important to him. But, if the woman needed a bodyguard, why was he smiling? She apparently had a different problem he seemed determined to solve, with his protégé's help.

"So, how's the side?" His eyes flicked there. "You good?"

"I'm fine," she replied for what seemed like the umpteenth time that day, though spared him the athletic exercise she'd demonstrated for Jan. "Good as new."

"Great!" She noticed what appeared to be mirth in his eyes, as if only he held a special secret. He turned toward the conference table, drawing her with him, his arm positioned gingerly around her waist. "Samantha Wells, this is Francine Markham, my mother's dearest friend."

She walked over to accept the older woman's outstretched hand. "It's nice to meet you, Mrs. Markham."

"Please, call me Francine." Her face took on a measure of relief. "You're an answer to a prayer, dear." To Bob, she said, "You've come through for me, again."

Samantha glanced toward her boss for guidance. "Really? I'm flattered."

"How would you," he began around a smile bigger than before, "like to go on a little trip?"

She looked from one to the other. "A what?"

He seemed to have taken on the persona of a game show host making the announcement of a grand prize to an uncertain contestant. "All expenses paid. Two weeks in the beautiful state of Alaska."

"Alaska?" she repeated.

"Several months ago," Francine explained, "as part of a group tour, I booked a cruise for two up the Inside Passage with stops in several cities along the way." She paused to take a short breath. "Then land travel across parts of the Alaskan frontier to Denali Park and ending in Anchorage."

"That sounds wonderful." It was the only reply she could think of.

"It is, dear. Or rather it will be. But now, unfortunately, there's a problem."

"And, that's where you come in," Bob noted.

Again, she looked from one to the other. "Me?"

It was Francine who retained a serious air. "Yes, dear. You. As you said, it is a wonderful trip with the promise of numerous good memories. But now, unfortunately, one of us can't go."

"Oh." Samantha understood now.

Though bodyguard might not be the proper term, chaperone wasn't either. This woman was looking for a traveling companion and, not wanting to risk contact with a complete stranger, she'd come to her friend who owned a security company for help. Either way, this would be an easy enough assignment. She'd worked bodyguard detail for state and local officials when she was on the force and knew the drill. Attending to details, adjusting schedules, coordinating connections, occasionally providing company.

Not to mention, the idea of a trip to a place she'd always wanted to visit appealed. "That sounds...interesting."

"It should be fun," Francine offered. "I've been twice already. The views are spectacular, yet each and every time the scenery is new, exciting and totally awesome." She clapped her hands together then held them in front of her face, fingertips touching her bottom lip.

Samantha got a kick out of her use of the teen-like expression. Traveling with this woman would no doubt be a treat, and she found herself actually looking forward to it.

"I'd love to go," she said, catching the older woman's enthusiasm. "It sounds like a lot of fun."

"It's settled then. Wonderful!"

While Francine's reaction was certainly flattering, the relieved look on Bob's face wasn't lost on her either. Two weeks out of the office, and a trip to Alaska, wouldn't be hard to take. She'd have to find someone to cover her refereeing duties for volleyball, but Michelle was good about adjusting schedules. Sadly, that was the only commitment she would have to take care of before she left town for two weeks.

"You've been talking about taking a vacation," Bob said. "Sick time doesn't count."

That was true. She'd often joked with him about needing some serious R and R. *I finished on the force on Friday; and you had me running surveillance Saturday night,* she'd teased. That was over eight months ago. In Bob's mind this assignment was a no-brainer, a reward for good service.

"Auntie Fran!" A girl all of fifteen or sixteen burst into the room.

Francine stood, then came around the table to pull her into an eager hug. "Good news, sweetie. I've found someone to go to Alaska with you."

Samantha's head shot up. "But, I..." she began, but no one paid her any attention. Aunt and niece spoke in excited rise and fall spurts. It was apparent they hadn't seen each other for awhile. "Oh, but I couldn't..."

Bob's triumphant expression turned to puzzled concern. Samantha looked at him with what she hoped was a smile of reassurance. She could do this, she was flexible. Traveling with a teenager couldn't be too difficult.

"Hey, Miss Wells." The girl turned her way. "Is it really you? Gosh I didn't know you were a detective."

Samantha's mind registered the brown ponytail first, then observed almond shaped eyes in a matching shade. She took in features she should recognize, and her memory leafed through a series of similar faces until a name clicked into place under this one. "Lisa?" The last name escaped her, if she had ever known it at all.

"Yeah, you remembered. Hi." The girl looked over at her aunt. "Miss Wells referees some of my volleyball matches."

"You two already know each other?" Francine exclaimed, hands coming together by her chin. "Well, this is too perfect!"

"Some girls from volleyball are going." The names she rattled off next were vaguely familiar. "Have you ever been to Alaska, Miss Wells?"

"Never."

"Then you two are in for a real adventure," Francine offered. "And, don't worry, dear, it's a very select group of National Honor Society members. Other parents and siblings are going too, but Lisa is the only one you'll be responsible for. By the way." She turned to Lisa. "Where is your father? I thought he was bringing you down here."

She shook her head. "I'm meeting him here. Mom dropped me off. She said she didn't want to trouble Daddy with having to drive all the way to pick me up."

"Nice of her, wasn't it?" A male voice spoke from the doorway. Only a fool would miss the sarcasm in his remark. He stepped forward to plant a kiss on Francine's cheek and sweep the teenager into a swift hug.

Samantha observed the family affection with

casual interest, until recognition dawned once more. Her mind again registered familiar features. This time with no series of similar faces, only one. And, this name clicked into place beneath the face with much more force than before.

Chase!

No one else in the room seemed aware of the explosions taking place at her discovery. She was surprised the entire building hadn't been vaporized with them in it.

This wasn't happening.

Her mind began to form a string of arguments to explain why she couldn't make this trip. Unfortunately, none of them sounded very convincing.

Certainly he had noticed her as soon as he entered the room, his eyes took in everything and everyone before coming to rest on her. Warm, compelling, intoxicating. Much like his embrace. Tiny jolts of thunder rocked her; it took a moment to recognize the tempo of her own heartbeat. By sheer will, she took a number of deep breaths to bring herself under control.

If he experienced any of the same emotions, his outward appearance didn't betray it. She saw no trace of it in his stance, no evidence in his expression. His only reaction was the slightest widening of his eyes in recognition and the brazen one two flick of his gaze down her form. The inspection was over in a second, with her the only one aware it even happened, shamelessly aware.

"Oh look at you!" Francine exclaimed as she took him into a fierce bear hug he accepted without complaint. He allowed himself to be held out at arm's length and inspected by a woman who was, at best, half his size.

"Chase. Buddy," Bob said as Francine released her hold on him.

She didn't need to watch Chase stride back across the room toward Bob. Every angle and plane of his body was remarkably easy for her mind to recall.

A handshake between the two men became the quick embrace of good friends. By their expressions, friendship ran deep. Chalk up one more reason she couldn't refuse the assignment.

"How were the lectures?" Francine said, then didn't wait for his answer. "Well received, I'm sure."

"They went well," Chase answered. "Good crowds."

"Good crowds?" She laughed at that, her voice full of pride. "From what I saw on the Internet, they were sold out within a day of being posted."

His reaction was a self-conscious shrug and slight blush which Samantha found oddly endearing.

"It's not exactly saving the world, Francine."

"You always were too modest, Chasen. And, it's *Aunt* Francine to you."

"Aunt Francine," he corrected, then added with a good natured smile, "any other faults of mine you'd like to discuss?"

"No, not yours. But some of mine. Where are my manners?" Francine looked over at Samantha. "You seem to already know my great niece." With a wave of her arm she indicated Lisa who took that as a cue to enter the adult conversation.

"Miss Wells is an official at my volleyball games. Thursday nights? I wrote to you about them." She paused to take a short breath. "She is one of the best refs ever, Daddy. She'll not only make a call, but explain things to us if we have questions."

Samantha barely heard the compliment, her mind locked onto *Daddy*.

Francine cast Lisa an indulgent smile. "My turn. My turn," she said on a little laugh, then looked over at Samantha. "Surely you have heard of Chasen

Canfield?"

"I have," she found enough of her voice to answer, remembering how Bob talked about a friend of his, a dedicated conservation officer, now retired. The man had taken on a corrupt local government in Alaska tied to a commercial fishing scam. Bob had supplied snippets of the illustrious career of someone he admired. Hearing the word retired, she had imagined gray hair and a paunch.

"In the flesh!" Francine's voice fairly sparkled as she went on to highlight her nephew's many accomplishments. "Chasen, this is Miss Samantha Wells."

Despite being at the mercy of wildly roiling emotions, Samantha called on every ounce of training to remain cool under pressure and held calm reassurance in her voice. "Mr. Canfield."

"How are you, Miss Wells?" Then as if he couldn't help himself. "Samantha. And, it's Chase."

He took her offered hand, slid his fingers suggestively along her palm. She had to concentrate to keep from jerking away and hold the shiver that took her as a result deep inside, where no one, including him, could find it. Dropping his hand, she met his eyes. A slight smile played at their edges, but never quite managed to take over his mouth. It didn't matter. Now in control of herself, she smiled for both of them.

"Chase."

"Have you two met before?"

At Bob's question the hairs on the back of her neck prickled to alert. Had she really expected his cop gut not to pick up on their obvious reactions to each other?

"Actually we have. Sort of." Though Chase's words were meant for the others, his attention remained on her. "We stood in line together this morning getting coffee."

His glance shifted to take in the three sets of eyes watching in silent expectation. Samantha held her breath as she waited for him to elaborate.

"We were both a little bored," he continued with calm reassurance. "And exchanged those little pleasantries like any two strangers would." His eyes ambled back to her face as if he dared her to argue with his practical summation, or deny it. Then something flashed across his features and another smile began to climb onto that damned appealing mouth. Teasing, self-satisfied, and much like the one she'd seen there after their kiss. "Actually, there's more."

He wouldn't dare!

She wasn't sure if he planned to share details of the kiss or the car incident. She decided to opt for the car incident, less shock value.

"It all happened so fast," she cut in then went on to relate the story as if getting pulled to safety happened to her every day. "You know how some of these Detroit drivers can be. I should have paid more attention."

"See, dear?" Francine said when she finished. "I told you he was a hero." She looked toward her nephew, then back at Samantha. "But, you knew that, didn't you?"

"Yes." Her lips made the admission before her mind could censor the thought. "I guess I did."

She hadn't seen Bob stand up and walk toward her, hands out in concern and alarm on his face. "You didn't tell me that! Are you sure you're okay?" He pulled out a chair, escorted her toward it, then forced her to sit before his troubled look landed on Chase. "She was...uh shot in the field, about a month ago."

In an instant, Chase stood over her as well. "I didn't know." His voice was tight with regret. "She didn't tell me." The hint of accusation wasn't lost on her. Like she could have yelled, *Careful! I've been shot!* the moment he grabbed her.

"It was minor, really." She waved her hand in dismissal. "A flesh wound."

"Did I hurt you? Did I..." He looked her over as if trying to determine where the wound was located. "...touch it?"

She shook her head. Though she could recite from memory every place on her body he had touched, the area of her wound wasn't one of them.

Standing up quickly, she was pleased when both men moved out of her way. Her regard fell from one to the other. "He saved me from a car, Bob. And, no, Chase, you didn't hurt me." She marveled at the familiar way in which she'd just addressed him, all formality between them vanished. With exaggerated purpose, she turned toward Francine and Lisa. "But, we're here to discuss another problem."

And mine too. Somehow she had to get herself out of what she'd agreed to.

Chase looked warily at Samantha then back at his aunt, as if he just now remembered there was a reason for his being at this meeting. "So, what's this all about?" Apprehension colored his tone. He appeared to be a man who relished control and didn't take well to surprises. "You said on the phone you needed to talk about Lisa's trip."

"That's right." Francine looked toward Samantha. "I've been helping put together this trip for Lisa's class as I told you. And I planned to go as well."

"Because her mother was too damned busy to be bothered," Chase muttered, before recognition of his aunt's exact words registered on his face. *"Planned?"*

"Friends of ours own a travel agency," she went on to explain to Samantha. The next was said to her nephew. "You know Clarence and Mindy Darling."

"Planned?" he said again. If he was growing

impatient, he hid it well. Samantha's anxiety was off the charts, and she already knew all the details.

"Yes, Chasen, past tense, I'm afraid. The trip starts in about a week now." She looked apologetically toward her great-niece. "It seems my doctors don't want me to go."

Chase moved to put a hand on his aunt's shoulder. "Your doctors? Is it serious?"

"They think it is." She flicked a wrist in dismissal before her arm fell to her lap. "According to them, my heart beat needs to be regulated. For crying out loud, the old ticker is close to entering the century mark. It has a right to stutter a little bit. You'd think they'd cut my heart, and me, a little slack."

"What do they say?" he prompted, his tone serious. "Exactly?"

"If you ask me, it's just so much silliness. Why at my age..."

"At your age, you need to listen to your doctors," he said gently, leaving his hand on her shoulder. "Maybe they know more than you think."

"The fact remains," she continued. "This is not fair to Lisa."

"Your well being is what's important." He reached down to touch her arm. "Lisa's a big girl who can deal with a little disappointment."

"So you admit she's growing up?" The matriarch cast a sly smile at her great-niece and ignored her nephew's huff of disapproval.

"You know what I mean." His voice was stern even as he kept a gentle hand on his aunt's arm. "Temporarily postponing the trip isn't that big a deal."

"D-a-a-a-d." Lisa stretched out the word in typical teenage fashion. "What about everyone else?"

He looked her way, confusion creasing his brow as she recited the names of other members of her class who were also making the trip. "They can't postpone," she reminded him when she finished.

"Oh. Yeah. I guess that could be a problem."

"On a more practical note," Francine noted, "I'm afraid I neglected to take out trip insurance. Everything is already paid for. Veranda state room for two," she looked over at Lisa and smiled.

"I'll talk to Monica," Chase said. "And take Lisa myself."

To Samantha it sounded like a wonderful idea, which would put her out of this situation, this room and this man's presence.

"Oh, Daddy, that is so sweet," Lisa replied while she cast a pleading look toward her great-aunt.

Even Samantha could sympathize. The last thing she'd want to do would be take a cruise with her own father. But, maybe that was just her.

"You know Mom wouldn't like that," Lisa said softly.

"You can't go anyway, Chasen. What about your lectures?"

"I can still honor the ones next week. The rest can be rescheduled."

"The good news is you don't have to do any of that," Francine declared, though he seemed rather skeptical of her reassurance. "There is no problem." She and Bob exchanged wide smiles then she looked over at Samantha. "Because Miss Wells here has agreed to go!"

Brown eyes widened, shot to his aunt then ricocheted back toward *Miss Wells*. His face contained all the elements of intense shock, and would only have been enhanced more if his jaw dropped open. A part of his expression he managed to control only by drawing his lips into a tightly held line.

The reflection of appreciation Samantha enjoyed from his gaze earlier in the day was now replaced by the wariness of distrust, and she was surprised at the thousands of tiny daggers stabbing her heart.

Though no one else in the room knew the content of his thoughts, they surely picked up on his reluctance

"Why so glum, Chasen? It's the only way Monica will allow Lisa to go," Francine offered kindly. "You know that."

"My mother couldn't...is too busy to go herself," Lisa explained to Samantha with a brave face. "But she wants me to go with someone besides my father."

"Monica likes to control things," Chase added. "Especially as they pertain to anything I try to do with our daughter."

Lisa gave her father an apologetic glance. "That's just...Mom."

"I know, honey." Coming to his daughter's side, he put a possessive arm around her shoulders.

He continued to stare at Samantha, who, unlike the others, knew exactly what he was thinking, recognized the bombshell he was about to drop and was sure after he did, she was going to have to be the one to explain why.

Chase opened his mouth.

Samantha closed her eyes.

"I don't think that will work," was all he said.

Chapter Three

Francine spoke first. "Oh, why not, Chasen? Of course it will work. All I have to do is call the travel agency to replace my name with hers."

Lisa joined the assault. "Won't work why?"

"Because it won't."

"I knew you'd do this." Francine said flatly. "I thought if I had a viable solution for you, one I'd even cleared with Monica, you'd allow Lisa to go. I should have known better. You can't keep her a little girl forever you know, Chasen. You must let her grow up sometime."

As Samantha listened, she heard another conversation from her own adolescence, between her father and her mother, about her.

"Mom doesn't have a problem with it." Lisa spoke with all the strength of teenage defiance. Samantha recalled how she'd used the same tactic in her own youth.

"I don't imagine she does." There was no malice in Chase's voice this time, only the slight hint of defeat.

"Let her go, Chasen," Francine said again. "She will be sixteen in a few weeks and I'm sure she'll be just fine with Samantha."

He splayed his hands out in a motion of self defense. "When did I become the villain here?"

"When you started to argue," his daughter replied, as if that explained everything.

"When *I* started to argue?"

"Yes. You," she responded with the assured

indignation of her age. "If you'd just let me do what I want..."

...*my life would be fine,* Samantha finished for her.

She had a feeling this discussion, or one similar to it, had taken place within this family unit before. She heard the yearning in Lisa's voice, the decisiveness in Chase's, the pleading in Francine's.

Chase stared at Lisa for a long moment. He wore the definite look of a parent trapped in a losing argument. Wanting desperately to do the right thing for his child, required to protect, yearning to please, and unable to reconcile any of it. Suddenly, all Samantha wanted to do was protect them both. In part, because she felt responsible. Chase was no villain, but given the first impression he had of her, she could understand why he didn't exactly consider her nanny material.

She wondered if it would be best to confess the truth behind their first meeting.

"She shouldn't be going with a stranger." His sharp remark brought fresh dagger points against her heart before she had a chance to speak.

"She's not a stranger, Daddy."

Hearing Lisa come to her defense, she couldn't shake the desolation crawling through her at his straightforward comment.

"She isn't, you know," Francine added quietly. "Our good friend Bob knows her. Lisa knows her." She paused as if she were about to reveal some sacred secret. "And, you know her as well."

Only Samantha knew why surprise, then guilt, crossed his face in quick succession before practiced composure prevailed.

"We've planned this all out, Chasen," Francine said, all traces of weakness gone. "You're scheduled to fly to Seattle five days from tomorrow on your lecture tour. The cruise ship leaves from there the following day."

"I can go with you, Daddy. Attend to your lecture." Lisa said, as if the offer were added incentive for his agreement. "Then you can take me to the boat dock."

Chase found his voice at last. "What about her bullet wound? What if she's not yet a hundred percent?"

For her part, Samantha would grant him only one excuse for being obstinate, the man cared about his daughter. That did not give him the right to question her ability.

"Don't make assumptions about me until you know me better." She didn't care how her words sounded, he could take them any way he liked. "I do my job."

"What's not good about the idea, Chasen? Lisa won't miss the trip." Francine gazed up at him, her eyes intense, "and I won't be forced to jeopardize my health."

He winced at the low placed emotional blow; even the others flinched in sympathy.

"Samantha tells me she's ready, Chase. That's all I need to hear." Bob's measured tone warned of the promise to follow. "You can trust her. She's damn good at what she does."

"I don't doubt that." His eyes flicked down her frame. "It just won't work."

"Am I interrupting?"

Samantha couldn't believe the intrusion of David Frank's irritating voice, knowing he could care less if he was interrupting or not. The self deprecating smile on his face may have fooled the others, not her. He greeted Bob with a calculated amount of respect and used appropriate charm as he acknowledged Francine and Lisa.

"Jan asked me to let you know Len Baxter is on the phone, Chief." Though he spoke to Bob, his eyes flitted to every other person in the room. "She thought you might want to talk to him right away."

Bob stood up and looked over at Francine. "I've been playing phone tag with this guy for a couple of weeks now. Do you mind if I take the call?"

Her hand was already raised in dismissal. "Of course. Go. Samantha and Chasen can go over a few details with Lisa and me. Right, dear?"

"Actually," Franks cut in, "I need to talk to Sammie for just a sec. If that's okay with everyone?"

Samantha almost gagged at the inane endearment. Nobody called her that, least of all him. She started to protest, to shake her head no. Whatever he had to say to her could wait until the end of their meeting. Or, the end of the century.

"That works." Chase rose, offered the newcomer a cursory handshake then looked past him to Bob. "Is there someplace I can make a phone call?" His glance slid over Samantha. "In private?"

"Find an empty office," Bob offered, walking with him toward the door. "Most of our agents are out in the field today."

****

Chase strode down the hallway unsure of where he was headed, only certain he had to get away. He silently cursed himself for so readily agreeing to Monica's no-way-are-you-going-with-Lisa terms. If he didn't do something, and fast, his daughter was going to end up on this trip with—*Her.*

The woman was not exactly his idea of a suitable chaperone. He leaned more toward someone who wore sensible shoes, full cut pant-suits and had gray hair done up in a no-nonsense bun with expression to match.

Images from the coffee shop flashed before his eyes. *Damn!*

He slipped inside the first empty office he found, and realized immediately whose it was. The place was infused with the scent of Samantha Wells. Moving slowly, he looked around her private space. A bookcase on one wall held the usual assortment of things he suspected women kept. The trophy seemed out of place. He strolled over for a closer look at a photograph where a younger, and grinning, Samantha stood between two adults. Her parents, he surmised. The father looked out at the camera, pride evident in his expression. Chase ignored a familiar hurt clutched in his gut as he turned his attention to the woman. An older version of the daughter, with the same laughing emerald eyes and full mouth.

His attention was drawn back to Samantha's face, struck by how much like Lisa she looked. Not so much in features, but in personality strong enough to be revealed in a photo. Same kick-ass attitude in the eyes, same I-can-take-on-the-world confidence in the expression.

He had no idea how long he stared at the picture before he glanced at the flowers on her desk then walked over to check out the card beside them. Curiosity overcame good judgment. He bent toward the larger arrangement, read the attached message, and wished he hadn't.

David.

Putting a face with the name, he was taken by surprise at the resultant rush of anger. At himself for being duped? Or at her for making him care? He wondered if this guy knew what his girlfriend was up to when he wasn't around.

So what? The woman's actions are none of your concern.

As he tried to convince himself of that, he also told himself confessing to everyone the real reason he didn't want her to be responsible for his daughter's safety would solve everything, at least for him. Aunt Francine would no doubt be properly appalled; Lisa would be disappointed but she'd bounce back. Surely Bob had another female on staff available to go with Lisa. What did it matter anyway?

Because it wouldn't be—Her.

Taking a seat behind the desk, he snatched the cell phone off his belt. He'd said he wanted to make some calls, best get to it. There were still people in Alaska who would come through for him if asked.

Right now he planned to ask.

****

The moment Chase left the room, every muscle in Samantha's body sighed with relief. She feared her legs would buckle if she didn't sit down soon. Too bad sitting down wasn't an option when dealing with David Franks.

She followed him a few feet into the narrow hallway, stopped, but he kept going. "That's far enough. What is it?" Though she wanted to grind the questions out from between clenched teeth, she kept her voice light in case anyone happened to overhear.

He said nothing for a moment, placed his hands against the wall, essentially trapping her and let his knee bump against her thigh. On the outside she didn't flick so much as an eyelash; inside, her stomach turned.

If they'd been anywhere but the office, she would have slammed her knee up between his legs. Instead, she kept up a bland expression when he brought his face closer to hers.

"Nothing really. I just missed you."

Her voice remained as flat as her expression. "That's nice. But, I really need to get back."

"I wondered if you'd reconsider going out for drinks if I added dinner to the mix?" His voice was husky, his hot breath an unwelcome intrusion.

"Can't."

Huskiness gave way to irritation. "Can't or

won't?"

"Can't."

Though the thought of spinning him into a choke hold was tempting, she saved it for fear of making a scene with a co-worker. This was Bob's agency, something he'd worked his butt off for. With that in mind, she stepped to one side, then levered her arm upward to push his out of her way. The maneuver reversed their positions, bringing his back to the wall, with her standing in front of him.

His attempt at confident bravado failed as he angled his head toward the conference room. "So I was right about the new assignment." When she didn't respond right away, he offered a possibility. "Probably because of the Kleins."

She stiffened at the glib reference to the PSI case she'd worked just before the shooting. The Kleins were in the middle of a contested divorce when the husband side of the mess tried to handle Samantha. All because she'd demonstrated compassion when she showed him graphic evidence of Mrs. Klein's infidelity. Turned out the guy was a slime ball in his own right and the wife's affair was in retaliation. Samantha threw out every counter measure she knew to discourage the man's advances, but nothing worked. Finally, to protect the integrity of the agency, she took herself off the assignment.

Though she never divulged every sordid detail, Bob said she handled the situation like a pro. It appeared Franks viewed the incident in a different light and assumed she was now being punished. On the up side, she'd viewed the entire Klein fiasco as a learning experience: don't get caught up in private family issues on any case, again.

It was so like Franks the jerk to bring up old news.

"Nothing's been finalized yet."

His hand latched on to her upper arm when she

moved to walk away. "I don't know why you have to be such a bitch to me all the time. I said I was sorry about the..." She knocked his hand away when he made a move toward her injured side. "Even the state boys concluded accidental discharge."

"And that makes it okay?" Referencing the fingers still clutching her arm with narrowed eyes, she said, "Do you mind? I have a meeting to get back to."

He offered no resistance as she pulled free, but kept his contentious stare trained on hers. But when he ended visual contact to glance over her shoulder, his angry expression cleared to one of polite acceptance. She tilted her head at the change in him.

"Okay, then. I will see *you* later." He sounded like a second-rate lounge singer finishing his act. The inflection on the *you* was well placed, no doubt to bring up illusions of a hot steamy night. Her stomach lurched again.

"Fine." She choked back rising anger. *This guy did not merit a screaming fit.* "I'll see you later, too."

Wanting only to be away from him, she made a hasty turn toward the conference room, colliding with a hardened form that charged out of nowhere. She pulled up short before teetering backward, but Chase had already reached out to keep her from falling.

In the split second he held her, she felt a tension in him she hadn't picked up on before. Her gaze swept across his face, along the rigid set of his jaw, the severe line of his mouth. Before she had the chance to step free, he'd set her away from him and backed off.

"Sorry to interrupt." The tightness in his voice suggested otherwise.

"Don't worry about it." Her response was equally tight as she continued walking, eager to get the events of this day behind her.

He fell into step at her side. "That was cozy." He nodded toward Franks' retreating form.

Indignation and annoyance fought to become her primary emotion. She discarded them both in favor of a healthy dose of good old fashioned anger. "Only because he tries to make it look that way."

"You sure about that?"

She grabbed onto his arm to halt his progress, along with the mistaken content of his thoughts. "David Franks considers himself one of God's rare gifts to women and is determined I be a grateful recipient."

"Really?"

He made no attempt to hide the sarcastic inflection announcing he wasn't convinced, and she wondered why she even cared one way or the other. Then she quickly figured out why. Chase Canfield believed her behavior with him that morning carried over to David Franks, and any other man she had occasion to have contact with. Understanding how wrong he was provided the strength to set him straight.

"Never in a million years." She went on before he had a chance to dispute her again. "Those kinds of things are based on trust. My trust of *him* has been compromised big time."

"Because...?"

"Because he was with me when I got shot! With his gun!" She hurled the information at him like the sharp report of rifle fire, then waited for his reaction.

To say he looked stunned to silence was an understatement. A certain sense of victory was hers in the eerie calm following her revelation. His mouth flattened into an even grimmer line than before, his hands balled in and out of fists.

"I was helping him serve a warrant," she hastened to explain, alarmed by the intensity of his response. "The target went for Franks' gun. It went off in the struggle."

"Like that's an excuse."

"It was an accident. Accidents happen." Her tone became matter of fact. The same one she'd used to give details of the incident to the Michigan State Police troopers who came in to complete their mandatory investigation. She'd been a fountain of cooperation, only so Bob didn't lose his PI license. "I've seen recruits on the firing range shoot themselves in the butt while trying to draw their side arm out of the holster. Same thing, sort of."

She was relieved to see his posture relax, then decided he'd best not plan to relax too much, because she wasn't finished with him yet. This charade had gone on long enough; the time had come to end it. Not so much to ease his mind about her competence to protect his daughter. That was a lost cause. She merely wanted to reclaim her good name, or as much as she had left. Because, like it or not, she cared what he thought of her.

Fingers still gripping his sleeve, a slight tug forced him to face her. "We need to talk." Her voice held the raw edge of frayed emotions. "Alone."

"Okay." He glanced around the empty hallway and through the windows along one side of the conference room. Bob, Francine and Lisa stood engaged in animated conversation, unaware they had returned. He brought his gaze back to her. "We're alone. Talk."

"I don't know what you think of me and, quite honestly, don't care." *Liar!* She pushed the protest away and swallowed quickly. "I might have been a little blatant in...my response to you earlier. It's uncomfortable to admit this," she went on in a voice hushed more by her unexpected embarrassment than his obvious antagonism. "You were a convenient diversion, and my coming on to you was...just me...fooling around. A way to blow off a little steam."

"Congratulations."

"Congratulations?" she repeated. "I don't..."

"You had me fooled."

His gaze roamed down her neck to her breasts and lower. "I didn't think anyone could come on as strong as you did without having something..." His gaze paused, then held just below her waist. "...to back it up."

Though her mind chose to ignore his comment, her body refused to obey the message as a flutter deep inside responded to the touch of his eyes.

"I'm sorry if I misled you." She placed intellect back in control over hormones. "The entire encounter really meant nothing." When she glanced up, he had looked away as well.

"Meant nothing," he repeated before his eyes caught hers again. "I can accept that."

"I do apologize, but this really should have no effect on either one of us any longer. Make no mistake, Mr. Canfield, I am quite capable of taking very good care of your daughter."

She waited for him to respond, but only the silence returned. His lack of a comeback meant one thing. If he wasn't going to accept her justification, she needed to go a step further. To the choice she'd tried to avoid, but was now obliged to take. "Under the circumstances, I can understand your reluctance to trust me with Lisa. And it's clear you never will." She was struck by a sharp jab of disappointment, not so much for herself. She wanted this for Lisa. "How about we go with the truth?"

"The truth?"

She swallowed hard. "The truth about us."

"Which is?"

His tone gave her pause. She said truth, and was about to explain truth away with another lie. "That there is nothing between us. Even though our first meeting...," she forced herself to look back at him again. "...would dispute that. There appears to be only one option left." She took a hasty breath and dove in. "You can reveal whatever you want to Bob, your Aunt Francine...even to Lisa. Explain everything. Tell them why you don't consider me a good choice for this assignment." She lifted a chin which, by sheer force of will, did not tremble. "After you do, your family will no doubt accept your decision not to use my services, and you'll be free to seek another solution."

He stared at her as if trying to absorb the full extent of what she just offered. "You realize you're handing me the chance to be, if not a hero, at least not the bad guy in my daughter's eyes?" He looked away from her, then back. "What will Bob say?"

"He won't like it, but he'll understand." She lifted her chin again as she released his arm. "You choose. I promise not to argue."

Without another word, she turned, took a few steps forward and opened the door to the conference room.

"We may even go international," Bob was saying as she entered, and she knew he spoke of their dream for PSI. "There's a lot of work for well trained agents in the private sector." He gave Samantha a pointed look. "Capable, well-trained agents."

"That's very nice." Francine's attention focused on Samantha. "It's always refreshing to find a person wanting to do something for others."

She acknowledged the compliment with a small smile and calmly took a seat with her back to Chase. "Too many good cops retire early," she said, picking up on Bob's earlier comments. "When they still have a lot of productive years left. Bob and I want to change all that. At least that's our plan. To franchise the agency and provide employment opportunities outside of municipal police departments."

"Samantha talked me into tying into an Expo which is coming up in a couple of months," Bob said.

The Expo, he explained, was the brainchild of the head of a Bring Back Detroit commission that had been formed a few years before in an effort to revitalize the more blight ridden areas of the city. Trade shows for all manner of vocations had been held in those years. This year for the first time, law enforcement was one of those professions, which fit perfectly into PSI's franchise plans. Vendors and speakers from all over the country were invited to attend and *sell their wares* as it were to the assembled professionals.

"Sounds like a lot of work." Francine noted.

"Probably," Bob admitted. "But, with Samantha's help, I'm committed to seeing it through." He glanced up at the doorway where Chase, no doubt, remained. "So, what's the good word, Buddy? What did you decide?"

Her body locked into defense mode awaiting the inevitable reply.

Bob would understand.

So what if her last case for PSI ended on a sour note? This one had turned sour before it even began. How many more times would Bob stand by her? How long until he started to doubt she was an innocent bystander in these situations?

In the Klein matter she *had* been innocent. In the Canfield matter, anything but. She readied herself as best she could while her heart seemed to cease all movement in preparation to plummet to some unknown and empty abyss.

"I've decided to let Lisa go to Alaska with Ms. Wells."

Breaking a rigid posture she wheeled around, unable to keep her gaze from flying toward a face which revealed nothing more than distinct, or practiced, disinterest.

"Way to go, Daddy!" Lisa flung herself into his arms. The smile on his face as she hugged him the only betrayal to an otherwise stoic expression.

Francine clapped her hands. "I knew you'd come around, Chasen." She looked to Samantha, her face beaming. "I don't know what you said to him, dear, but, he obviously listened."

"Well this has certainly turned into a win, win situation." Bob stood up, beaming in much the same way, and reached for the older woman's hand.

"We're done then." Accepting his assistance, she rose to her feet, then reached toward Samantha as she passed by. "And, I want to hear about each and every thing you do when you return, dear," she said, clasping frail fingers around hers.

"Of course," Samantha agreed, gripping her hands a moment longer.

"Lisa and I are going to do some shopping while we're downtown. Pick up some things for the trip." She mentioned the names of a couple of stores in the promenade area of the building a few flights below. "We'll meet you later for dinner, Chasen?"

He nodded.

"I'll go down with you," Bob said. "I want your advice on a purchase I plan to make." He walked briskly over to Chase. Pumping his hand, he added a quick slap on the back. "You won't regret this."

Chase ran guarded eyes over Samantha. "I hope not."

Oblivious to a look she'd clutched to her heart, Bob placed his hand on her shoulder next. "I'll leave you to work out the details with Lisa's dad."

"Of course."

Lisa's dad. Which was precisely how she would consider Chase Canfield from here on out. The father of someone she had been hired to provide a service. A customer, an assignment, part of the job.

As the small entourage of Bob, Francine and

Lisa made its way toward the reception area and a waiting elevator, their excited voices trailed off. Standing side by side, Chase and Samantha were once more engulfed by thick, choking silence.

"Why did you do that?" she asked, hoping his explanation would allow her to sever some of the unwanted emotional connection she still retained. Like a butterfly not able to break free of a trap.

"I figured it wasn't worth it." A shrug accompanied his words while his gaze avoided direct contact with hers. An action her cop instinct discerned made his answer just shy of the truth. "As you said. What happened..." she felt her pulse rate pick up. "...didn't mean anything. Right?" He looked to her for clarification.

"Right," she managed, her stare straight ahead, as the butterfly sought to escape.

"However, I have a question for you."

She looked at him now. "Yes?"

"This morning, when we first met. You didn't tell me you were an ex-cop. Why?"

Because at the time, I didn't want to lose you.

"It was a detail. We were dealing in the shallow stuff. You didn't tell me you were a former conservation officer," she countered. "A highly decorated former conservation officer."

"You're right. I didn't." He paused for a moment as if deciding how much of himself to share next. "I like to concentrate on what I do now. Study the environment. Look into the effect of ravenous human consumption on mother nature."

"Sort of like the world and our place in it?"

"Something like that. Sometimes it's nice to slow things down. Appreciate the moment."

"That's a nice way to think."

"The world has a lot to offer. We tend to forget that sometimes." Softness entered his eyes and the tenor of his voice lowered "Listen. This morning.

49

With that car. Things got a little rough."

"Out of necessity," she reminded him.

He gave her a half smile of appreciation. "None the less." He reached out and she held her breath as his fingertips stroked the length of her arm. "If I hurt you, I'm sorry."

"Sorry?" she whispered. Giving into the shiver brought on by skin against skin, she met his eyes. "You did what you had to do. It's okay. Really. You didn't hurt me."

"I want you to know, I would never do that." His voice remained a gentle caress as the hand broke contact and returned to his side. "Hurt you, I mean."

Crossing her arms, she rubbed the places he had just touched. "My struggling didn't hurt you either?"

His smile snared the butterfly back into the net. "Actually, more than I'd care to admit. But, I'm fine." He watched her for another long moment. "That in itself is proof you can take care of yourself. And, my daughter."

In the course of their conversation, he'd gotten closer. She, in turn, had shifted her body toward him. No longer side by side, they were now face to face, eye to eye; and, almost, but not quite, mouth to mouth.

"A gut reaction. I thought you were a...well, you never know what you'll run into on a busy downtown street."

He watched her lips move, his concentration deep, and she wondered for one wild instant whether he planned to kiss her again. She couldn't let that happen.

"Your Aunt Francine and your daughter are very nice people." She spoke up fast, in an effort to divert his attention.

It took a moment for him to lift his awareness from her mouth. "Aunt Fran is amazing," he said when he was finally able to meet her eyes. "Hard to believe she'll be eighty soon." He smiled with true affection. "And, Lisa." The smile broadened. "Amazing doesn't even come close to describing her."

She began to tell him about Lisa's prowess on the volleyball court, and enjoyed the resulting pride on his face.

"I've rarely seen her play." Regret tinged his voice. "Work has kept me away."

"She's good enough, you know. She could play in college." She warmed to this connection with his family. "I did. It was fun."

"Just fun?"

She couldn't lie to him about this. "Actually playing sports at the college level comes with some pressure. Along with a crash course in time management," she added on a laugh. "But, I thrived on it." What she had enjoyed most was the scholarship money that made her less dependent on her domineering father for support. Especially since she's majored in criminal justice, her choice; instead of pre law, his. "It's nothing Lisa couldn't handle."

"I already know where she's going and what she's taking in college."

"Oh." She closed her mouth to keep from blurting, *your idea or hers?*

His response was like a splash of cold water, but she quelled the urge to launch into a lecture about parents allowing their children the courtesy to decide their own futures.

Let it go, her now weary, and slightly overworked inner voice warned. *This isn't your fight.*

"So." She pushed away every argumentative thought that entered her mind. *Time to drop the personal revelations and take control of the assignment.* "Since we have to make some arrangements regarding your daughter's trip, shall we uncomplicate matters and start with an agreement?"

Caution imbued his features. "Which is?"

She extended her hand, professional demeanor intact. "Friends?"

"Friends," he agreed.

Chapter Four

Samantha arrived ahead of time to meet Chase and Lisa at the embarkation terminal on the Seattle waterfront. The place resembled an airplane hanger, immense, square and flat roofed. A single room inside consisted almost entirely of chairs. Gray, molded plastic and, for the most part empty, they stood in evenly spaced rows. Obligatory restrooms graced each end of the huge open area. Glass paneled teller windows covered the back wall, with metal stanchions, strung with royal blue velvet cord, providing a well defined maze leading toward them. Blazer-clad staff members busily laid out papers, pens and clipboards on a few pedestal tables, stopping to assist any incoming guests who sought them out.

A series of glass and metal doors, at the moment propped open, faced a busy downtown street where cart pushing porters collected the luggage of arriving passengers. Samantha waited just inside one of those opened doors, a carry-on tote at her feet. She was early on purpose so her newest client had no chance to doubt her competence.

Dressed for comfort more than style, she wore pale green linen slacks, a darker green tank top, and had a light weight sweater with embroidered flower patterns down its front, draped across her shoulders.

Much as she had a few days before, Mother Nature provided a warm summer day of clear skies, balmy winds and sunshine. Though the outdoors was picture perfect, Samantha preferred to be in. A warm Pacific breeze swirled through the door behind her, lifted her hair to flutter several strands across her face, then dropped them back around her shoulders. She absently pushed the wayward tresses behind her ears as she reviewed, again, details for her newest assignment.

Preparation was the key to successful execution, and she was definitely prepared. The events of this, the first day of said *assignment* had progressed exactly as planned. If she'd been one to make up to-do lists, she could tick off each completed item.

One flight across four time zones, check; taxi ride to the waterfront, check; bags properly signed in, check; passport in order, check; cruise ship ticket in hand, check.

There was only one thing she hadn't been able to as easily check off her imaginary list. Put anything about the man involved in the *assignment* out of her mind. Since she'd met Chase Canfield, he had set the notion she carried of herself—as a rational adult—spinning madly out of control, until it landed in a cockeyed heap in some far reaches of her psyche.

On the up side, the previous week had afforded her the time she needed—rather, her body needed—to heal. The bruising had faded, the soreness was gone, physically, she was mended. Only her heart remained in question. During the day, thankfully, she stayed busy screening and interviewing potential franchise candidates, keeping thoughts of him at bay. During the day.

Work was useless at night; nothing could help at night. When she had been able to sleep, which wasn't often, he stole into the privacy of her dreams. She shifted in her chair to dislodge the distracting thoughts of his kiss, fleeting in time yet permanent in memory. Caught in a cop's mind trained to retain the details, and a woman's mind bound to recall the passion.

"Coffee?" Rodney, one of her seat mates on the trip from Detroit, held out a white Styrofoam cup. "I don't know how good it is."

She accepted, smiling her thanks.

"Now, we wait. Right?" He took a seat beside her. "Until they tell us we can board the ship."

"That's right." Having at least taken time to read the instructional letters from the cruise line Francine had forwarded to PSI, she knew that much for certain. "With time for paperwork in between."

"Ah, yes, paperwork," he replied. "Gotta love it."

Shortly after getting on the plane in Detroit, she met Rodney and his friend Brad, then learned they were all booked on the same cruise. In the interest of efficiency, cost and company, they'd shared a cab ride from SeaTac airport.

"At least if we get lost, we won't be alone," Rodney had joked at the time.

From the moment she met them, he had been the one to do most of the talking, as he was now. Fussing about how Brad had spent an inordinate amount of time in the bathroom since their arrival at the terminal.

"Pre trip jitters?" she suggested, taking a careful sip of coffee.

"I hope that's all it is. I'd hate for him to be sick the entire time we're here."

Trying to assure him that probably wouldn't happen, she continued to scan the latest group of arriving travelers. She hadn't told Brad and Rodney who her cruise partner was, only that they were meeting in Seattle. On her next visual pass around the room, she spotted Lisa and Chase enter by a far door.

They were both dressed for comfort, much like her. Lisa wore cropped pants and a striped tee shirt under a light jacket. Chase had traded his suit for khaki slacks and a blue pull over shirt. On him, the casual clothes provided even more evidence of a trim, well muscled body. When her heartbeat tripped up a notch at the sight of him, she knew trying to curb it was futile.

"There's my group." Cup set aside, she stood up. Rodney rose along with her to look where she looked. "Blue shirt. Striped tee," she offered.

"Oh." The single word said it all. "I see them." He gave Lisa a passing glance, then spent considerable time in a critical assessment of Chase. "Is he your boyfriend?"

"Just a friend," she answered honestly. "And, his daughter."

"Too bad." Rodney's eyes remained on Chase who had just spotted them and was guiding Lisa their way. "You'd make a nice couple. Oh, there's Brad. See you on the ship." With a quick air kiss aimed at her cheek, he was gone.

Nice couple. She considered the possible truth of that comment. Because Rodney thought it, or she wished it? Dismissing both options, she watched her *friend* and his daughter approach. Chase's initial expression of recognition, even pleasant expectation, had turned guarded. She saw his gaze follow Rodney's retreating form, then focus back on her and the scowl on his forehead posed a definite silent question. A question he had no right to ask and she had no inclination to answer.

Better to concentrate on Lisa. The teenager's face was a transparent reflection of her joyful mood as she took in their surroundings with open-mouthed wonder. Catching the girl's eye, Samantha lifted her arm in a wave of welcome.

"Hey, Miss Wells." She engulfed her chaperone in an unexpected hug. "This is going to be so awesome."

Grabbing hold, Samantha hugged back, enjoying the warm, solid feel of human contact. This was real;

this was her purpose for being here. When Lisa released her, she kept her hands on the girl's upper arms simply to hang on. "How are you Lisa? I agree, it's awesome." She hadn't yet found the strength to look over at Chase. "Did you check your bags? Do you have all your papers?"

"We checked the bags outside. And, yes, in here." She patiently indicated a fringed leather pouch strapped around her waist then fairly shook with uncontained excitement as she leaned forward. "I am so looking forward to this. Daddy used to work in Alaska, you know. He's told me so much about how beautiful it is."

Samantha had no choice then but to acknowledge Chase. No, she corrected, Lisa's dad. How she needed to think of him from now on, as the father of her current assignment and part of her job. "Mr. Canfield." Assuming almost a caricature of good old professional demeanor, she extended a welcoming hand.

His expression had softened to one of indulgent pride as he'd watched the exuberant behavior of his daughter, and hardened slightly—but only for a second—as his attention focused back on her.

He took her hand lightly, fingers touching palm, exerting only the mildest pressure, but she might as well have been held in a vise. She was that powerless to pull her hand away and just as powerless to tear her eyes from his. "It's Chase, remember? Samantha." His voice was deep, almost lazy, as he drew out the syllables of her first name in a way that sent an expectant shiver down to her toes.

"You're right, Chase." Her own voice sounded strange, infused with the uncertainty born of a reflexive response to him. A physical surrender she always tried to keep hidden and he always managed to pull out of her.

"Did you have a nice flight?"

She nodded. "Very smooth. And you?"

"Smooth."

"Let's get in line while we talk." Samantha watched Lisa grab her tote from the floor at the same time as she felt her hand being released by Chase.

Had he been holding it all that time?

"Good idea!" Turning from him, she hefted the bag Lisa handed over onto her shoulder. "It's nice to see you both again," she said as they headed for the now fully staffed teller windows.

"It's nice to see you again, too."

****

Chase almost fell over from the force of that understatement. Nice didn't even begin to describe how he felt about seeing her again. She appeared the same as she had just a few days before. But, why shouldn't she? Those looks had been etched in his mind since the first moment on the street. Even before he'd made physical contact, she'd taken over his mind and been with him ever since. Both in his dreams and out. He'd come to the conclusion there was nothing he could do to change his reaction to her, so he decided he may as well sit back and enjoy it.

She'd taken his hand in greeting and, as it turned out, his breath in one movement. He had everything he could do to grasp her there and go no further. To behave like the friend he agreed to be. That day, when he'd watched her walk toward the conference room, head high, shoulders squared, ready to accept whatever life, or in this case, he had to throw at her, he knew he'd refuse her offer to reveal everything. Not so much because he wanted to, but because he had to. She deserved better than that, especially from him. Whatever he would have gained from a full disclosure, she would have lost more.

If he had his way, and if they'd been alone, his grip on her hand would have served as a lever he could use to pull her into his arms. And he knew exactly what to do with her once he got her there.

Back off, his mind demanded. *She came out and told you that you're nothing special to her. Live with it.*

But, he didn't want to *live with it.* Something deep inside of him wanted to be a part of her world, whatever that looked like, wherever it led. Something deep inside of him even believed they may have a chance at some form of a future.

Or so he thought, until he arrived here to find her with *him,* whoever the hell *he* was. He had to admit he was damned put off seeing her with some other man. One who seemed to have an inordinate amount of interest in *him.* Sizing *him* up. As in sizing up the competition? It had taken all he had to not demand, right then and there, she explain herself. Since she hadn't been inclined to offer an explanation, he had no intention of asking for one. The guy was all wrong for her anyway. Too thin and flighty. She needed someone more stable and substantial.

Someone more like me.

"Let's get in line!" Lisa's voice broke in to drown out his thoughts.

The newly formed threesome joined a row of other passengers making their way to the back counters. Moving then waiting, moving then waiting. Samantha inclined her head toward his daughter, and their whispers and occasional bursts of laughter evidenced some secretive and high level girl talk. Chase quickly made a conscious decision not to try to join in. Girl talk was way out of his league, and he knew better than to subject himself to such pressure. Instead he decided to spend his down time watching the woman who had taken over his thoughts, and his life, the past week.

She wore her hair to one side today. It looked fine to him, but she continued to push it behind her ears as if she were trying to alter the style. Her eyes sparkled as she laughed at something Lisa said. He remembered those eyes. A potent blue green, they took on the bright color of emeralds when she laughed and the deep and mysterious tone of jade when she was provoked. He found himself wondering what their color might be when, and if, she was ever consumed with passion.

"Here you go, sir." The strong female voice made those thoughts screech to a halt as a fast moving clerk handed him a clipboard. "We need your paperwork filled out and signed at the bottom. We imprint a credit card for purchases on the ship," she explained to him and the line in general, her voice sounding like a well worn recording. "There's no cash exchanged on board."

Chase nodded his understanding, as did the others. Then, head bent to the task, his fingers guided the pen quickly and efficiently across the pages as he provided the requested information. Soon his paperwork was completed and it was time for him to wait once more. Left on his own to pass more idle time caused him to wonder again about Samantha and her male companion.

A woman like her, he told himself sternly, *just naturally attracts the opposite sex. Any man who wants to be a part of this woman's life had better be willing to stand in line.*

He exhaled a frustrated breath. This, he noted wryly, was exactly what he was doing now. Standing in line all alone.

"Daddy."

"What is it?"

"They need your credit card."

He reached into his back pocket to produce the piece of plastic from his wallet. The clerk ran its unique magnetic strip through a small machine that gurgled in acceptance.

Seeing Samantha had just approached the next available clerk with her completed paperwork, he quickly retrieved his credit card and offered it across the counter. "Use this one."

"No, thank you." Pushing his card aside, she handed over one of her own. "My personal charges will go on here, please."

****

Her small smile and the negative shrug of her head were meant to mask the torrent of emotions roiling inside. Using his credit card would generate a list of her purchases, and an insight into her she would rather he didn't have. No way would he learn any more about her than he already had. Anyway, most of what he did know, or thought he knew, wasn't true.

Concentrating on Lisa's incessant chatter, she couldn't help but wonder when he planned to relinquish the care of his daughter to her. *Probably at the boat after the check-in process,* she concluded as they walked through the back doors of the terminal toward the Windstar, their home for the next few days. The huge black hull raised the ship like a small skyscraper above the pier in a shining expanse of whitewash and windows. A stunning, four-star hotel on water, all stately, elegant and inviting.

A maze of metal ramps, enclosed by two-tiered metal railings, zigged and zagged up one side of the luxury liner, to end at an open doorway on the ship three stories up. Assorted passengers climbed at all levels along the temporary inclines. Couples arm in arm, parents holding the hands of little children, small groups containing older children and adults.

As they began their own ascent, Chase lifted Samantha's bag off of her shoulder to slide it over his own.

Those already on board strolled the decks or leaned over gleaming wooden railings waving to everyone down on the pier. Catching their excitement, Lisa threw back enthusiastic greetings.

"I can't wait to get started! So when we get to Alaska, Daddy," she asked without taking a breath. "Do you think we'll see a bald eagle?"

Chase regarded his daughter with a loving smile. "Where you're going? Probably at least a dozen."

"Oh!" Her eyes widened even more. "That would be incredible!"

He and Samantha exchanged indulgent smiles.

"Tell me something," he said, as he turned his full attention back to Lisa. "Why this interest in Alaska?"

"Oh, Dad." She rolled her eyes with the impatience of a teenager faced with having to respond to the unnecessary query of a parent. "I wanted to go where you've been, see what you've seen."

He stared at her with a mixture of awe and satisfaction. "You remembered the stories I told you?"

"Of course," she replied over her shoulder. "Why wouldn't I?" Before he could answer that, she yelled, "Oh! There's Susie. Susie! Wait up!"

Chase and Samantha could only watch her dodge around an elderly couple to hurry on ahead of them, as the girl she'd called out to stopped and waved. The two older people with her, no doubt her parents, looked back at Lisa, said something to their daughter, then continued walking toward the ship.

"I guess you made an impression," Samantha noted.

"Yeah." Though he nodded in agreement, remnants of disbelief remained on his face as he watched his daughter bob and weave a path toward her friend. "I guess I did."

Lisa's lead on them grew as she and Susie, spied, then joined more of their friends. At first Chase and Samantha tried to catch up with her, but, hindered by others on the ramp, had to be satisfied keeping her in view.

They watched as she and her friends approached two ship's photographers who were set up in a corner of the huge structure taking keepsake pictures. Caught up in the festivities, the girls began to strike some good natured poses, their laughter and chatter drifting back across the pier.

"Lisa seems like a real people person," Samantha remarked. The stream of other passengers had slowed, leaving the two of them alone. "You must be very proud of her."

"She's always been friendly and curious," he answered, his eyes still trained on his daughter. "When she was younger, I worked overtime to impress stranger danger on her."

"I'll bet." She understood exactly where he was coming from. As a cop, she'd seen the consequences for children who trusted too much. "One of the most important jobs of any parent."

"It's been hard to let her go. Especially since her mother and I aren't together." He fell silent at the exact moment she wanted to learn more about his life. Non-stop questions circled in her brain about his relationship with a woman he'd been close enough to, at one time, to father her child. Did he still love her mother? Why were they no longer together? His choice or hers?

Looking again toward Lisa, she noticed a man— a boy really—approach. He was probably Lisa's age, maybe a little older. Then a woman came up to single her out, and Samantha's questions about Chase and the mother of his child vanished. Chase keyed on the situation at the same time, and both picked up their pace. But Samantha, not Chase, moved faster and, Samantha, not Chase, arrived at Lisa's side first.

It was then she noticed the strangers wore matching jackets with an eagle crest above the right breast pocket. Below that, stitched in script, were the words *Darling Travel*. Each jacket sported its wearer's name, stitched in smaller script, across the pocket itself.

True to what must have been strict training in proper protocol, the boy immediately greeted her with a small salute. "Welcome aboard, ma'am. Darling Travel, our agency booked your group." His pride at that even exceeded his politeness. "If there's anything you need while we're here, you just let me know."

"Thank you." She checked out the name on his chest. "Ethan."

"Welcome! Welcome!" A cherub of a woman with short, curly blond hair grabbed Samantha's hand. "We were just telling Lisa we know her Aunt Francine. I'm Mindy Darling and you must be..."

"I'm Samantha Wells. I'll be traveling with Lisa."

"Oh," the response was guarded until she smiled at a place behind and to Samantha's left, her eyes reflecting recognition. "Mr. Canfield, right?"

Samantha felt his arm come around her shoulder as he offered his hand. "Chase." His breath fluttered by her ear.

"Yes, Chase. Mindy Darling here. Welcome to you as well. We were just telling your daughter we know her Aunt Francine." She edged closer as she looked over to where her son stood talking to Lisa. "Well, our kids seem to have hit it off." She glanced back at him with a wink. "And don't they make just the cutest couple?"

"Mindy!" A man standing a few yards away called out.

The woman turned toward the sound of her name. "What?" she asked, missing the look of shock crossing Chase's face.

"Could you come over here, please?"

She glanced at the man who had called to her, then back at Chase and Samantha. "It looks like Clarence needs me. This is always a busy time for us. Have a nice trip!" she added over her shoulder as she hurried off. "I'm sure we'll see you all on board."

"How are you, sir?" The boy Samantha identified as Ethan introduced himself to Chase. "I was just telling the ladies about the Denali Park leg of our trip." His manner became more animated as he began to describe the upcoming excursion. The *ladies* he spoke of, primarily Lisa, hung on every word. "Of course, there can be danger." His voice took on a serious tone.

Chase issued a vague cough; the *ladies* leaned forward.

"I'll show you what we call *bear etiquette* before we get there," Ethan promised.

Samantha's cop's radar had long since relaxed, satisfied this situation and the people within it posed no threat to anyone, and she was surprised when Chase moved to put himself between Ethan and his daughter. Anticipating his intention, Lisa outmaneuvered him by pivoting slightly.

Good for her, Samantha thought, as Ethan, followed by the *ladies* continued up the ramp. Thinking only of diverting an overprotective father, she reached for his arm at the precise moment two photographers descended their way.

"Okay, now let's get a shot of the happy parents," one said.

"Oh, but, we're not...," she began.

"Here you go on a dream vacation! How about your first souvenir?" the second photographer joked, keeping up a stream of good natured encouragement as he positioned them for a picture.

Photographer number one brought the camera lens to his eye then lowered it to look directly at Chase. "Put your arm around your wife, sir! This is a happy occasion!"

Samantha felt his arm come around her waist as instructed and his fingers begin to close, hesitantly, on her side.

"It's okay," she whispered, thinking he was conscious of her bullet wound. "You're not hurting me."

A subtle yet strong motion on his part swept her against the length of him, and she wished she hadn't just given him so much reassurance. Heat surged through her at the unexpected contact. Her knees wobbled and the ground moved beneath her as if the ramp itself were swaying in the wind. She wrapped her arm around his waist more to steady herself than anything else.

"Probably concerned about the money you'll be spending, huh, sir?" the second photographer continued in what was probably well rehearsed banter. "Relax. Enjoy yourself!"

"Oh, I plan to."

The exchange struck her as odd, until she concluded it would have been rude of Chase to enter into a long winded explanation about how he wasn't taking the trip, just seeing them off.

Flashbulbs hindering her vision, Samantha kept hold of Chase a moment longer as they continued along the ramp. An action he didn't seem to mind.

"Ethan says they offer a tour of the ship in half an hour," Lisa announced when they caught up with her a few moments later. "Can I go?"

"We'll see," Chase replied.

Stepping away from him, Samantha entered the ship first. Coming to a stop in yet another line, they began to pass through necessary security screenings. Setting their belongings on a conveyor belt to be x-rayed and walking through metal detectors themselves.

"Can I go on the tour?" Lisa asked again, as the three of them, now cleared to board the ship, started down a large hallway.

"I don't know, Lisa," he responded absently, preoccupied checking the numbered signs which provided arrowed directions to the various levels and state-rooms.

"Why not? My friends are going? Julie. Susie...Chad."

He shot her a pointed glance at the teasing mention of a male name. She cast him an innocent smile in return.

"The state rooms should be around this corner," he said, still studying the number signs.

"Then can I go?" Lisa asked.

While Chase inserted the key card in the door they stopped in front of, he answered a definitive once and for all, *No!* She quickly responded with *Why not?* By the time they were inside their assigned state room, a father-daughter argument was in full bloom.

Quelling the urge to intervene on Lisa's behalf, Samantha quietly followed. She wanted to advise him to let up and allow her to go on a perfectly harmless tour, all part of the ship's carefully planned schedule. Instead she said nothing, leaving him to make the decision and, suffer the consequences. Silently, she resolved to handle Lisa's future requests in a different way. After she was left in charge, of course.

She walked over to where their suitcases were

neatly set in one corner of the room and hefted the smaller of hers onto one of the beds. Behind her, Chase's voice rose in frustrated anger. "I just don't think it's necessary for you to take off right now."

Lisa pounced. "Not necessary? Why?"

"Because we really don't know the Darlings. They're neighbors of Aunt Francine, not long time friends. And anyway..." He looked around the small room. "You need to get settled in here."

As if to comply with those instructions, Samantha began to unpack the bag she had slipped unnoticed from Chase's shoulder. Leaving the argument where it belonged, between father and daughter, she took time to scope out the set-up of their room, or rather rooms. A suite of sorts, two rooms with a common balcony, was connected by adjacent doors now standing open. Twin beds, desk, small couch and dresser were fit into this room. She thought about stepping to the doorway to see what the sitting room looked like, but didn't.

"...or do you want to keep yanking my leash? All my friends' fathers are supportive of them. But, not mine!"

Lisa's words made her look up in time to see Chase glance her way. She could tell by the confounded expression on his face, Lisa's latest statement made his resolve begin to falter. She also gathered he sought some form of support—or at least an indication he was making the right call—from her. Unfortunately for him she couldn't do that, because she didn't believe he *was* right.

Her decision to stay out of their argument made, she continued to ignore them both as she busied herself arranging a few personal items in one of the dresser drawers. Next, she hung some of her clothes in the closet with extreme care, remaining there to space them just so as if the task required her undivided attention.

"I'll unpack later. I promise," Lisa said.

"You'll unpack now," was the stern comeback.

"Fine!" Flouncing toward her suitcases, she unzipped the garment bag on top with uncalled for force then, sensing her actions were overdone, she calmly lifted out some dresses and slacks, already on hangers. Settling them very carefully on the rod, so she wouldn't disturb Samantha or her things, she turned to face her father.

"I am almost sixteen. Are you always going to treat me like a baby?"

Samantha detected hurt behind the defiance and wondered if Chase did, too. For his own good, she hoped so.

Can't I ever live my own life? In her mind, she heard herself as she listened for Chase's response.

"A tour can wait until everything is settled."

Holding an armful of sweaters above an open drawer, Lisa tried again. "This is a *guided* tour, Daddy! As in properly supervised!" She was on the verge of tears, every father's downfall. Samantha wondered what Chase would do next.

Lisa made a show of snuffling back her tears. "I promise you, I'll be careful. Please?"

"Okay. Okay. Yes. You can go on the tour. And, take your time," he added as if to add half-hearted proof he really did trust her.

Hearing his consent, Samantha backed out of the closet.

The teen didn't need to be told twice, she was out the door with a quick wave to her chaperone and an even quicker peck toward her father's cheek. "Thanks, Daddy. I will."

Samantha watched the door close, thinking it hadn't been much of a good-bye between parent and child. But, then, she supposed every family was different. What she'd just witnessed resembled the type of farewell she often gave her own father.

From the other side of the room, Chase looked downright battle weary. "She really does love you, you know," she offered gently.

"Does she know that?"

"Yes, she does."

"Why do I feel I can never say the right things or make the right decisions with her?"

One hand raked through his hair as he seemed to ask the question of himself. Knowing he wasn't really seeking an answer, she waited in silence for him to continue. "I've screwed up with Lisa before. More times than I care to admit. I know it; I'm sure she knows it, too. But, I can't change that now. All I can do at this point is just plow ahead and hope I get some things right." By the time he finished the self observation, his arms were at his sides, hands balled into fists.

If nothing else, Samantha knew he cared deeply for his daughter. And, she imagined, he could be hurt deeply by her too. He seemed so utterly miserable, her heart went out to him. Meaning to offer friendly comfort, she crossed the room. Once beside him, she lifted her fingers to touch his cheek. Eyes locked with hers, the fists relaxed, and, with measured slowness, he reached up to cover her hand.

Her fingers flexed as if she were about to pull away.

"Don't." They whispered as one, each having an opposite meaning.

In one motion, his free hand slid under her hair at the base of her neck and she moved toward him. Part conscious decision and part subconscious surrender to the pressure that beckoned. His other hand dropped hers to circle her waist and, having her firmly in his grasp, he fit her against him. She reached her arms around his neck in response, making the connection between them complete.

His lips drew nearer until she could feel light wisps of his breath on her mouth, and she was lost. Her only purpose in life became to possess the warmth and comfort those lips offered. The last thing she heard was her own moan of acceptance as his mouth came down on hers.

Yielding was instant, her response urgent. She might have starved for years; nourishment had finally arrived. At last he pulled his lips from hers but still he held her close, his cheek resting against her hair. After a long moment he moved his hands to either side of her face.

"I've wanted to do that all week." He rested forehead against forehead as he let out a contented sigh. "And, it was better than I remembered."

He searched the features still held in his hands as if seeking confirmation she remembered too, and agreed with his assessment. As if her physical response hadn't been enough assurance of her need for him. She saw the dark shades of desire smoldering in the depths of his eyes, and the discovery stole breath from her lungs as surely as if she'd been plunged into a deep and forbidden pool. Then his arms pulled her tighter, and again her lungs were robbed of their breath. But by now she'd decided breathing didn't matter, she'd survive without it.

Head cradled on his shoulder, she closed her eyes as she took in the feel of him, the scent of him. Hers to keep as memories for when he was gone. Devastation ran surprisingly deep as the thought of their upcoming separation began to take hold in what remained of her conscious mind. "I'm so sorry you have to leave."

"I'm not going anywhere."

****

As the statement played over in her brain, each word grew louder, more distinct.

I'm not going anywhere.

She spread her hands across his chest, then pushed hard to break free of his embrace. "You're what?"

"I'm not leaving." He seemed less sure of himself the second time around—as if he sensed he wouldn't like her reaction.

"Why?" Even as she asked, she knew why. Chase had gone back on his promise to trust her. Yet she asked the question anyway, needing to hear what he had to say for himself.

"They were looking for an on-board naturalist for this trip and I volunteered. It was...convenient."

"*Convenient?*" The sensible, reasonable side was back and roaring with indignation. "So, regardless of what you said, you didn't trust me after all."

"I thought this would be an opportunity for us to get to know each other better. To..."

His attempt to dispense a little bit of personal information only fueled her fury. "If you think we'll pick up where we left off last week..." She took another step back. "Think again."

"That's not it at all. You're twisting my motives."

She turned on him then, much as Lisa had done a few moments before. "Am I? Or are your motives just twisted all by themselves?"

"I also came along for Lisa."

"Don't you ever trust?"

"When it's been earned." The seriousness of his tone gave her pause, but she refused to let his unending suspicious nature impact her ability to do her job. Which had just become her one and only purpose for being on her way to Alaska.

"Trust is also built by keeping one's word. I gave you the courtesy of keeping mine. You're daughter will be...would have been fine with me. Does Bob know you're here?"

If her boss, friend, mentor did know, would he

think her incapable of earning his friend's confidence? Worse, if he didn't know, what would he say when he found out?

His responsive grin was playful. "I won't tell if you don't."

She could tell he regretted the playful comment as soon as it was out of his mouth. Now was *not* the time to be playful.

Feet splayed, hands on hips, she sized him up. "I don't suppose your quarters are downstairs with the rest of the staff?" *That would be way too easy.*

"Not exactly."

She wanted to scream. Didn't the man understand the impact of his actions? Or feel anything? Then it hit that maybe he didn't—feel anything—at least for her. Maybe the whole situation, this trip and that kiss, was all part of the same little game. "You need to go."

He strode toward what she thought was an attached living room. She wasn't prepared for him to turn abruptly to look at her. "Just for the record, I didn't ask for the room next door." He raked a hand through his hair again then dropped his arm. Something in his manner told her, at least on that point, he spoke the truth. "Someone must have thought I might like to be near my daughter."

"Don't you?"

"Of course I want to be near her!" he said over his shoulder and walked away.

But not near you. She finished what he hadn't needed to say out loud.

Not moving, not looking his way, she waited until she heard one of those doors close behind him.

Though she listened awhile longer, she never heard the bolt slide into place. Moving quickly, she shut the door on her side.

Unfortunately, the sharp click as she slid the lock home brought meager comfort.

Chapter Five

Peaceful coexistence became the order of the day. Samantha and Chase endured each other when necessary, avoided each other wherever possible.

For her, avoiding him proved easier than expected. A celebrity of sorts in Alaska, he took headline billing on the cruise liner's daily newsletter, and stayed busy with the duties of ship's naturalist. When the three took a pre-scheduled land excursion into Ketchikan on day two, he was recognized wherever they went, and subsequently was interviewed, by a television crew which happened to be filming short news segments at a local bird sanctuary.

As a result, she and Lisa were able to spend more and more free time together. Samantha discovered the warm and friendly young person inside the shell of recalcitrant teenager with a definite sense of what she wanted out of life. Lisa planned to become a veterinarian; she and her father had already picked out the school. She also confided her parents never had gotten along, yet provided no details, except to say her mother made things hard for her father whenever she had the chance. She was currently on husband number five, a successful real estate developer whom Lisa didn't care for. All show and no substance was how she described him. Samantha couldn't help but agree. Well known throughout the Midwest, the name of Monica's fifth husband was not famous for his humanitarian causes. From what little she knew about Monica, the two sounded like an even match.

Lisa was understandably upset about her mother's determination to have her newest husband formally adopt her daughter in what sounded like an *in name only* type arrangement. At least Samantha surmised as much, given everything else she'd been told about the girl's home life.

Like the detail she'd disclosed about Monica devoting most of her time to the new man in her life and his two young sons. Though Lisa didn't come out and say so, Samantha gathered, this came about at the expense of time spent with her daughter. Monica sounded like someone who was either overwhelmed by the pressures of raising an adolescent, or had simply lost interest in the task. Why didn't she turn the girl over for Chase to raise? Unless he'd already turned down the offer, a situation she found hard to imagine, judging by the way he doted on Lisa—when he wasn't handing down restrictions.

Whatever the underlying reasons, the ambivalent behaviors of both parents caused Lisa to reach out to her chaperone. In that sense, they grew close, and took to sharing heart to heart chats, slumber party style, just before they fell asleep each night.

Like the one they were having now.

"Mom says I should be grateful to be in a real family where we all have the same last name." There was no mistaking the confusion in her voice. "I guess I don't see it that way. She even wants me to call this new guy Dad." Her voice grew thick as if to hide tears. "I can't do that. I only have one Dad."

Samantha understood the reluctance. She sensed hearing his only child call another man *Dad*, even if she didn't mean it, would wound Chase to the core.

"...and he's so much fun to be around."

Lisa was already on to a different subject. Her

inflection, which spoke of teenage infatuation, caught Samantha's attention. She didn't need to ask to know the different subject was Ethan Darling. Lisa had talked about the boy non stop since day one.

"Don't you think he's cute?"

"Yes." She had to smile as she recalled the young man's blond haired, blue-eyed good looks. "He is."

Having no doubt they would be seeing, at the very least hearing, a lot more about Ethan, she wondered how Chase would take to the news. It was a good thing she'd looked into the Darling family's history through contacts she still had on the Job back home. True background checks, though a matter of course for bodyguard detail, weren't exactly proper protocol for a simple chaperone situation, so she'd blurred the edges.

"He seems nice," she noted out loud.

"What do you think my Dad will say? Do you think he'll accept Ethan?"

Chase would not be pleased at the prospect of his daughter being involved in a ship board, or any other form of, romance no matter how innocent. Then, what father was ever pleased at his daughter's attraction to someone of the opposite sex?

"Accept him as a friend of yours?" she said lightly to avoid the real question. "I don't see why not."

"I mean, do you think he'll approve of me seeing him? You know. Hanging out?"

Hanging out. Translation: the state of being connected in a socially accepted manner, said manner being more than friendship. "Do fathers ever approve?" she hedged.

Lisa sat straight up to face her. Though she couldn't make out a clear expression in the dimly lit room, she certainly read the body language. With her torso angled forward, and arms slightly outstretched, Lisa definitely exhibited the characteristics of someone determined to get answers.

"No, I mean really?"

"What do *you* think?" Samantha asked, clinging to evasion a while longer, as she sat up too. Body guard duty rarely required personal involvement; she'd underestimated duties of a chaperone might.

Lisa's form retreated slightly, though she maintained an upright position. "I think he would eventually." The comment was made with a wistful air. "Approve, I mean. But my dad's kind of a hard sell when it comes to me and boys."

"Most fathers are." She was stalling. In her personal opinion—one she had no intention sharing—Chase was just a little too possessive, and too much of a hard sell when it came to his daughter.

"I mean. He's a great dad," Lisa said as she lay back down. "He's always been a part of my life. When my mom lets him." Her voice lowered at that. "Even more so than some of my friend's fathers who live with them all the time." She sat up again. "And I know for sure that he loves me."

Samantha had to agree the man possessed the capacity to love. Lisa was evidence of that in more ways than one.

"Sometimes I just wish he'd give me more credit."

To find my own way, Samantha finished for her.

"...to know what I'm doing. To find my own way." Lisa concluded. "You know what I mean, Coach."

The room quieted as each became lost in thought. Samantha's were of the struggle she had fought to gain independence from her own father. If Chase knew what was good for him, he'd back off and let his daughter truly find her own way.

Unfortunately, the man hadn't shown himself to be a master of knowing what to do where his daughter was concerned.

Unlike Lisa, she didn't require her father's approval where boys or, in her case, men were concerned. She knew her mother would approve of Chase; what would her father's reaction be to her choice? Stiffening, she stopped herself right there. Chase was not her choice—as a man or anything else—yet in the privacy of her thoughts, she felt her cheeks flame.

"Do you think you could talk to him for me, Coach?"

You don't know what you're asking. Protests spun in her head like a string of Roman candles, lit but not quite ready to go off.

"I don't...I think you should talk to him yourself," she argued gently.

"Oh, I know," Lisa replied quickly. "And I will."

Samantha lay back down. "I think that's best."

"Eventually." Her hands dropped to her sides. "I just thought you could, you know, explain to Dad that I'm growing up. That I may be interested in boys...that..."

Judging from your father's first impression of me, he would probably not take too kindly to my being your romantic advisor.

Lisa deserved a better answer.

"I'm not sure he'd listen to me." She hoped the reply would take her off a hook she felt digging in more deeply as she struggled to break free.

"Are you kidding? The way he's tuned into you?"

Samantha's eyes widened at the unexpected revelation. She heard the rustle of sheets as Lisa settled deeper into her bed, clearly unaware of the bomb she'd just dropped.

"I know my dad. I can tell when he likes someone." Her words slowed, her voice laden with impending sleep. Finally, with a contented sigh, more rustling of the covers, and one last, "G'night, Coach," conversation ended.

"Good night, Lisa," she whispered, then lay there for a long time, trying without success, to get comfortable.

Eyes closed, mind alert, she went over a request that would be impossible to fulfill. Of course, Lisa had no idea anything existed between her *coach* and her father outside a business relationship, and certainly no inkling of intimacies already shared.

Intimacy which could never, ever, happen again.

Squeezing her eyes shut, she willed herself to *not* remember his kiss, and failed miserably. She still felt the pressure of his mouth on hers, inviting and seeking, asking for nothing more than she was willing to give. Settling on her side, she nestled her cheek against the pillow, not wanting to relive any part of his kiss. And, if she could admit it, the yearning inside of her that went with it. Forcing herself to think of other things, she remembered how Lisa talked about Chase as a caring and involved parent, then compared the image to the one she held of her own father.

Take for instance their most recent contact, a telephone conversation earlier in the day. She'd tried to call her parents when she first arrived in Seattle. When they'd been out, she'd decided against leaving a message. Then, in the flurry of getting settled and dealing with Chase—Lisa's father—she'd neglected to call again until that very afternoon. After she'd hit the speed dial button assigned to their number on her cell phone, she imagined the radio signal bouncing over the tree tops, hitting tower after tower along the northern plains until it arrived at the city in the lower peninsula of Michigan where they lived. After a few seconds of dead air, the other line began to ring.

She was disappointed when her father answered.

"Hi, Dad." As always, she tried to keep the apprehension out of her voice.

"Samantha?"

Before he could say anything more, she explained the reason for her call and told him about the trip to Alaska.

His response was almost comforting in its predictability. "Alaska? What the hell for?"

Closing her eyes, she'd tightened her hold on the phone, unable to imagine Chase talking to Lisa in such a way. "It's an assignment, Dad."

His response to that was a non-committal grunt. "Well bring your mother a nice souvenir. Make her happy. It's the least you can do."

The least you can do.

Why did every request her father made, even the most minor ones, have to be delivered like a command? "I already have." Her response was laced with rebellion.

Not my job to make her happy, Dad, it's yours. Try it some time.

"I don't know why in hell you insist on traipsing all over the country."

"It's what I do, Dad."

"Well, it shouldn't be." The reply was gruff. "If you'd gotten your law degree like I wanted, you could be in practice with me now."

Samantha held the phone at arm's length. Maybe if she studied the instrument from a distance, she could make sense of this conversation. Working with her father; now that was a frightening thought. They couldn't even have a civil phone conversation when they were hundreds of miles apart. How would they do working together on a daily basis?

Does he realize this is a courtesy call? Does he realize that he can't dictate what I need to do anymore? Part of her wanted to tell him what was in her mind, to explain to him she was an adult and his control of her life was now officially over. "Is Mom there?"

As she waited for her mother to come on the line, she recalled the way Lisa always spoke of Chase. She tried to imagine having that same kind of feeling for Edwin Wells, and couldn't conjure up anything close. Those feelings simply didn't exist between the two of them, and certainly never would.

She went through much the same explanation of her current activities with her mother. This time, though still predictable, the response was a total opposite. "That's nice, sweetheart. Alaska in the summertime sounds marvelous." That was so her mother. Always accepting, never questioning her or whatever she chose to do. "Have a great time."

"I will." She almost uttered the automatic *love you, bye*, but she wanted to hang on to the comforting sound of her mother's voice, wanted to share her jumbled thoughts about a man she'd just met. The man who had stolen his way into her life and now refused to leave.

She needed her mother's advice.

What's happening to me?

In the end, she had quelled the urge to delve into a long description about the man and how he made her feel to *Love you, Mom. Bye*, and ended the conversation.

Her eyes flew open as she rolled to her other side and quietly punched the pillow in frustration. She'd now come full circle with her thoughts, back to Chase Canfield and her feelings for him. Unreturned feelings for him, she added as a sort of figurative cold shower. It didn't help. Tossing aside the covers, she grabbed her robe from the foot of the bed, pulled it quickly over her pink satin pajamas, and slipped out onto the veranda.

The peaceful Alaskan night was a welcome contrast to the turmoil of her thoughts. Soothing waves whispered against the ship's hull, a mild reverberation in the stillness. Strands of multi colored lights, strung stem to stern on the decks above her, reflected in shining ripples on the smooth surface of the water. Beyond that faint light, a blue black haze hid any landscape they might be passing.

Elbows resting on the short railing, she allowed the surrounding darkness to bring her into the comfort of its folds, until thoughts of where she was going and who was along started up again. Serenity vanished, and she lifted her eyes skyward, huffing out a sigh of annoyance. The restless toss of her head from one side to the other did little to dispel her irritation, then a movement to her left caught—then held—total awareness.

Too late she discovered Chase was out there too. Reclined in a deck chair, feet propped up on the railing with a blanket across his lap, he looked to be asleep. As far as she knew, she hadn't bothered him—yet. Not wanting to disturb him now, for his sake as well as for hers, she turned to go inside.

"Don't leave."

The softly spoken words stopped her progress and stilled her heart. She glanced toward the avenue of her escape, the room she shared with his daughter. Their ship's light cast a muted shadow on the girl's peacefully sleeping form. Torn between her two options—retreat to the safety of that room, or do as he asked and remain out here with him—she hadn't been able to budge to do either.

In the end, he made the choice as he set the blanket aside and walked over to stand beside her. "Please."

"I didn't want to wake Lisa." She spoke as if she owed him an explanation for being out there. "I couldn't sleep."

"Me either."

Tufts of sea chilled air blew upward in response to the ship's movement, yet his closeness, not the cool night breeze, caught her in a shiver. Saying nothing, he retrieved the blanket and settled it around her shoulders. She snuggled into the plush material which still held his warmth, and his scent.

Delicate waves continued to whoosh a tranquil cadence as they brushed along the side of the ship, and made her hesitant to speak. Not sure how to open the conversation and not wanting to disturb the peaceful setting, she said nothing.

His question broke into the silence. "What does Lisa think for far?"

She had an easy and truthful answer. "She loves everything."

"How about you? Are you having...enjoying yourself?" He turned slightly toward her as he spoke. The lights from his room allowed her to see his face, though she hoped her own uneasy expression remained in shadow. He could have no idea she needed to lie again, this time to cover up what she truly wanted to say.

Not with you so close and tempting every night and every day.

"Yes. As a matter of fact, I am. Lisa is a lot of fun to be around."

"I'm glad. Alaska is a beautiful place. You won't regret making this trip."

He turned toward her again, causing goose bumps to rise on her skin. She burrowed more deeply into the blanket, his blanket, as her eyes met his. "No. I shouldn't." *But, why do I?*

"At least the sight seeing part," he amended, then his gaze moved down her form, stopping momentarily as it slid over her exposed legs. For the first time, he seemed to notice she wore only short pajamas and a robe. "Still cold?"

"Really. I'm fine. I'm not cold."

Suddenly, she recalled the sweet pressure of his kiss, and a warm flush crept up her neck to settle on her cheeks. She ducked her face further into the blanket before he could notice.

"The glaciers out here are incredible," he said, and she was relieved their conversation was taking a safe, neutral path. "I learned a lot about the beauty of this place when I lived here." He went on to expound about vast resources and beautiful landscapes before he spoke again of Lisa. As she listened, she began to see the man he was inside emerge. Beyond Lisa's father or her boss's friend, even beyond her shallow notice of his physical attributes that first day in the coffee shop. She saw him as a man devoted to family, who cared about his child.

A man she could grow to love.

Once more she shivered as the strength of that particular notion shot through her. At the same moment, another of equal strength bounced back. *Loving him isn't an option.* Not now and not for her. She had a job to do. Period.

"How long did you live here?" It was her attempt to remain on the safe and neutral path.

"Five years."

"What did you do?"

He turned back to stare out into the night. "Worked for the Forestry Service."

"What did you do for them?" she prompted, not wanting to miss an opportunity to learn more about him.

"Conservation mostly. It was my job, with others, to catch the poachers before they did too much damage. At first, I thought I was enforcing the US Forestry Laws."

His comment surprised her. "You weren't?"

He shook his head. "The Indians who originally

settled this land believed animals were to be killed for food and clothing only. The carcass scraps and bones, what was left after man had what he needed, were always to be burned so the animal's spirit could recover." He looked directly at her. "I was simply enforcing beliefs here long before we were. I incorporate the gist of that philosophy into my lectures. There's a lot of bad inherent in this land, but also a lot of good. I want Lisa to see the good, while I protect her from the bad."

"You should be able to do that," she offered, not understanding why he couldn't. "This ship seems like a pretty safe place."

"Lisa's a very impressionable young girl. I hope you're right."

He had given her insight into his job, then shared with her his concern for his daughter. Now it was her turn to share information with him about how she was doing hers, on both fronts.

"I had the Darlings checked out. Ethan, too." She managed to bring up her most professional voice. "If that's any consolation. You said you didn't know them very well. I thought I could help put your mind at ease if I told you they're pretty solid citizens. No wants, no warrants. No customer complaints or rap sheets on any of them," she finished in a lighter tone.

"I appreciate you did that." His voice was so earnest and sincere, she had to remind herself his thoughts were for his daughter, not her. "But, can't you get in trouble for that kind of thing?"

"I still have friends in a number of police departments." It was all the explanation she felt compelled to provide. "Anyway, someone once said you only get in trouble if you get caught. And I don't plan to get caught."

There, she'd done her job. Stuck to business and kept the conversation on a reliable neutral path. She was feeling pretty good about that, until his next words changed the direction of that good old comfortable course, and pushed her off guard in the process.

"I owe you an apology for...my actions our first day on board."

She looked at him, not sure what her response should be, but he went on before she had a chance to form a thought.

"I should never have kissed you. I regret that." He studied her for a second then averted his gaze.

"That's okay," she managed, a little sad he could be sorry for a kiss which had come to mean so very much to her.

"We sort of got off on the wrong foot." There was no need for him to reach out and touch her; he'd already secured her undivided interest with his eyes. "I'd like to change that." His voice was barely above a whisper. "I also owe you an apology for barging in on your assignment."

"Then why did you?" The question was out before she could stop it, but she wanted to know why he didn't trust her.

"When I ran the idea of my coming along by Lisa, she seemed okay with it. I guess I should have run it by you as well."

"It would have been nice." She glanced out over the water then back at him. "There was no emergency call for a naturalist was there?" To her surprise, and a small amount of perverse delight, she watched him drop his chin to his chest then back up.

"Do you have to ask?" His response was suitably sheepish, and she recognized the admission was hard for him.

"I guess not."

"I called in every favor I'd ever earned around here to get assigned to this particular cruise ship on short notice."

She turned to lean her back on the railing. "It's been a long week."

"And, it's only Tuesday."

They both laughed and the simple, companionable sound echoed like a peace offering between them before silence descended.

Chase's voice broke into the night. "There must be a way to make this easier."

"I'm sure we'll find it." Her words rode a delicate mist that rose up to touch his cheek.

He'd moved so close, his body was at risk of making direct contact with hers. Light contact, but then, any contact would be too much. Need and desire danced along every fiber of her skin until she was sure sparks must have been flying out of her. Shooting skyward in tiny electric bursts, only to become harmless smoke on a waning hiss as they hit the water below. One more time a shiver took her.

"You *are* cold." He put his arm around her to draw her close, much as she'd seen him do so many times with Lisa. "And, I'm keeping you out here. Talking." He turned both of them toward the door to her room. "I should get to bed anyway. I have an early lecture tomorrow."

"I'd like to hear what you have to say."

She said it more out of nervousness at his touch than anything else. Maybe if she kept talking, she wouldn't have to deal with the physical sensations coursing through her. At the same time, she honestly did want to hear more. What little he'd already shared just now about this land fascinated her. "I'd like to attend one of your lectures."

"Eight thirty sharp." He sounded genuinely pleased by her interest.

"Oh, I'm sorry. I can't." She was surprised at how disappointed she really was.

"Really?" Was that disappointment she heard in

his voice, too?

"Lisa and I have plans. Mindy Darling has arranged a work-out class for some of the daughters and their mothers." She hurried on to dispel the unexpected intimacy that simple statement conjured up. "So many points are given for certain activities. I guess you can earn prizes. Tee shirts. Sweatshirts. That kind of thing. I thought Lisa might enjoy it."

"Oh."

"After all," she added, to cover their mutual disappointment. "Lisa is why I'm here."

"Of course." He cleared his throat. "Maybe the next one. I have three more scheduled this trip."

"Same time every morning?"

"Same time," he answered smiling.

She reached up to pull the blanket from her shoulders and found it trapped under his arm.

He put his hand over hers. "Keep this. For now." He pulled the wrap more tightly around her. "No sense you getting more of a chill than you already have."

His eyes indicated a sense of caring, yet she was certain an unnamed intensity filled them as well. His lids lowered slightly, much as they had before— twice before—each time before he'd kissed her. She felt herself start to lean forward, waiting to feel his fingers as they came up to caress her cheek. Waiting for his hand to cup the back of her neck and exert the slight pressure that would draw her face to his.

She closed her eyes as the gentle night air fluttered between them.

"Goodnight, Samantha."

She heard his words without feeling his touch, and her eyes opened again.

"Pleasant dreams, Chase." His name came out in a breathless whisper.

Then he was gone and she was back in her room. She stood just inside the door holding the blanket, his blanket, tightly around her. Finally, she placed it carefully at the foot of the bed next to her robe, and crawled under the safety of the covers.

For a long while, she lay very still, shielded by darkness, with the comfort of sleep just beyond her reach. Memories of his kiss had kept her up before. The fact he hadn't kissed her tonight, as she'd expected—and wanted—kept her up now.

Staring at the ceiling, she could do nothing more than contemplate this latest encounter with someone she didn't want to get to know. Someone she kept learning more about, and found herself, against all rhyme and reason, beginning to actually like as a person. Love as a man.

Chapter Six

Samantha glanced around the classroom designated for Chase's lectures. The term *state of the art* came to mind. An impressive array of silvery white projector screens and multi-colored maps lined all four walls. Additional high-end technical equipment sat on the front table beside a microphone fitted podium. The only commonplace furniture was the round, backless stool to one side.

Nearly all of the chairs, arranged in auditorium style seating, were filled. She was a bit surprised, and pleasantly impressed, at the number of people who were actually interested in what he had to say. Though a few empty places remained up at the front of the room, she purposely chose to sit toward the back.

After walking several laps around deck number four with Samantha, Lisa opted out of attending her father's talk in favor of breakfast with her friends, then the splurge, courtesy of her father, of a full spa treatment. Chase had offered Samantha the same indulgence but, suspecting he was only being polite, and feeling a little uncomfortable at the intimacy of the offer, she declined.

Truth be known, she preferred being here to watch him work.

Throughout the room, murmured conversations revealed shared expectations and experiences already enjoyed. Most of them, she discovered, at the suggestion of their ship's naturalist. Those conversations quickly ceased as Chase entered with a cheery, "Good morning, everyone."

Most, including Samantha, answered with a collective return greeting. The rest of the audience members merely positioned themselves, and their attention, toward his voice.

The naturalist they'd come to hear threw a "We'll get started in a moment," over his shoulder as he began to pull maps and charts out of a side cupboard. A few of the previous conversations resumed in response.

Having nothing better to do, Samantha found herself watching Chase. Not having seen much of him the day before, she hadn't expected to miss him as much as she had.

He wore jeans and a crew neck sweater. The jeans could well have been custom made, considering the way the supple denim material molded to his hips and legs. They fit tight enough over his backside to receive more than a few appreciative looks from a number of the female attendees, as she'd noted when he walked in. He turned to pull the scrolled map of Alaska into view then bent over to pick up a dropped pencil, and she caught herself taking in a quick breath. Along with half the other women in the room, she acknowledged, with a small flicker of indignation.

Shifting in her chair, she forced herself to concentrate on the sweater he wore instead. Brown with flecks of silver, and a perfect match for his eyes, it fit well across his shoulders, bloused slightly at his torso then covered his arms. Arms which held the strength to hold her close.

She shifted in her chair.

"You wanted a little intra-ship culture too, I see." Samantha glanced up as Rodney sat down beside her and smiled at the welcome distraction. "So how's the trip been for you so far?" He didn't give her a chance to answer before he asked another question. "Isn't the ship just absolutely spectacular? Totally fabulous, fabulous, fabulous!"

"It is beautiful." She managed to get that much into the conversation before Rodney took over again.

"Did you hear about the Captain?" He put his hand on her arm and leaned toward her as if she were his co-conspirator in some highly-classified covert operation. "As I understand...," his voice lowered as he cupped his hand against her ear then quickly brought his mouth there to reveal what he had prefaced to be a secret.

It seemed Brad and Rodney indulged in visits to the ship's spa every morning. Much like barber and beauty shops everywhere, the spa was a prime source of local gossip which, today, revealed a story about their captain having a mistress in Juneau and every other port of the Inside Passage. True or not, Samantha couldn't help but be tickled at Rodney's secretive manner. To him, everything and everyone was a great adventure to be explored with child-like wonder. A trait she enjoyed in him, and sometimes envied.

"Welcome to today's class." Chase's voice projected easily over the room and she only half listened to the balance of her seat mate's story.

He granted the attendees a uniquely special smile to accent his words and, even from a distance, that smile was able to raise her pulse rate more than she cared admit. He continued to glance around the audience and, as that glance settled briefly in her direction, the corners of his mouth dipped downward just enough to make her wonder if he wanted her there after all. Maybe his invitation had been meant only as a hollow courtesy, much like the over-used, *let's do lunch*. Whatever the reason for his apparent displeasure, she was here now and couldn't very well get up and walk out without drawing undue attention to herself.

"Erosion of a glacier is termed calving," he said to begin his lecture. "Most of you have probably witnessed the event, or something like it, on television. A portion of a glacier collapses into the water. It's a spectacular sight. But, up close and personal," did his eyes skim over her just then? From this distance, she couldn't be sure. "...it's truly breathtaking," he went on. "But, don't get the idea such beauty doesn't come without consequence. A calving glacier displaces water and releases a backlash of energy as the separated chunk of ice goes down, and can be devastating to whatever happens to be in its path."

Rodney shivered at the descriptive word picture. "Sounds frightening."

Still facing his audience, Chase turned their attention to the map behind him. "We are now entering Tracy Arm on the way to our next port of call, Juneau." His eyes drifted back to Samantha, then narrowed as they slid over Rodney. That she saw for sure. *What was his problem?*

"Over half a million acres make up the area. Six hundred thousand acres, to be exact, of relatively untouched," again his attention was drawn to Samantha, "Alaskan back country."

"He's quite the possessive sort." Rodney spoke close to her ear. Then, personal comment delivered, he pulled away to straighten in his chair. "I certainly got the message." He lifted his hands in the air, splayed open as if to signal surrender. "She's all yours, Fella," he mumbled.

"Rodney," Samantha admonished with a harsh whisper. "Shhhhh." She made a hasty, and veiled, survey around the room. If anyone had been bothered by their exchange, they didn't show it.

In the rest of his lecture, Chase relayed more facts about the region, the respect he held for the land evident in his tone. He wrapped up by urging guests to take the opportunity to explore the many sights in Juneau later that afternoon, then invited questions from the group.

"And, where might you be going?" A woman sitting in the front row posed the question, her inflection leaving no doubt there was an open invitation to accompany her if he were free.

He smiled at that, and again, Samantha's heartbeat notched up. "My plans haven't been set yet," he laughed, then his expression turned serious as, once again, he glanced at Samantha.

As some participants began to file from the room, others surrounded Chase to ask questions. Perfectly at ease, he lounged on the stool, one leg braced on the floor, the other foot resting on the bottom rung. He talked patiently to everyone who approached him, answering questions and offering advice.

Naturalist Conversations. Samantha remembered the term from the daily newsletter publicizing Chase's lectures, which was exactly how he conducted them. As intimate and relaxed conversations with friends. He had Lisa's same people skills, or, more accurately, she had his. He also had a special patience she hadn't seen in him before which was evident as he dealt with some of the more obtuse questions directed his way. Judging by the comments made and expressions shown by the people who had already talked to him, he seemed to have a way of making everyone who sought him out feel important.

She noticed women, more then men, tended to seek him out. *Natural order of things,* she told herself. It had nothing to do with the fact he was *brutally tall, dark, and handsome,* as she had heard one of the older women who was leaving comment. Females just naturally asked more questions than males, especially in relation to the environment. It was right up there with the well known adage about men never asking for directions.

On impulse, she reached for Rodney's arm. "Come on. I want you to meet him."

He made a feeble attempt to jerk free. "I'm supposed to meet Brad by the pool."

"Please." On her second try, she connected, circling her fingers on his forearm.

"Brad doesn't like it when I'm late," Rodney warned as he allowed himself to be pulled toward the front of the room, and Chase.

The last participant who lingered to talk was a younger woman with long blond hair and big baby blue eyes. Claret tipped fingers stayed on Chase's upper arm as she told him about the excursion she and her girlfriends were planning to take. From what Samantha could overhear, the event included a salmon bake and native Indian performance.

"You're welcome to join us if you like." The invitation was issued in a coy, but sultry voice, complete with the innocent batting of make-up extended lashes.

See yourself, Samantha? A nagging little voice intoned. *No!* she answered quickly, then just as quickly amended. *A little.*

"Thanks. I'm afraid I won't be able to make it," she heard Chase reply.

"Is he blushing?" Rodney had quit struggling against a very determined Samantha. "He is blushing. How cute!"

Still wearing an easy smile, Chase caught their approach and stood up. But, that was where, she noticed sadly, his smile ended.

She finally loosened her grip, releasing Rodney's arm in time for Chase to pick up his hand as she made the formal introductions. Acting the true tourist, he began to ask the naturalist's advice on the best ways to get the most out of their current trip. He even mentioned Brad's weak stomach, tendency for seasickness, and the problems that caused in choosing itinerary.

"Whale watching is out for us," he joked. Reciting from a printed brochure he held out in front of him, he went on. "Lovely small boats shuttle you, safely, into noted coves and inlets in search of spectacular views and the huge, gentle mammals." He glanced up. "Brad would spend the entire time hanging over the railing."

Chase let out a good natured laugh.

"We'll probably just do a more sedate clam bake and Indian dancing," Rodney finished, his tone indicating long suffering disappointment.

"Salmon bake," Chase corrected. "And, I'd say that's your best choice."

"Well, Brad is waiting." Rodney peeked up at the large wall clock above the door. "He hates it when I'm late." With an air kiss for Samantha, and a *nice meeting you* for Chase, he was gone and, as it turned out, so was everyone else who'd come to attend the lecture.

Chase began to stow the maps and charts he'd used in a side cabinet. "Your friend seems nice." His back to Samantha robbed her of the chance to view his true expression.

"Thanks. Your friend does too." She couldn't resist a reference to his salmon bake invitation.

He paused with his hand on a partially rolled up projector screen to cast her an easy over his shoulder glance that turned into a don't-even-go-there look of pretend warning.

"Breakfast?" Coming to her side, he turned her around with one hand on her shoulder, snapping off the light switch and closing the door with the other.

"Sounds great."

As they made their way toward the ship's cafeteria, she filled him in on how she had come to meet the duo of Rodney and Brad.

"It was nice to have the company," she said as she finished the explanation.

"I'll bet."

His hand rested at the small of her back, an action becoming so natural, she barely noticed its presence until he exerted more pressure to direct her through the door of the spacious dining room.

The distinct and strong aromas of frying bacon and sausage greeted them first, then mingled with the lighter scent of sweet baked goods. The rise and fall echoes of clattering dishes and shouted orders burst toward them next.

"How about an omelet?"

He guided her toward the appropriate line before she had a chance to answer one way or the other, but his choice turned out to be a good one. They quickly polished off made-to-order dishes, complimented with toast and juice, then, neither having anywhere to be, lingered over a second cup of coffee. Their table, in one corner of the noisy dining room, was near a bank of tall windows, affording them a spectacular view of the passing scenery.

As the ship approached another inlet and drew closer to the shore, the indistinct landscape of hazy mountains and blurred shorelines emerged into clearer focus. High-masted fishing boats dotted the water front, and an uneven cluster of log homes appeared in the valley between two hills. Here and there a cabin huddled close to the water.

Chin resting in her palm, she stared out at the stunning display. "Kind of gives new meaning to the term sparsely populated."

"When I worked for the Service I saw a lot of that territory."

"It's so expansive. How do you keep from getting lost?" She saw no roads leading either toward or away from the shore line, no rhyme or reason to the positions of the dwellings.

"Landmarks. You learn to read the mountains. Their shapes change, depending on what direction you see them from." He made the off-hand comments as he picked up his coffee then turned his attention away from the landscape. "So, you and Lisa seem to be getting along pretty well." He took a slow sip from his mug, watching her over its rim. "You get along with her better than I do."

"It's easy for me. I'm not her parent."

"It's different with you." He set down his cup. "We've had our disagreements." He pointed at himself then at her, and his brow furrowed and his eyes took on a worried cast. "But, at least when you get angry with me I know where I stand. With Lisa, I'm lost."

If nothing else, she appreciated his honesty as she recalled how she had seen him struggle to do the right thing by Lisa. This was not the time to launch into a *you need to do this, this, and this with your daughter* lecture. Still, she recognized an opportunity to fulfill the promise she'd made to Lisa a few nights before, to bring Chase around in the most sensitive way she could. Help him see his daughter was growing up and maybe needed just a little more freedom to accomplish that growing up. Except two things held her back. One, she wasn't exactly sure where to start and two, she and Chase were getting along remarkably well for a change and she hated to ruin the moment.

When she reminded herself this trip was for Lisa, not herself, she jumped feet first into giving advice. "You two have a very good relationship. From what I've seen."

"You think so?"

"I do." She softened her voice to show him understanding. He sat back, the anxious unease lifting from his features.

This was good. At least he was open to some discussion.

"Sometimes I believe I'm incapable of having a real relationship with her," he confided then glanced to the side. "Sometimes I think it will be better if I don't even try."

Lisa had one parent who had given up trying; Samantha couldn't stand by and allow the other to do the same. "You always have to try. Even when everything that's going on in your life seems to be saying otherwise." She wanted to make him see, on some level at least, Lisa was coming to such a time in her life. A time where she still needed him to be there for her, but needed him to trust and let her go. "There comes a time in everyone's life when they need to move beyond their day to day experiences. When they need to grow."

"I guess I can understand that."

That was painless. Bolstered by this first successful step, she took her advice a pace further. "And, it's usually when a special person comes into someone's life that those needs take on a special significance." She had decided not to name Ethan; she would leave that up to Lisa.

He angled her a sidelong look. "Yes?"

"It's not always easy, but when that happens sometimes action needs to be taken. And it's not always a painless action to take." *If I can, I want to spare Lisa making the same mistakes I did.* "I know these things."

He reached across the table to cover her hand. His thumb rubbed gently across the tops of her fingers, and she had to force herself to concentrate on what she was going to say next. Each time he touched her, a tiny spark flickered to life and found the strength to burn into a full fledged flame. If he had any idea of the effect he was having on her, he gave no indication in his expression.

"How would you know?"

"I learned from my own father. In my case, I was never able to please him." The words came out flat, devoid of emotion, as if never having her father's approval no longer mattered to her. Because it didn't.

She went to pull her hand away only to find his grasp tighten slightly.

"I never would have suspected that." He finally released her hand as leaned back in his chair.

"It's true." She gathered up her cup between both hands, more to warm the surfaces which now felt cold at the loss of his touch.

"It just sounds strange to hear you say that. I guess I didn't expect it of you."

"Maybe you don't know me as well as you think you do."

"Oh really?" His eyes flashed an emotion which passed too quickly for her to read then his gaze settled on her with amused scrutiny.

"Yes, really." It was the only comeback she had, and before she could pull away, his hand took hers again.

The flame, never completely extinguished from before, rekindled, flared anew and began to grow, causing a dangerous heat to spread through her limbs. And, all he had done was touch her hand. What else was he capable of doing to her? She had a feeling she wasn't ready for the answer.

"Maybe I should work on that." She heard this last statement and wondered if, lost in her own thoughts, she'd missed words that came before. Maybe those words were proof she'd gotten through to him after all about his relationship with Lisa.

"Work on what?" she asked without thinking.

His other hand came across the table to capture both of hers, and he leaned toward her.

"Getting to know you better." His voice was a

low, intimate whisper that made her want to close her eyes and willingly offer herself up for his continued touch. She was sure the emotions playing across her face at that moment must have been transparent enough to broadcast the fact loud and clear. The only control she somehow managed to exert over herself was to keep a sigh of acceptance from escaping her lips.

"Does that scare you?" he asked as if picking up on, and enjoying, her reaction to him.

"What?" She began to look away and he squeezed her hand, forcing her to look back at him.

"That I want to get to know you better?" His voice was so low she could do nothing but push forward to hear him. "Does it scare you?"

"Should it?"

"Not at all."

All thoughts of her speaking on behalf of Lisa slipped far, far away. Somehow he had managed to turn their conversation around, yet again, back to the two of them. In addition, his smile as he spoke almost unhinged what little platonic resolve she had been clinging on to. It was all she could do to remain in her seat, to not jump across the table into his arms, and overwhelm him with her kiss.

"There you are! We've been looking for you."

The distinctive sound of Lisa's voice brought her fantasy up short, and she could only hope the expression on her face wasn't a beacon of her thoughts. Chase released her hand at the intrusion as they both sat back. Ethan was with her, and Lisa bounced down into the empty chair beside Samantha, leaving him no choice but to take the seat beside Chase, which he did with shy caution.

"How was the spa?" her father asked. "Did you enjoy yourself?"

She cast a surreptitious peek up at Ethan. "Yeah, I did."

The boy's face became tinged with crimson. "I told her she was beautiful, spa treatment or not."

"You did?" Chase said.

Ethan's guilt-filled eyes shot his way. "Yeah. Uh, I hope you don't mind, sir."

Chase glanced over at Lisa's glowing face. "Not at all," he replied with a look of mild consternation. "Not at all."

"Did Coach tell you how we did in volleyball yesterday?" Lisa asked. She picked up a half eaten piece of toast from Chase's discarded plate, studied it intently, then set it back down.

"No. She didn't." He sat forward as if eager to have another chance to learn something else he didn't know about his daughter's chaperone.

"We won!" she answered proudly, striking a spontaneous high five with her *coach*. "Every match!"

"Really?" As usual, his open expression showed how amused and pleased he was Lisa was having a good time. Samantha was happy to think part of that pleasure might be because of something she had done.

"Coach is just awesome as a player. Digging out passes. Spiking the ball over the net. You should watch her play sometime, Daddy."

"Yeah," he agreed, the suggestive air of mischief in his expression for only Samantha to pick up on. "I should."

She made a half hearted attempt to ignore the implied proposition as she explained the matches had taken place, impromptu style at the end of their work out session. "The net was there. We were there," she concluded with a shrug, conscious Chase still watched her. "But me? You should have seen your daughter. She had a phenomenal run...seven points...on one of her service positions."

"Only because you cheered me on. Telling me I

could do it," the girl replied on a grin. "With that kind of encouragement, anyone could have done as well."

"You're the one who did," Samantha replied. "So what else have you been doing?"

Lisa proceeded to rattle off a laundry list of activities she'd recently been part of, then her tone grew serious. "And tonight is our next to the last night here." She glanced around to indicate the ship itself. "On board."

"The day after tomorrow we take to the land, huh?" Samantha looked to Ethan both for confirmation and to draw him into the conversation. The poor boy had been unusually quiet since he'd arrived.

"The bus leaves at ten thirty am," he responded.

"One small bag is all we're allowed. Right?" Samantha asked. "Two nights on the road. Whitehorse. Denali Park. The rest of our bags will be sent to the hotel in Anchorage?"

"If you're lucky," Ethan started to joke, then like Lisa, his tone turned serious. "No. I'm kidding. This line is very good about keeping track of luggage." He seemed to have a hard time looking Chase in the eye. Finally, he took a deep breath and turned toward Samantha. "Did you get my mother's message? She said she was going to call you."

Something in his manner told her this wasn't good. "She might have," she replied. "I haven't been in our room since early this morning. Why?"

When Ethan hesitated, Lisa spoke up. "You can tell them, Ethan. They won't bite." She looked over at Chase, a small smile curling her mouth. "You won't bite. Will you, Daddy?"

"I might," he deadpanned. "Depends on what it is."

Ethan said nothing, just looked at Lisa as if his mouth had suddenly been molded shut. The crimson surge returned as he tried to look back at Chase.

"What's going on, son?"

"We have a slight problem," he blurted, dropped his eyes then raised them again. "Ma'am. Sir," he took his time looking at each adult. "It seems the Denali excursion, the land part of this trip, was overbooked." He gulped a nervous swallow then continued. "When the name change was made at the last minute," he indicated Samantha, "the reservation was sort of deleted. And you, sir," he rotated toward Chase and swallowed again before he went on. "Never had a reservation in the first place. My mother was going to talk to you about all of this." The boy raised his hands, palms out, obviously uncomfortable being the bearer of bad news. "She was going to call you."

"So the three of us will just figure something else out," Chase responded simply as if there were no problem at all. "There's a lot to see in this state."

Ethan faced him head on. "Actually, sir,"

"Actually?" Chase echoed, then straightened in his chair.

Ethan did the same. "Lisa's reservation is intact. Along with everyone else in the group. It's just yours, and," he seemed to cast around for the right name to use for Samantha before settling on Lisa's choice, "Coach's."

Chase sat forward, Ethan leaned back.

"So what you're saying is..." he indicated Lisa with a lifted finger, "she's in and we're out." The finger pointed to him and Samantha in turn.

Ethan's initial response was a meager smile he quickly strengthened. "Your reservations were made at the last minute. I know that's no excuse, but...I'm sure my parents will be happy to provide you with some form of compensation. Pay for alternate transportation. I..."

Chase put up a hand to, gently, cut him off.

"That's not necessary, son. Mistakes happen."

"But, I can still go. Right?" Lisa broke in.

"I'm not sure about that...,"

Here we go again! Samantha thought.

"But, Dad I...," Lisa began then clamped her mouth shut at her father's sharp look.

"I'm not sure, Lisa!" His no nonsense voice was strong enough to catch her attention, along with the awareness of some people at a few surrounding tables.

The girl completed an adolescent perfect eye-roll, heavy sigh maneuver. "There you go being my non-supportive father again."

Chase could only look back at her, releasing an exasperated sigh of his own, minus the eye-roll. Samantha regarded him as he seemed on the verge of yet another heated verbal exchange with his daughter. *Hadn't he gotten anything out of their recent conversation?* Up until now she had stayed out of their minor confrontations, had tried to stay neutral. Until Chase made the decision to join this trip, Samantha had been charged with taking care of Lisa on her own. If he hadn't been here, her decision would be to let Lisa go. She made that decision now, and decided to speak up on Lisa's behalf.

"I think you should let her go." There, she made her opinion known. Now, she just had to drive that view home. "It certainly sounds like enough parents will be with her. And her friends."

Bolstered by this new ally, Ethan raised his head to bring himself eye to eye with Chase. "I've taken the trip twice, sir." To his credit, the gaze didn't falter. "It's perfectly safe."

"I'm sure Lisa will be fine, Chase."

"My parents will be there," Ethan offered.

Reaching across the table, Samantha carefully placed her fingertips on Chase's arm, meant to provide reassurance, she wanted so badly to will him into making what she knew his daughter would consider the right call.

"The rest of your group is going. Right?" He looked directly at Ethan. "All the parents? Right?"

"Right, sir."

"Oh, right, Daddy," Lisa agreed, an amiable bundle of cooperative energy.

"Okay then, you can go."

"Thank you so much." She leaned toward Samantha, arms extended, inviting—or asking for—a hug. Samantha readily complied, squeezing with the added fervor of their shared victory.

Chase looked expectantly at his daughter. But when she made no move toward him, he dropped his eyes, and Samantha almost wished Lisa hadn't hugged *her* quite so readily.

"I'll go tell my parents," Ethan said. "I'll let them know they will be in charge of Lisa. Of course they already know that. And, I promise you, sir, they'll take really good care of her, sir."

"I hope so," Chase replied.

"I'll go with you," Lisa exclaimed. She and Ethan stood up in one motion, then both looked quickly toward Chase who nodded his assent. This time, she wrapped eager arms around her father who clutched her close in response. "I'll see you guys at dinner," she finished over her shoulder as she and Ethan rushed off.

Chase watched them for a moment then pushed his cup to the middle of the table.

"That went well." He rubbed the back of his neck as he cast questioning eyes toward Samantha. "Do teenagers ever quit?"

She kept her tone casual as she quelled a nervous laugh. Now that she'd convinced him to lighten up on Lisa, she hoped it was the right thing to do. "Quit what? Being teenagers? Yeah. When they reach twenty."

"So only four more years of this?" Though his tone was hopeful, the worry in his eyes told another story.

"Something like that," she replied. "If my experience is any indication."

"Experience as..." His gaze shot over her. "You don't have any kids, do you?"

"No." She laughed at the thought. "I haven't even come close. Not yet, anyway," she added on another laugh, this one rather strained. She did want children, at the right time, and, of course, when the right person was in her life.

"That's too bad. I've seen you with Lisa. I think you'd make a good mother."

"I was referring to my experience as a daughter," she continued quickly, wondering one second if he'd read her mind, then, the next, convincing herself there was no way he could have. "My father and I would go round and round like that. Like you and Lisa. Sometimes we still do."

"So," he gave her a slow look as if he were measuring her ability to advise him about the perils of parenthood. She shifted slightly under his stare. "Speaking as an experienced daughter. Does she know that I love her?"

"Deep down, she does. And I'm sure she loves you too. It's just easier at this point in her life to sort of deny it, to pretend she doesn't." Her nervousness caused her to ramble. "Love you, I mean."

So why are you denying your own love? Her pesky inner voice made the challenge. *You with your lofty ideas and proclamations about life.*

"So if you deny love, pretend it isn't there. Try to convince yourself it doesn't exist? Then it's easier. Is that it?" Somehow, as he talked, he'd leaned across the table, shrinking the space between them and finishing his questions with his face very close, dangerously close, to hers.

She tried to ignore her pounding heart as it struck a pitter patter beat up to her throat. "Something like that," she managed.

"Interesting. So if you deny love. It's just easier. That doesn't mean it isn't there. Right?"

"Right," she admitted, wanting only to close a conversation which had become decidedly too personal. "I hope Lisa has a good time."

She also hoped she'd just guided Chase into the right decision.

Guided? She'd practically railroaded the man. Spur of the moment and in front of Lisa to boot. Not one of her better planned out reactions to a personal and private situation. And what if her response turned out to be wrong?

She'd been so caught up with helping Lisa, she'd forgotten all about helping herself. *Concentrate on the assignment. Complete the job.* Those phrases had been her mantras of survival. Now she didn't have those. Her *assignment* was moving on without her.

Plus, she'd done precisely what she'd sworn to never do again. Gotten personally involved in a case. She'd been so sure of herself, and so proud of her ability to obtain background checks on the Darling family. They'd been so squeaky clean, she hadn't even entertained the notion it wouldn't be a good idea for them to be responsible for Lisa.

Her decision, right, wrong or side-ways, wasn't all that was important, she told herself now. The fact remained; she'd crossed a self-imposed, but still forbidden line. She'd become personally involved in a private family matter. An assignment's family matter.

Would she never learn?

Chapter Seven

Samantha studied herself in the full length mirror mounted inside the closet door. Tonight was the captain's dinner and, for many of the passengers and crew the formal evening was a highlight of the cruise.

Her dress for the event was a strapless sheath of black scalloped lace over turquoise satin with the skirt ending mid calf in a row of more black lace. She wondered briefly if the strapless style was too daring, then, caught in a flare of devil-may-care recklessness, decided the dress was just fine. Fastening a delicate choker of pearls suspended on thin gold wire at her throat, she hooked matching pierced earrings into place. With a slight shake of her head, she sent the delicate dangles swaying as she gave herself one last look.

"What do you think?" Lisa appeared from behind a short curtain she'd drawn between the two beds, her face a glowing mix of unconcealed excitement and shy anticipation.

The dress she wore was all pink and flowery and sweet, with a matching ribbon to catch up her hair. Tiny spaghetti straps formed a criss-cross pattern over her shoulders and down her back, while the long airy skirt flowed to just above her ankles. Samantha smiled as this girl on the verge of womanhood walked toward her.

"You'll turn heads tonight. I only hope your father can handle it."

"Daddy helped me pick this dress out," she noted

with an air of pride as she peered into the mirror Samantha had just stepped away from.

"Really?"

Maybe Lisa's Daddy isn't so off base after all.

"You look awesome, Coach! You'll turn heads of your own."

Samantha checked her image one last time. "Thank you."

At least the affirmation from Lisa helped quell the butterflies which once more took up residence in her mid section. They'd moved in the first day she'd set eyes on Chase Canfield and had been with her ever since. Relatively quiet tenants, most of the time, they really came to life during those occasions when he kissed her. How many times was it now? Twice—almost three?

Kisses aside, all he had to do was be near. The man had such a tremendous power over her emotions and she had absolutely no idea what to do about it. Check that, she did too. When in doubt, de-escalate the situation, take control. First and foremost, she needed to avoid being alone with him tonight. Which should be easy enough to accomplish, since most of the passengers and a good share of the crew would be around. And Lisa would be with them, she'd be careful to make sure of that.

"Ethan said he'd look for me tonight." Lisa cast her a backward glance, wide eyes gauging her reaction. "He's asked me to sit with him and his parents for dinner. Daddy already said it was okay."

She calmly folded her hands across her middle to keep the butterflies from jumping through her skin. "Really?"

****

Damn!

For the umpteenth time, Chase tried, and failed, to fasten the last button at the top of his heavily starched tuxedo shirt. One part of the formal outfit, rented from the ship's stores, he was now trying with some effort, to get into. Mouth set in grim resolve; he fumbled once more with the offending button, before he heaved out a frustrated sigh and dropped ineffective hands to his sides.

Not even dressed yet and already he was a nervous wreck. *Bad sign.*

Dressing up under any circumstances was just not his style. Jeans and a flannel shirt, he could identify with those clothes. Not tonight though; tonight he was stuck with this damned monkey suit.

It's the tux. The damned tux was the cause of all his problems. It was no doubt the wrong size and, therefore impossible for him to wear.

He knew that wasn't true even as the idea hit him. It wasn't the tux or the shirt or anything other piece of clothing that had his nerves on edge, it was her and him, and this damned uncooperative body of his. Every time she was around, he felt like a horny, hormone driven teenager, and there was absolutely nothing he could do about it.

This wasn't exactly how he had planned his life. And yet, this was how he'd always dreamed his life could be. Or at least imagined how it was supposed to be. It felt so right to him being with Samantha. Being anywhere with her and his world was complete. What happened between them so far had been perfect, a part of his life he wouldn't have missed for anything.

But, something, ego perhaps—or fear of failure—kept him from sharing these newly discovered personal revelations with her. What if she didn't agree with his—assessment?

Damn. As usual, memories of her and vivid imaginings of what they might become came to mind without much effort. Then, to make matters worse, the harder he tried to ignore the images, the more they insisted on recognition.

He remembered his first glimpse of her, all softness and curves and beauty. His mind replayed the sound of her voice, the sparkle in her eyes when she smiled. As thoughts of Samantha took over his brain his body jerked to alert. The lower part, in particular provided a purely physical and typical male response to such suggestive mental stimulation. He looked quickly down below his belt for any outside evidence and, to his relief, found none. Luckily, the trousers that went with the tux were loose enough to provide him some privacy, which was something. If he had to walk around all night with the unwanted reaction, no one would know but him. And boy, would he ever.

The couple of kisses he'd managed to claim from her so far just weren't making it for him anymore. And there was nothing he could do about that either.

Damn! His fingers were like ineffective clubs as he tried again to close the top button on his shirt. Giving up if only momentarily, he slipped on the shiny black wing tips. Just a little bit snug. Good, they'd provide a diversion of sorts. If he concentrated on his feet hurting all evening, it would spare him having to concentrate on other parts of his body.

A collage of uncalled exposés of Samantha came to mind as if his subconscious sought to torment him even more. Unfortunately, the pictures his mind brought were of her paired with any number of other partners. The guy in her office, the duo she picked up on the plane. Not caring for the offered set of mental pictures, he conjured up an illustration of his own.

One which had her paired with him and naked.

"Dad?" A knock sounded on his door between the two rooms. The knob rattled. "This is locked. Are you ready?"

"Almost." Absently, he walked over to let her in.

"The reception starts at six. In twenty minutes."

As usual, mouth going, she bounded full blast into the room. "We need to get going."

"I'm just trying to get this...confounded..." The sight of his daughter, and what she was wearing, cut him short.

Momentarily forgetting his wardrobe dilemma, he took his time absorbing her appearance, emotions moving between pride and sadness. She was young, she was beautiful and she was growing up way too fast. So fast, the speed of it sometimes took his breath away. He wanted only to do what he had done when she was just a little girl, wrap her in his arms and keep her safe from the world, while, all the while knowing in his heart, he couldn't make her stay a little girl forever.

"Honey, you are gorgeous."

"Thanks," she said with uncharacteristic shyness. "Wait until you see Samantha."

"You like her, don't you?" Asking the question was just a formality, he already knew the answer.

"I do," she replied. "I'm glad you do, too."

He shot her a look at the last comment. *Was he so transparent?* He tried to come up with a suitable reply, but Lisa spared him the trouble.

"Oh wait!" She jumped up from the bed she'd just plopped down on. "I forgot my necklace. I'll be right back!" With that, she disappeared into the other room.

Fingers to his collar, he turned back to the mirror beginning to hate—actually hate—the top button of his shirt. This inanimate object causing him so much trouble. Maybe he could somehow fashion a neck tie over the damned button and no one would notice it was undone.

He reached for the clear plastic bag he'd torn open then tossed at the foot of the bed. The package contained cuff links and matching studs. At least he'd been able to connect those items together at all the right spots. Searching the bag again, all he found was a thin, single strand of black cloth.

Great! They didn't even have the decency to provide a simple clip on style tie.

He muttered yet another curse as he started to bring the thin piece of material to his neck, not at all sure what he was going to do next.

"Can I help?"

At the sound of her voice, his fingers froze mid trip. He should have known she was behind him before she even spoke. Should have recognized, as he did now, the sweet, tantalizing smell of her which was becoming more and more familiar to him.

He turned around slowly and, one look had his breath stolen away again. Seeing Lisa, he'd felt pride and love. Seeing Samantha, he felt something else mixed with the love. Something warm and comfortable spread through him as the L word so easily entered his mind. But then, he really shouldn't be surprised.

She was all lace and satin and beauty. Her dress clung exactly where it was supposed to and draped everywhere else. The curve of her neck, the slant of her bare shoulders, begged to be caressed then kissed. The pulse at the side of that beautiful throat seemed to quicken in response as he regarded her. She was dangerously close. That, mingled with the scent of her, was enough to send all his senses careening out of control. At that instant, he wanted more from her than anything he had taken before. More than just the warmth of her kiss, he wanted all of her. No barriers, no restrictions.

If Lisa hadn't been in the next room, he swore he'd gather Samantha into his arms, lay her across his bed and follow her down. He'd make love to her with all the passion and need he had in him, giving her the pleasure and consideration she deserved.

An involuntary tension just south of his

waistline reinforced his private thoughts. He closed his eyes on a sigh; he couldn't worry about that now.

"If you would." It was all he had in him to say.

"Hold still. Please."

He could do nothing but drop his hands, the tie left to dangle, limply, from his fingers. She stood on tip toe, her focus not on him but on the button beneath her fingers. As her lips pursed in concentration, his mouth twitched in response. Her breath was warm as it fluttered across his neck and the term weak in the knees became more than just an expression for him. He flexed his legs slightly, fearing they would give out on him if he didn't. In the process his thigh brushed against hers.

Eyelids lowered in distinct reaction, she pushed the errant button into place as if she'd been infused with a sudden burst of efficiency and strength. Had her breathing quickened when she reached down to take the tie from his fingers? He couldn't tell. His own breathing had become so ragged, it took a resolute effort on his part to bring it under control.

Concentrate. Inhale and exhale. Inhale and exhale. On the last exhale, he watched his breath lift a wispy curl at the side of her temple.

She leaned up and into him as she brought the tie around his neck. On tip toe again, her body barely skimmed over his with a tortuous slowness. He silently cursed the tuxedo with all its elaborate trimmings, along with his inability to even dress himself. Then he went on to curse the current effect she was having on him, in a purely primitive way, at another involuntary rise below his belt he was powerless to prevent. All he could do was shift that area of his body away from her. Now, before his secret was revealed.

His thought to move away came too late, the actual action even later still. At that precise moment, she swayed against him and her sharp gasp said it all. Eyes growing wide, they met his in recognition and mutual understanding, then her lashes fluttered down to shut him out.

She fashioned the tie into place with a touch so delicate, so shattering, it caused him to suck in his breath. The very breath, only moments before, he'd held so consciously under control. Now he was in control of absolutely nothing, not even himself. Especially not himself.

"There." She completed one final adjustment and, thankfully, moved away from him.

His desire was only to maintain physical contact, wrap her into his arms, and hold her tight.

"Looks good. Thanks."

Making a show of readjusting the tie, in reality, he was trying to readjust his life. He felt as if he were choking, gasping for air, fighting like a drowning man through a maze of unknown channels and uncharted rivers.

"I'm ready!" Lisa's voice helped him break to the surface.

"Shall we go then?" he said, pleased to hear, though his lower body had betrayed him, his vocal chords had not.

Meager consolation in the scope of things, but he'd take it.

****

Lisa was out from between the parting elevator doors as soon as they arrived on the eighth floor. It took a moment before Chase and Samantha could follow. Although strategically spaced signs indicated the way to the reception which preceded the Captain's Dinner, they needed only to follow the other formally dressed patrons going in the same direction, and caught up with her a few moments later.

"We wait here for our chance to meet the captain," she announced with new found authority as they joined her in line. "I asked."

They stood in a wide hallway, its walls rimmed by thick, heavily lacquered banisters, one on each side. As the human column snaked around the final corner, they came into an open area, where an intricate crystal and gold chandelier winked and twinkled its lighting from a plush carpeted floor to an arched cathedral ceiling.

The captain and top officers, in the full formal dress of starched white jackets replete with colorful insignia, made up a reception line to one side. An attractive young woman, perhaps a few years older than Lisa, stood to the captain's left.

"Name please," she requested as they approached.

"Canfield, " Chase said, then went to introduce Samantha, but never got the chance.

"Captain Dorsair, may I present Mr. and Mrs. Canfield. And daughter Lisa," the girl finished as Lisa gave her name.

"Mr. Canfield, our naturalist. Nice to finally meet you." As expected, the ship's commander emoted abundant charm and confidence in keeping with his position.

"Captain." Chase reached out his hand which the older man pumped with enthusiastic zeal.

Drawing Samantha forward, he opened his mouth to properly introduce her, but Captain Dorsair was already clasping her extended hand in both of his. "And, Mrs. Canfield, lovely to meet you as well." He brought the back of her right hand to his lips.

"Samantha," she said simply. "And, actually, it's Wells. I'm not Mrs. Canfield."

"Ah, even better, Samantha," the man repeated, his close set eyes registering obvious approval. "A pleasure."

She had the bizarre image of a black and white

movie clip with the mustachioed villain touching his lips to some poor damsel's hand, then running a trail of lascivious kisses up her arm before he buried his face in the curve of her neck. As he kept her hand poised below his mouth, she wondered if Rodney's spa-gathered rumors might be true.

"You command a beautiful ship," she murmured. Well aware of the slight swell of his chest and stiffening of his posture, she smiled her most blameless smile before pulling herself free, taking Chase's offered arm to help her move away from him.

Her first thought, as they made their way down the rest of the reception line, was how nice it was to have the security, and strength, of someone like Chase—no, to have Chase—beside her. Before she could thank him for the subtle rescue, they entered the carefully controlled chaos of the formal ballroom.

This area was larger and more impressive than any other part of the ship. Another gilded and crystal chandelier, this one at least three feet in diameter, descended from the vaulted ceiling to shower the guests below with a kaleidoscope of twinkling illumination. Identical fixtures, though smaller in scale, were affixed to each of the four corners, to glitter their own light show out and into the room.

The rise and fall murmur of so many different conversations became a muted roar as more and more enthusiastic passengers crowded into the festive room.

Uniformed wait staff moved nimbly about hoisting large round trays laden with delicate long-stemmed glasses, some filled with clear, bubbling liquid, others containing fluid a rich yellowish orange in color.

"Champagne and fruit nectar," one waiter explained as he stopped before them with a small bow then lowered his tray for their inspection.

Chase was careful to hand a glass of nectar to Lisa then, lifting two glasses of champagne from the tray, he passed one to Samantha and kept one for himself.

Eyes wide in adolescent awe, Lisa looked across the room. "There's Susie and Jenna. Oh. And, Ethan with his parents," she whispered, lowering those expressive eyes in demure shyness. "I wonder if he sees me," she murmured, before raising her gaze in expectation.

As it turned out, Ethan was of a similar mind. Catching her eye, he waved and, his mother, seeing the exchange, motioned for Lisa to join them. She made a move forward, then stopped to look questioningly at Chase.

"Go ahead," he said, smiling.

Lifting her glass to keep its contents intact, she swiftly made her way through the crowd.

Taking a substantial sip of champagne, Chase glanced over at Samantha. "What else am I going to do?"

"Nothing."

"In this case, I feel a little like I just set her up on a date."

Following his tilted head, she looked over to where his daughter had joined the Darlings. Mindy stood between Lisa and Ethan, large smile in place, one arm around each of them, talking non-stop. "Lisa seems okay with it."

Chase cut her a glance, then took a closer look. "She does appear to be enjoying herself, I'll give you that," he replied, watching Lisa laugh at something Ethan said.

"Isn't that what this is all about?" Samantha countered. "I mean, strictly from a parental point of view?"

He cast her another quick look. "Uh-huh."

"Mr. Canfield!"

Chase turned at his name, and Samantha recognized two women who had been at his lecture that morning. She remembered them because they sat in the front row, center chairs, taking what appeared to be elaborate notes.

"Mr. Canfield," they exclaimed in unison, faces reflecting eager anticipation.

"We had some things to ask you about the glaciers we'll be seeing tomorrow," the taller one explained.

"Sure," he replied. "But first, I'd like to introduce you to Samantha Wells."

The women each gave their names, offering her polite notice before turning their full attention on Chase and the subject they'd come to discuss.

More observer than participant in the ensuing exchange, Samantha set her almost empty glass onto a passing tray and stole a sidelong glance at her escort. Formal attire flattered him, but, as far as she was concerned, he would have looked just as appealing in a ratty tee shirt and cut off jeans. She watched his face as he responded to a litany of questions, his expression relaxed, and a congenial smile in place.

It felt good to stand beside him on one side of the huge room while, across the way, his daughter, bright eyed and laughing, was surrounded by friends. How, after only a few short days, had she become so involved in Chase and Lisa's lives? Easily and without conscious effort? She had no answer for that, but with Chase still involved in conversation, she simply took time to bask in the sheer joy of a special moment.

"Mr. Canfield," she heard one woman say after awhile. "Is there anything you don't know?"

"There's plenty I don't know." He chuckled, then looked knowingly at Samantha. "Just ask my teenage daughter."

"Don't listen to him," she joked, joining the conversation. "He's a great father." Only after she'd made the comment, did she realize how true her statement was.

She opened her mouth to elaborate, when the woman who had been doing most of the talking spoke up again.

"Oh! That's our song." She referenced a low-key melody the orchestra had started to play. "Harold will be looking for me. We always dance to this."

Excusing herself, her companion in tow, they headed back into the crowd.

"How about us?" Chase had turned toward her, still smiling. As his eyes came to rest on her face, he extended one hand. "Shall we?"

Nodding her assent even as he took her into his arms, she closed her eyes to rest her head on his chest. His body was solid and warm, his breathing steady and reassuring.

The song was *Unchained Melody*, originally recorded by the Righteous Brothers. The person singing now was doing a pretty good job of running up and down the scales with his lyrics, and hitting high notes the late Bobby Hatfield was famous for.

I need your love, I need your love,
The talented vocalist implored.
God speed your love, to me.

Was Chase holding her closer in response to those lyrics? Or was she allowing herself to indulge—again—in wanting him to? Right now, the reason didn't matter. Right now, it was so good simply to be as she reveled in the special feel of him and comfort of being held.

Their feet barely moved as their bodies swayed in perfect rhythm with the music; torsos and thighs playing a sensual game of catch and release. The physical contact was light, almost remote, yet each subtle connection held an intimate and unique signal.

Soft music, chilled champagne, the closeness of this man, proved to be a potent enough combination to engulf Samantha's senses. Everywhere their bodies touched, magic flared, making the new strange and unsettling sensation creeping over her all the more unwelcome.

This impression held no magic. This was sheer blue-gut intuition nagging at her that something was wrong. Standing in Chase's arms felt too right, too perfect, but the unease persisted until it became so powerful, she could do nothing but concede to it.

She lifted a reluctant head to watch others around them. Then instinct made her immediately seek out and find Lisa.

When she did, her insides seized; her body set up for battle. This went beyond a cop's suspicions. This was personal. An older man, an *unknown* older man, had pulled Lisa away from the group and now loomed over her like a vulture sizing up its prey. Samantha had noticed the mope standing alone against one wall when she and Chase entered the ballroom. Dressed in a plain brown suit with his tie loose and slightly pushed to one side, she'd seen him survey the room with measured disinterest, yet something about his posture alerted her he might bear watching.

Now she saw he held a second glass of champagne which he advanced toward Lisa. Though his mark smiled politely, her body language told Samantha she was uncomfortable. Maybe even a little afraid.

Without a word, she backed out of Chase's arms.

"What's going on?" he asked.

She was already hastening to Lisa's side.

The crush of party-goers prevented her from getting there as fast as she wanted. Not wanting to make a scene by calling out or ordering the man to stop his advances, she wended her way forward, all the while keeping Lisa in view. Continuing her struggle through the crowd, she was too far away to make physical contact, but close enough to hear what was being said.

"The northern lights are all ablaze tonight," the man was telling Lisa. Though he sounded completely sincere, her cop instincts registered a different motive. "By the stern at deck ten," he noted with phony nonchalance, taking a sip of his drink and indicating she do the same.

"Oh, I'd love to see them."

Samantha could only shake her head. That was so Lisa. Always polite and accepting—to a fault.

She made a mental note to arm her charge with some self-defense moves and letch evasion tactics the next time she got the chance. But then, letch evasion tactics didn't always work with determined perverts. Like Harvey Klein. Fresh anger at that recollection caused already high adrenaline levels to spike. Good. She'd need the extra power to take care of this creep.

"How can I ever thank you?" was Lisa's pleasant response to something else the predator said.

"Oh, don't thank me now. You can thank me, properly, later."

At his sinister little snicker, Samantha's back stiffened. She was sure there was nothing proper in the scenario running through this guy's brain— provided he had one. With a final surge of effort, she made her way past the last human obstacle.

"Northern Lights, you say?" She murmured as she stepped between the perp and his victim, intercepting the glass of champagne he'd been so intent on sharing. "That's nice to know."

She set the untouched liquid onto a passing tray when all she really wanted to do was dump its contents over his head.

The man's startled gaze shot over her at the intrusion. Mouth open, his now empty hand still poised in mid air, he cleared his throat as a crimson blush crawled from his neck, over his face and up his forehead to disappear far into his scalp.

"Yes." Though it was obvious he'd been caught in a lie, he seemed determined to convince Samantha of its truth. "Off deck ten."

Too bad she wasn't buying it. "Thanks so much," she answered with interest as faked as his. "We'll have to check them out for ourselves."

Turning to carefully steer Lisa away, they almost bumped head long into Chase and Ethan. Samantha was struck by the similarity of their expressions: concern and the grim evidence of suppressed anger.

"Just an over zealous vacationer," she said, using her calming cop's voice to defuse what could easily become a volatile situation.

"He didn't hurt you, did he?" Ethan grabbed Lisa's full attention before Chase had a chance to do the same. The boy held two glasses of the orange nectar, an unspoken explanation of why he'd left Lisa alone.

"No." As if all at once aware of what could have happened, Lisa's eyes grew round before a faint blush caught her cheeks, and she brought a hand to her opened mouth. "I guess I should be more careful who I talk to."

"You think?" her father asked sharply.

Appearing satisfied Lisa was safe with Samantha, Chase dogged the stranger's heels as he hurried toward a group of older patrons. She could only hope he'd hold his temper and not flatten the man when he caught up with him. Unable to make out what their conversation contained, judging from Chase's overpowering stance and the man's slumped shoulders, she surmised he had extracted an apology. Small compensation for what he'd done, but Chase seemed okay with the gesture.

"I'm going to the bathroom," Lisa looked toward her, face pale. "Is that all right if I go alone?"

Open fear remained in her eyes, evidence she was still very much feeling like the victim she could have become. Samantha knew unless she instituted empowerment tactics right now, Lisa would have a harder time recovering from the ordeal.

"Sure you can, sweetie. You don't need to be afraid."

Ethan, still holding the two glasses of nectar, seemed to want to follow her. Then as if realizing where she was headed, he looked helplessly toward Samantha. "I'm going to tell my parents what happened. See what they say," he said, setting off in the opposite direction.

She watched Lisa take a few tentative steps away, then seeming to sense she really was okay, her chin lifted and her spine straightened as she made her way across the room.

"Where's she going?" Parental concern permeated Chase's expression and elevated his voice as he returned from his revenge seeking mission.

"To the ladies' room."

"I want to talk to her before she gets there." Saying nothing more, he started to follow his daughter.

Samantha put her hand on his arm. "Right now, you need to leave her alone. Let her figure this out for herself. I'll talk to her later tonight."

His stance indicated he wasn't convinced, then his next words proved that. "She needs to know..."

"...that she wasn't remotely responsible for what just happened," she finished.

Rigid and well into fight mode, she wondered if the pervert had any idea what might have happened to him if Chase had gotten between him and Lisa first. "I still need to talk to her."

She tightened her grip. "So you can what? Reprimand her? Get into an argument? Another one of your father daughter tugs of war?"

"No, but..."

She rubbed her hand along the top of his forearm, much as a parent would soothe a child. "Unclench your fists," she told him quietly. "And your jaw," she went on after he'd complied with her first instruction. "Then you'll be ready to talk to your daughter."

Even as she convinced him to calm down, she knew how difficult calm down was for him to attain. His entire body seemed to vibrate with the effort it took him to relax. She wondered if he'd be able to hold on to his hard fought serenity as she saw Lisa head toward them from the bathroom.

"I need to talk to her." Though he made a direct statement, his tone suggested more of a question.

"You can. But talk. Don't accuse."

He shot her a veiled look. "Be, like she says, *supportive*?"

"Exactly."

"Come with me?" Even as he issued the request, his arm was around her waist as they made their way toward Lisa. "The bastard claimed he thought she was thirty."

"Maybe he really did," she answered, her own voice reflecting the disbelief they shared.

"So how are you doing?" Chase asked when they got beside Lisa.

Huge eyes looked up at him. "Okay, I guess."

He reached out to take her hand.

"Oh, Daddy, I am so sorry," she blurted before he had a chance to open his mouth.

"You don't have anything to be sorry for, sweetheart." He glanced back over his shoulder.

"That son of a bitch does."

Samantha's fingertips, brushing his arm in warning, curtailed further retaliatory comment.

"I shouldn't have talked to him," Lisa's voice shook and her lip quivered. "I shouldn't have let him get so close."

"Well, he's gone now," Ethan said as he came up, his face awash in guilt. "I shouldn't have left you alone."

"You're both wrong," Chase said. "That bastard should have left her alone."

"It's just...everyone has been so friendly...I just..." Lisa stopped speaking and put her head down.

Chase reached out a hand to smooth the hair back from his daughter's face. "It's okay, honey. You didn't know. But, next time..."

"I'll have taught her some things to say to put the jerk in his place," Samantha cut in before Chase could put the idea into Lisa's head there would be a next time. "Then I'll show you how to knock someone like him on their butt when you need to. Does that sound good?"

"Yeah," Lisa answered on a sigh, as a tiny smile flickered into a bigger one. "Yeah, Coach. Real good."

"My parents said we could report him if you want," Ethan spoke up, and Lisa looked expectantly toward her father. "Have him escorted off the ship."

Samantha hoped Chase wouldn't be inclined to go that far, but decided to leave the decision up to him. "That's not necessary," he said, much to her relief. "Let's just forget about it right now."

"Yes," Samantha echoed. "Forget about it right now."

The tight circle the four of them had created fell silent for a moment before Ethan cleared his throat and squared up in front of Chase. "Mr. Canfield?" As Chase glanced his way, Ethan might have stepped back, but didn't. "Some of us are meeting in the crow's nest, the lounge area at the front of the ship near the top floors, after dinner. I was wondering if Lisa could join us. They've set it up for a movie night. Coke. Popcorn." He mentioned a popular movie.

"Oh, I've wanted to see that one." Lisa's eyes held a quiet pleading as she looked toward the adults.

Her father checked his watch. "I don't know."

"I'll walk her back to her room, sir. After. And, I promise not to let her out of my sight," he added in a voice full of optimism.

His gaze held the same pleading look as Lisa's, and Samantha hoped the recent incident wouldn't make Chase's overprotective instincts kick in again. Once more, she couldn't keep quiet.

"That sounds like fun," she said, adding her own persuasive quality to the mix on Lisa's behalf.

Chase cast her a sharp look she met head on. There was no reason to penalize the girl for a momentary lapse in judgment. Especially in relation to something so not her fault. She tried to convey that message in her expression, but he was way ahead of her.

"Have a good time, sweetheart."

"Thanks, Daddy." Lisa's voice sparkled.

"Thank you, sir," Ethan echoed.

"I love you, Daddy." Impulsively, she wound her arms around his neck. Before he could respond, she'd pulled herself free and was hurrying off with her friend.

"She's growing up, isn't she?"

Though Samantha sensed by his tone he spoke more to himself than to her, she answered anyway. "Children seem to do that."

He glanced over to her at the verbal response. "Yeah, I suppose."

The band chose that moment to launch into a loud and boisterous swing number, complete with ear splitting blasts from the brass section.

"Do you want to get some air?" Running a finger inside his collar, he had to speak up and bend toward her to be heard.

"I'm ready to get out of here," she agreed in an equally loud voice, accepting his arm as they headed for an exit.

The deck was quiet and deserted as they stepped outside. Behind them were bright lights and blaring music, before them only inviting darkness and welcoming peace. A light breeze washed across the water, took on the coolness of its surface, then brushed back across the deck. Samantha hugged herself against the unexpected chill at the same time as Chase's tuxedo jacket fell over her shoulders. She pulled its comfort, more tightly, around her as the warmth from his body spread down over hers. They strolled side by side in silence, then stopped to lean against the smooth, thick railing. A full moon revealed the blurred outlines of sloping hillsides and high peaked mountains rising from the shoreline in the distant mists.

"That's twice now you've protected her," Chase noted quietly. "Once when we were boarding, and just now in there."

"I wasn't aware we were keeping track."

He glanced at her with a shrug. "I still appreciate that you did it. Twice."

She started to say *It's my job*, then stopped short. She would have done the exact same thing, job or not. "You're welcome."

It was a while before either spoke again then his voice broke into the silence.

"Her mother is trying to take her away from me. For good."

"Is she?" There was no need to disclose his

daughter had already shared the information. That revelation, and Lisa's reaction to it, were two things needing to remain private between a father and a daughter.

"She thinks it's important for Lisa to have her newest husband's last name." He turned to face her, his hard expression a sharp contrast to the calm tenor of his voice. "I don't agree."

Samantha searched her mind for the proper response. "I don't blame you."

So which husband were you? The thought shot through her mind, and she grabbed it back. That request was too far off the subject and none of her business.

He answered her unspoken question. "Her mother and I never married. I'm a little, no, a lot embarrassed to admit Lisa was the product of what turned out to be a one night stand." Regret tinged his voice as he went on. "I was very young, and incredibly stupid, but I'm not one bit sorry she's here. I didn't even know I had a child for a couple of years. I met my daughter for the first time when she was almost three." He didn't wait for her response. "I had to fight for every moment with her. First, I obtained a court order to be able to submit to a paternity test. Then it was back to court to fight for visitation rights. Monica sure doesn't make it easy." He paused, lost in some private reflection. "I'll never forget the first time I saw my little girl." His voice was a mixture of pain bolstered by sturdy resolve. "Do you know what it's like to look at your child for the first time and see fear, of you, reflected in their eyes?"

Samantha shook her head. She'd seen fear in a child's eyes before. Usually when she was responding to a domestic dispute and had to call in a social worker to care for the children while their parents were hauled away. But not from a child of her own, and never directed at her as its cause. She could only imagine how devastating that would be to a parent.

"No." Her voice was charged with emotion she made no attempt to conceal.

"I hope you never do." He said it on a sigh then recovered himself to add, "Lisa is growing up on me. I will admit to that."

She wanted to provide some form of comfort to ease the suffering so evident in his voice. "Daughters never really leave," she told him. *Unless fathers push them away.* She cast off the unbidden thought. This wasn't about Samantha and Edwin, this was about Chase and Lisa. And she was beginning to see the difference.

"So how did Lisa come to have your last name?"

"At one time, I was, or rather I should say, my income potential was rather attractive to Monica, so she agreed to change the birth certificate from father unknown to...me. Then she made no secret of the fact she was only doing it for the money."

"You're kidding."

"I wish I were. My career was getting a lot of press. Our department was thriving in the public's view. Government had a lot of money in those days. As its employees, we were paid well, and the raises came through on a pretty steady basis." He looked out over the water, his face grim. "I guess Monica thought the paternity suit was just some kind of macho endeavor on my part with no feelings behind it. She figured I'd be happy enough to keep sending out the checks...from a distance...and have very little to do with Lisa in person."

"Boy was she wrong!" Samantha made the remark before she thought about it. "I mean...I'm sorry, that just slipped out."

"No. It's okay. I'll take that as a compliment. I'm proud of being a hands on dad. Though my job didn't always cooperate."

"Child support has to come from somewhere."

"The new custody hearing is scheduled for a couple of months from now." He looked down at her, and his voice took on the same quiet resolve as before. "Which I plan to fight with everything I have."

She already knew that.

"And I plan to win."

She knew that, too.

The double doors behind them swung wide, spilling the echoes of trumpets and drums, along with a tight group of senior citizens, out onto the deck. Amid the unexpected noise, the sound of dinner chimes rose up to float toward them.

Chase glanced over his shoulder. "That reminds me. We haven't had dinner yet." Straightening, he placed his arm across her shoulders more for direction than anything else, as he turned them both around. "Shall we go inside?"

"We could." She was unable to keep the reluctance from her voice. Evening mealtimes on the cruise were a big production of lavish menus in a formal atmosphere. Lisa, Chase and Samantha had experienced two such dinners already, and she wasn't sure she was quite up for a third. The prospect of another round of eager to please waiters and their equally eager assistants held little appeal. When she didn't move immediately toward the door with him, his arm slid off her shoulder.

"Or, we could go down to the Bistro for burgers."

Once more, he'd read her thoughts. *Perfect.* "With fries?" she asked lightly.

"With fries."

"You're on."

Chase's tie was off and in his pocket before the elevator opened on a lower floor of the ship.

The casual dining area was practically deserted

as they walked inside. Its clientèle consisted mostly of parents with older children, a few couples and larger families. All of whom, like Chase and Samantha, had opted out of the formal dining experience. They were the only two people in the place clad in full formal attire, which earned them a few curious, if not indulgent, looks. Oblivious to those looks, they each picked up trays from one end of the cafeteria style line before heading toward the grill.

The hamburger, for Samantha, became a grilled chicken patty, though she gladly accepted the plate of sizzling fries passed her way. Iced tea and an oatmeal cookie completed her meal. Chase opted for bread pudding and an extra large coke with his double deluxe burger and fries.

Conversation came easily as they found a booth in a back corner. They talked of everything and nothing, then shared a laugh at the antics of a toddler who wandered by their table, and smiled in understanding at the mother who followed quickly behind.

They talked about the beauty of Alaska and the opulence of the ship. Chase told her about his days working as a conservation officer in the frontier and how it had kept him away from Lisa. The one regret of his entire career, he admitted. Samantha shared her story of burn out while on the police force and Bob's rescue of her sanity. She also told him of her deep affection for their mutual friend, an affection she learned he shared. Then he wanted to know about their plans to franchise the agency. As she continued to answer the number of questions he had, she became aware those plans which were, at one time, a driving force of her existence, held little of their original appeal as she recited them now.

After awhile, from the far side of the dining room, a vacuum cleaner began to drone a constant rumble and chairs were turned upside down on top of tables by fast moving waiters.

Pushing his chair back, Chase slowly stood up, offering her his hand. "I guess that means we need to leave." The reluctance in his voice matched a similar feeling in her heart.

"I guess it does."

Words were no longer needed as they headed back toward their rooms. Walking slowly, they purposely took their time, neither wanting to reach the end of their short journey, when they would part company, to spend the rest of the night alone.

Despite a perfect evening, Samantha fumbled with the key card out of sheer nervousness when they finally arrived at her door. With Chase so close, she could feel his breath on the back of her neck. It was just naturally time for the good night kiss she was trying with all of her might to avoid. Not because she didn't want his kiss, but because she wanted it so badly, she wasn't sure she'd be able to stop at one. Those thoughts diminished as the door finally clicked open, but then new thoughts, bewildering thoughts, took their place.

She knew she needed to turn around and at least say good night to him. Closing her eyes, she made the swift move. Backed against one side of the doorway, she found herself all but in his arms. The warmth of his breath brushed against her cheek. She could almost taste him already as she watched him stare at her lips for one long, drawn out moment. A moment filled with a confusing mix of crushing temptation and silent longing.

The rise and fall of voices coming toward the narrow hallway made them each take self-conscious steps back.

"This has been so much fun!"

The voice was Lisa's, and, judging from the laughter within it, the old Lisa was back.

Then a deeper voice spoke something so low, they couldn't distinguish what was said. The comment was followed, once more, by Lisa's laugh, and she watched Chase smile along with her.

When the young couple came into view, Samantha was sure as soon as *she* noticed, he saw they were holding hands.

"Oh, good evening, sir, ma'am. I brought her back." Ethan lifted his arm, and Lisa's, in a shared victory.

"I see that," Chase responded, watching until the boy released his daughter. "Thank you."

"We had a good time, Daddy," Lisa began, then slightly out of character, she provided only an abbreviated report of their evening, all the while looking at Ethan.

A combination of relief and apprehension on his face, Chase stood looking at them both.

Samantha only smiled.

"Well. Good night then," Ethan said when every bit of finishing-the-conversation had been used up.

"Good night," Lisa whispered.

He looked somewhat nervously at Chase, then back at Lisa where his expression changed to one of impulse and determination. Leaning in quickly, he brushed a kiss across her cheek.

"Sir. Ma'am." With a small salute toward each of the adults, he turned to head back down the hallway.

Lisa wrapped her arms around Chase's neck and held on tight. "Thank you so much for all of this. For everything. For being my dad."

"Oh, sweetheart, you are so welcome." He caught her in a fierce hug.

"Goodnight, Daddy. Coach." She pulled herself out of his arms. "I'm really tired," she explained, walking into their room.

Samantha remained in the open doorway,

moving to slip his coat off of her shoulders. "She is having the time of her life." She said handing him the garment.

"She is, isn't she?" Hooking the jacket over his shoulder with the finger of his left hand, he reached for Samantha's hand with the right. "Thank you."

"Me?"

"You're a big part of this too."

"If that's how you feel, you're welcome."

Still holding her hand, he slowly inclined his head toward her. She closed her eyes, then felt his lips brush her cheek in a sweet kiss much like Ethan had done with Lisa.

"Goodnight, Samantha," he said, before he turned and, also as Ethan had done, continued on down the hallway to his room.

Chapter Eight

With the ship securely docked in Skagway Harbor, the cruise portion of the trip came to an end. A tour bus that carried Lisa, Ethan, and their group to points north left before daylight. Soon after the departure of the bus, Samantha made quick work of packing the rest of their things because all passenger luggage was to be out in the hall for pick-up later that morning. Though she tried not to notice, a strange sense of loss tugged at her heart. Despite initial misgivings and their rocky start, bittersweet memories had been created for her here. Memories she would take with her forever.

Her immediate plans were to fly to Anchorage, spend time there exploring until it was time to escort Lisa back to Detroit. She had no idea where Chase would be going next. With his job as the ship's naturalist fulfilled, he was free to go wherever he chose, especially since Lisa wouldn't be around for a few days.

She hoisted the largest suitcase off the bed and was in the process of wrestling it through the door and out into the hallway when a firm hand ended her struggle. "Can I help?"

She looked up to see Chase's face lit into such a huge smile, she had to smile back. "Thanks. These seem to be twice as heavy now as they were when we got here."

"Mine seemed to grow, too."

"That happens to me when I take a trip." She meant the comment as an opening to engage him in easy small talk, maybe reminisce with him about the souvenirs and other purchases the three of them had made, both on the ship and during their dockside excursions. "I always end up with way too much baggage."

Uprighting her suitcase against the hallway wall, he looked back at her, the remnants of some strange and unknown emotion evident around his eyes. "Or not enough."

Neither her mind nor her heart held a quick answer as her attempt at an easy give and take conversation vanished.

He leaned the last suitcase beside the door then came back into the room.

"Lisa seemed excited this morning." Standing at the foot of her bed, she spoke more to fill the silence and calm the ever present butterflies in her midsection than anything else.

"She did." He regarded her for a long moment before speaking again. "Thank you for helping me to make the right decision for her."

Unsure how to respond to his unexpected expression of gratitude, she decided on the most basic reply. "You're welcome."

He glanced away as if to measure his next words. When his eyes took hers again, the smile was gone. A solemn expression had taken its place, and her heart, all the while maintaining a slow and steady cadence, slithered from her chest to her stomach. The butterflies already in residence in the area fluttered to alert at her heart's arrival.

He was preparing to tell her good-bye.

"We've been doing a lot of talking about trust since we've been here." Before she could respond, he took both of her hands in his. "I just have one question for you." He spoke so low, she had to lean closer to hear him.

"What's that?" she asked, just as low.

His mouth quirked into the beginnings of a wry smile even while his eyes retained a hint of trepidation. "Do you trust me now?"

"I trust you, Chase." It was the truest statement she had made to him in a very long time.

"Good!" His face broke into another wide smile, this one almost of relief. "Because for today at least, I have a plan for us."

****

The rest of the morning became a non-stop whirlwind. After a plane ride from Skagway, Samantha found herself in the small town of Whittier, which, Chase explained, was just one hundred miles south of Anchorage, then said, "We'll be at the hotel there tonight."

Once on land again, a short taxi ride took them to a warehouse type store tucked into one of the many coves along the shoreline. A billboard across the front listed kayak sales and rentals along with frontier supplies. Lettering below offered specially guided tours. In addition to the lofty promises made on the sign outside, the inside of the store seemed to have it all.

Kayaks, standing upright, lined one entire wall with the opposite wall containing paddles, tie up lines, life jackets and the like. All sorts of brightly colored wilderness clothing hung on a series of round metal racks situated on the floor in between. Chase seemed right at home among them, selecting gear as if he were choosing items in a grocery store off of a well thought out list.

"Gortex jackets are a must out here. And a water-proof pack is essential for keeping personal belongings dry." He held the now unzipped square pouch open for her inspection. "Not that we'll actually go into the water," he added at what must have been the slightly alarmed expression on her face. "It's just good to be prepared."

It wasn't until they'd each chosen jackets, both in bright red and orange, and taken them up to the counter along with an assortment of equipment she had no idea how to use, she even felt able to catch a breath.

One of two bored looking clerks, a boy of about twenty or so, smiled automatically as they approached. "This do it for ya?" In a series of quick and practiced motions, he scanned the black bar codes printed on white tags and packed part of the merchandise into a plastic bag.

"This is it," Chase replied, handing over his credit card.

"I'll need to see some other ID." The clerk intoned the request without looking at his customer, then his eyes widened and his head shot up. "Wow!" Boredom evaporated, he studied the name on the card, stared up at Chase, eyes still wide, then back down at the card. "Wow!"

Chase began to pull his driver's license out of his wallet.

"Keep it. I know who you are, Officer Canfield."

"I'm retired. It's just mister, rather Chase, now."

The kid gave a low whistle as if he hadn't heard.

"Officer Canfield. The boss said you were coming. Wow! Officer Canfield. I've heard stories about you all of my life. My name's Danny Wild." He offered a quick handshake. Still holding Chase's credit card, he stared at it as if to reassure himself who actually stood before him. "He told me to get a two man kayak ready for special unguided rental." Aside to Samantha he added, "now I know why."

If Chase felt any pride at the recognition, he didn't show it. In fact, he seemed a little embarrassed by all the attention as a couple of customers who stood behind them in line listened in on their conversation with a curious interest.

"The boss said to give you one of the new open-topped models," the kid said, stuffing the rest of their purchases into a second plastic bag he handed to Chase. "This way, Mr. Canfield, sir."

Chase and Samantha followed him through a heavy metal door into a warehouse of sorts as he continued to ask Chase a ceaseless line of questions about his days with the Forestry Service.

"That was awhile ago," Samantha heard him say after making polite responses to the barrage of questions.

"My sister just got a job as a reporter on the newspaper here in town," Danny said. "Her bosses would love it if she got an interview with you."

"Sure." Taking a business card from his wallet, Chase scribbled something on the back. "This is the Anchorage hotel where we have reservations for tonight and tomorrow. Have her call me there."

Danny's face lit with a definite case of hero worship. "I will, sir. Thanks."

Then they were outside, following a crowd of people boarding a two tiered ferry boat tied up at the dock. Several kayaks were being loaded on the lower decks.

"They drop you off at the head of Blackstone Bay, sir...," their self appointed tour director said after another quick, if not reluctant, hand shake. "You know where you're going from there."

"Yeah, I do. Thanks."

Once the charter got underway, the professional guides were easy to discern from the tourists. They were the ones sporting brightly colored jackets bearing a logo of the store. The little group clustered together conferring over some papers attached to a clip board before one of them picked up a wireless microphone to welcome everyone and give an overview on their upcoming journey down the river.

"We have separated all of you into smaller groups," the announcer noted. "And, we'll each read the names of the kayakers in our group. Please congregate around your guide when the boat docks at Blackstone Bay. We'll distribute the prepackaged lunches and kayaks at that time."

Samantha listened to the lists of names being read off as each guide took their turn at the microphone. Occasionally, an unusual or difficult name would be mispronounced followed by a spate of good-natured laughter.

She still hadn't heard her name, or Chase's, announced as the last guide finished. When their boat pulled up to a narrow dock and stopped, the others met with their designated guides and were provided last minute instructions. He walked her, with the lunches and kayak they had been given, a ways down the river bank.

"Shouldn't we be finding our guide?" she asked as they continued along a gravel path. "Shouldn't we be prepared?"

"Your guide is already here." He took his wallet from his back pocket and deposited it into the waterproof pouch he'd just purchased, his cell phone followed. He held the receptacle opened for her. Without being told, she did the same with her wallet and cell. "Now we're prepared," he said as he zipped the pack closed and fastened it securely around his waist.

She wasn't sure if he was serious then remembered he had asked her before if she trusted him. And she did, with all of her heart. Still, the lengthy preparations, especially filing a route plan with the kayak rental company, seemed a little extreme. She had been so thrown when she'd been handed an emergency contact form to fill out, she'd hastily listed Bob and the agency. Not knowing as much about the land as Chase, she wondered, foolishly perhaps, if he were being overly cautious.

"Anything else we need to do to be...prepared?"

"Just an open mind. And a calm body," he quipped. "And, don't worry," he assured her with a wink. "I used to be a Boy Scout."

"I was a Girl Scout, too." She looked out across the clear, meandering river that suddenly seemed very wide and very deep. "But that was a long time ago."

His chuckle in response did little to quell her burgeoning case of nerves as they stopped near a stand of trees. Ducking beneath them, they came out on the water's edge at a shallow inlet where she helped him set the kayak, their only mode of transportation for the day, into the water.

The first thing he taught her was how to get into the surprisingly sleek craft. The second thing he taught her was how to get out.

"In case it overturns," he said then added with measured caution, "which probably won't happen."

Despite repeated assurances she wouldn't necessarily use the knowledge, she obliged herself to pay close attention while he explained how to get out of an overturned kayak.

"Skim your hands forward along the sides of the cockpit until you find a toggle latch. Tug on that to release the spray skirt, the piece that covers your legs. Once that's released, you'll be able to slide out of it. Like taking off a pair of pants," he finished with what she assumed she was supposed to identify as a smile of encouragement.

She got the hang of kayaking with unexpected ease and, soon with Chase's help, was able to maneuver the craft, for the most part where she wanted it to go, by dipping the paddle along one side, then the other. Of course he sat in back to do most of the actual steering, or there was no telling where they might have ended up.

"We'll go down the river this way for about eight miles, then turn around and be at the our pick up point by six this evening. Seven at the latest," he promised. "I told them I'd call when we got back there."

Samantha could only nod her agreement as she joined him in the kayak, for real this time. An hour later, smoke-blue mountains with snow white caps, towered above them only to disappear into the endless mists of the clouds. Dark green fir trees which grew up against the shore were so dense; they appeared to be huge blades of thick grass on some massive suburban lawn. The beauty and sheer size of the land she'd viewed from the far away deck of a ship couldn't compare to this up close and breathtaking panorama. At times, Samantha became so caught up in watching the passing scenery, she forgot to paddle.

"This is how Alaska should be seen," Chase said. "Just like this."

She knew exactly what he meant, watching, in open-mouthed awe, as two bald eagles—looking more like small gliders than birds—dipped and soared on the wind currents above them. Even Mother Nature seemed to hold her breath out here, in quiet respect for the overwhelming beauty.

For a couple of hours, they paddled slowly, falling into an easy rhythm, their oars barely needed to break the water's surface to propel them along. The soft, soothing echo of the river flowing by the only sound around them, until the roar of rushing water, from somewhere off in the distance, broke the peaceful setting.

"We're not about to go crashing over a waterfall, are we?" She cast a nervous glance over her shoulder at Chase then back toward the sound.

"It's a waterfall. But not one that will affect us."

"Okay." She did trust him. *She did.*

"Over there," she heard him say after a few moments. "To your right."

As directed, she looked up. White foaming water tumbled and gushed over cliffs and crags, toppling and tripping as it made its way down the mountainside. Furious and wide at its source, the flow was eventually constrained into a narrow stream that dribbled and angled peacefully into the river—their river—hardly disturbing the smooth surface as it did so.

Samantha watched the spectacle with mouth open and eyes wide. She was totally out of her element in this wilderness—his wilderness—and for the first time in her life, didn't mind not being able to control what happened to her.

The afternoon had turned breezy but sitting in the kayak, Samantha was surprisingly warm what with sunlight reflecting off the water. As sweat gathered where the life jacket clung to her back, she toyed with the idea of asking permission to free herself from the confinement, but had a feeling Chase's careful precautions wouldn't allow it. She was relieved when a cove like shoreline where the river widened provided a perfect landing spot, and the opportunity to take off the oppressive vest.

Chase pulled the kayak out of the water while Samantha laid out the content of their box lunches. Some kind of sandwiches, small bags of chips and relishes, apples and plastic bottles of water. After they ate, she watched him collect the remnants of their meal, then stow the carefully wrapped package in their kayak. To be disposed of later, he said.

"Leave the land as you found it," he noted as he came to sit beside her on the sandy bank. "Clean and untouched. As if you'd never been there at all." He cast her a secretive look, a smile climbing onto his mouth. "And to keep the bears away."

"Bears?" Sitting upright, she did a three-sixty scan of their surroundings. "Are bears really a danger out here?"

"Anything can be a danger out here, if you don't treat it with respect."

"Are there a lot of them around here?" She inched closer. "Bears."

"A few. This is their home." He indicated the wilderness around them. "There isn't a lot of competition for them out here. They don't have too many natural enemies either, so they thrive." He smiled as her eyes grew large then put his arm around her shoulders. Instinctively, she nestled against him. "They basically keep to themselves. And, as long as we don't provoke them, they'll leave us alone, too."

"Are you sure?"

"Don't worry so much." His hand caressed her shoulder then slid down her arm, the words flowing out to drift along her temple as he pulled her closer. "You're safe with me."

She closed her eyes. *Safe.* Without intention, or conscious thought, she turned her face toward his. Eyes still closed, she felt his warm breath, the brush of his lips against her cheek.

"You know that, don't you?" His voice was low, almost sultry, as he asked a question which needed no spoken answer.

His fingers traced lightly across her cheek and down her neck as he spoke, making her skin tingle, and a surge of anticipation spiraled through her. Opening her eyes, she looked directly at him. She hadn't moved or pulled back, and he seemed to take that as an invitation to continue. Slowly, cautiously, still giving her a chance to escape, he began to lower his mouth toward hers. To her own surprise, and delight, she met him half way.

Then the kiss she had been awaiting for so long found its way to her mouth. Her moan of acceptance was more vibration between them than sound around them. The arm across her shoulders guided her down to the warm sand, while his other arm moved across her. A hand came to rest at her hip, then flexed only enough to fit her body against his. She lifted her arms to wrap around his neck, her fingers at first taut with uncertainty, now relaxed and sure as they moved lower to stroke the hard planes of his back. Boldness caused her to reach under his shirt until her fingers connected with the smooth texture of his skin. Slight moisture dampened fingertips which traced up the line of his spine. Reaching his shoulder blades, her palms skimmed back down his back then came around his stomach and up to lightly caress his chest. His muscles were hard, not from tension, but from release. A small surge of triumph was hers as she felt him shudder at her touch.

Sliding his hand at the bottom of her top, he pushed aside what clothing remained between his hands and her skin. The world and everything within it slipped to an indistinct and distant background as their personal universe came to consist only of the two of them, alone together, with nothing else around them but urgent needs and unfulfilled desires. As it had the first time they kissed, the ground beneath her began to sway and tilt. But, this time, she allowed the swaying sensation to take her up and sweep her away, free and unfettered, to a place from which she never wanted to return.

Kiss after kiss after kiss took them further away from the solitary existences they'd known for so long, and nearer to a place designed only for two. His lips left her mouth to trail feather soft kisses down her neck to the tops of her shoulder. Her skin was even more sensitive through the thin barrier of her tee shirt, and tingles of desire followed in their wake. Climbing and building, longing sensations rose up in her only to plunge—sharp and white hot—to a place deep inside she was now ready at last, to share only with him.

The interruption of a cell phone chime cut off further thought. Thought but not action as his lips continued their sweet contact with her skin. Then a repeat of the persistent chime cut off action as well.

She looked at him in absolute disbelief.

"It amazes me too," he replied to her silent question. "What Alaska lacks in physical closeness, it makes up for in virtual reception." He dug into the pouch at his waist, pulled out both phones for inspection, then with an expression she couldn't read, handed over hers.

With her mouth still swollen from his kisses, she made a half hearted attempt to readjust her clothing, fearing the caller would be able to observe what must have been her disheveled appearance if she didn't. She spoke into the receiver after checking the screen for caller ID. "Oh, Bob. Hello."

Her eyes flicked over Chase, hoping he had the good sense to keep his presence unknown. No doubt sensing her unease, he soundlessly got up to walk further down the shoreline.

"Am I interrupting anything?" The tone in Bob's voice suggested he was only half kidding.

"No. No, you're not." She watched Chase's retreat then purposely turned her back to raise telling fingertips to her lips again. "Nothing at all."

"I just had a few quick questions on the franchise contract our lawyer drew up."

She listened as her boss went on to detail some specifics he was having trouble understanding then answered him quickly. Aware of Chase's gaze on her, even from a safe distance, she was even more aware of her body's continued response. A response which hadn't been curtailed by the cell phone interruption.

"So, how's the trip going?" Bob's question signaled an end to the business side of their conversation. "Are you enjoying yourself as much as you thought you would? Isn't Alaska beautiful?"

"Great. Yes and yes," she answered, being careful to keep her voice from becoming over the top enthusiastic. A sure sign to any cop, retired or otherwise, of a lying witness.

If he only knew.

"And Lisa. How is she doing?"

Once more Samantha glanced over at Chase. "Lisa is doing fine."

As far as I know. Not really a lie, just a mild stretching of the truth.

"So you're off the ship now."

A pang of shame—or was it alarm at being caught—shot through her. *How could he know that?*

"Yes." *But it's not what you think.* Her mind started to form a list of excuses for her actions but found none Bob, or she, would find acceptable.

"Francine sent me a copy of your itinerary." The explanation removed the need for those excuses, and she let out a thankful breath. "The interior of Alaska. What do you think?"

She cast another quick look in Chase's direction. "It's...awesome."

"When you get back home," the heavy sigh he released as he spoke the phrase was an odd sound to come from the always on top of things and in control Bob Anderson. "We can finalize our initial business proposal with the lawyers."

"I'll look forward to it." For the first time in her life, she was lying to her mentor.

"I'm finding this franchise thing is a little over my head. I didn't realize until you were gone how much I had been depending on you to handle all the details for me."

Samantha closed her eyes. Another time, another place, she would have welcomed that kind of praise, but not here and not now.

As Bob went on to lay out the problems he was having with the *details* he spoke of, Samantha listened, her impatience growing. Apparently, David Franks had struck again. Surprise! Not only had his holier-than-thou attitude turned off some of their applicants, his lack of expertise in police procedures and protocols had made PSI appear to consist of incompetent amateurs. From what Bob said, Franks had all but alienated one of their most important prospects and was in the process of screwing up his part of the program.

"I should never have given him so much responsibility," Bob said, the weariness in his voice bordering on desperation. "I thought the guy just needed a chance."

"I'll be home soon," she promised, and was unprepared for the disappointment—no the absolute desolation—the acknowledgement brought out in her.

Be home soon.

As the unwelcome notion echoed in her head, she said good-bye to Bob and disconnected the call.

Chase came up beside her before she'd fully closed her hand to shut off the phone and, without a word, she handed the device back to be put away.

"I guess he misses me," she offered weakly. "He says he needs me back there."

"I'm sure he does." His voice held an uncharacteristic flatness. "Your job is important."

"Extremely." The reply was automatic though uttered, she realized at that moment, without its customary conviction. "David Franks is at his usual games: messing things up for the rest of us. The one thing he does well," she added with a shake of her head.

"So, other than that, how are things going at PSI?"

"Bob didn't say. He was pretty focused on the

franchise...problems." She shrugged off any further explanation.

She didn't want to think about her job, or Bob, or anything else not directly related to the two of them. She desperately wanted to reclaim the closeness she and Chase had shared moments before, now impossible to achieve because it was too late. The call, and its unerring reminder of her responsibilities, made sure of that.

"Cell signals are iffy out here." He still hadn't returned her phone to the all important waterproof pouch, and she resisted the urge to grab the tiny instrument and fling it into the river. "Ten or twenty feet in any direction," he went on as she watched her phone disappear for safe keeping. "No signal." He zipped the pouch. "You were lucky to be in the right place at the right time."

"Yeah. Lucky."

"Well." He made a show of scanning the sky. "We need to get moving if we're going to make it to the end of our tour and back to the pick-up point before dark."

Both willing to concede the romantic mood was broken, if only to themselves, they collected their gear while making polite, but distinctly distant, conversation, then continued their trek down the river.

Rounding a particularly tight bend, they came out on an open area the size of a small lake, and even the assortment of pictures she'd seen in travel brochures and guidebooks did nothing to prepare Samantha for the astounding image before her.

The massive glacier rose from the water, its millions and millions of ice crystals winking and sparkling in the brilliant sunlight, reflecting not the expected white of ice and snow, but the bright clear blue of a cloudless sky.

Chase used his paddle to bring them to a dead

stop on the glass calm surface. "What do you think?"

She could only shake her head, unable to speak or utter an intelligent sound about the sight which had taken her breath.

"I thought so."

They sat very still in the quiet reverent face of nature with the only sound an occasional plink, plink of the paddle atop the water as Chase worked to keep them from drifting too close or too far away.

"And this is one of the smaller ones."

She could only nod her recognition as she continued to stare at the natural giant.

Then chaos hit. Swift and devastating.

One moment she stared at the silent beauty of the glacier. The next, with a heart stopping roar, the front tip crumbled. A huge chunk crashed and heaved before tumbling a free fall into the river. Vaguely aware of Chase's loudly uttered oath, she was unable to move and could only watch this new spectacle in rigid fascination.

Water and foam flew upward as the river received the unexpected weight. A huge wave, frothing wildly, climbed halfway up the glacier wall. In immediate response, a second wave rose up, rolling and foaming like the first. Then, still rolling and foaming, the surge reversed course. Like energy released from a giant catapult, the thrashing wall of water swelled outward. Gaining strength and size, it sought the most resistance free path across the smooth river.

Directly toward Chase and Samantha.

"Get back!"

Sensing his shouted command rather than actually hearing it, she had already plunged her paddle in the water. Frantically she pushed forward, knowing all the while, any evasive action was futile. The force of the water was too strong, their efforts too weak. Escape impossible.

Shoreline and mountain tops disappeared as the huge, surging wall took over Samantha's line of vision, until all she could see was white, frothing water, bearing down on her from above. Within seconds, she was a part of the thrashing and churning force. Still in the kayak and, lungs burning, hopelessly upside down.

Somehow remembering Chase's instructions, she grabbed the back of the cockpit, ready to push the kayak off. Easily, like a pair of pants. She waited for her release, but her body didn't budge and, worse, her legs were drawn back into the craft. Fighting panic, she tried once more with the same result.

Push, nothing. Push, nothing! PUSH! NOTHING!

The kayak lurched and jerked at the mercy of the angry water. Terrified, still submerged with her lungs on fire, she fought to quiet her mind and forced herself to review the instructions yet again.

Maybe for one final time.

Slide, push, release. Nothing. Then reason hit her with the same strength as the unrelenting stream. *The spray skirt.* The spray skirt had to be removed! Thankfully, a quick tug on the toggle switch did just that, she slid free of the kayak, and her float vest took it from there.

Breaking the surface, she gulped madly at the air as instinct caused her to scream Chase's name. The sound recoiled back down her throat to become a gasp then a cough as another wave of water engulfed her. She had time only to take in a lung filling breath before she was sucked back down and under. The roaring was more muffled than before and somehow reason stayed with her, giving her the presence of mind to scissor kick her legs and down stroke her arms. She kicked and clawed her way upward. If she didn't reach the surface soon—the rest of the thought vanished as cold air hit her face. She hauled in a quick gulp of air in anticipation of being pulled under again. Then thought became reality as the ice cold water staked its claim to consume her into its depth.

Scissor kick, arm stroke, scissor kick, arm stroke. She maintained the presence of mind to match thought with action until those efforts, coupled with her life vest, brought her to the surface for good.

The small tidal wave had passed with only a few remaining wavelets dispersing their energy along the top of the water. She became the violent force of nature as, head flinging water from side to side, she searched for Chase, growing frantic when she saw no sign of him.

Had he—?

Before she could finish the thought something bumped, hard, into her back. For one wild second, she was sure some creature in the water had mistaken her for a meal. Did alligators live in Alaska? She braced herself, ready to fight.

"This way." His words sprayed her neck, his arm clamped around her angling her body out in front of him. "We need to get to shore fast."

Side by side, floating easier now, they rode the current which was about to deposit them in the middle of a natural dam, a cluster of branches and tree limbs jutting out from the shore. His quick grab at one of the sturdier branches stopped their progress with a jerk. Hand over hand, they made their way across the natural bridge until they could climb onto more solid footing. Shifting their weight, they hauled themselves up until they sat on top of a log, their feet and legs remaining submersed.

She rested her head against his shoulder, her breath still coming in short, jolting gasps. He held onto the tree with one arm, while wrapping the other around her waist. His body shook with the effort of holding them both until Samantha could place her hands beside his. A mutual sigh of relief was all they had time for as they hoisted themselves further up. Still side by side, half lying, half sitting, they watched their kayak bounce and bob on top of the water until it caught the same current they had ridden, then drift to rest against the far shore.

"We have to get out of the water," Chase instructed. "Hypothermia can take hold in as little as three minutes."

Lolling her head back, Samantha let out one final gasp. "Can't," she managed to breathe out. The rest of her comment—*too much effort,* formed only in her mind.

"Now!" The strength of his voice startled her. Grasping her waist, he pushed her up on the bank then hiked himself up beside her before they collapsed backward on the hard packed dirt.

Panting, shivering then panting again, she felt heat from the sun radiating out of a cloudless sky begin to flow through her. Chase lay motionless beside her, the tempo of his breathing already returning to normal.

"That was stupid," he gasped out at last, his voice the deep and raspy evidence of his exertion. He struggled to lie on his side and face her. "I should have known better. I am so sorry."

She made a move to roll toward him, but found the effort to be just too much. "Sorry for what?" she managed to say at last, having the strength needed to turn only her head, but not her body, to look at him. "That couldn't have been your fault."

"But, it was." His voice was tight with anger. Anger she knew he directed at himself. "Glaciers can calve at any time. I should have known, did know, getting that close to a glacier in that little boat was too dangerous."

"You didn't know...," she argued back, but he cut

her off.

"But, I did. I was so damned anxious to show off. To bring you up close to a glacier." He lowered his voice in the same self anger. "To impress you, that I disregarded your safety. And did a lousy job of executing the do you trust me crap I gave you this morning."

He turned his face away as he spoke, wiping his chin against his shoulder, and she was on her knees with new found energy.

"It's okay." She reached her hand over to touch his arm. "We're okay." She patted hasty hands down her front and sides. "No harm done. See? One piece. I'm still in one piece." She touched his arm again. "And so are you."

The glimpse of relief was all she saw on his face as his lips neared hers to touch them gently, briefly, much too briefly. "Thank you for that."

He lifted his mouth and his kiss was gone before she was even able to fully enjoy its sweet pressure. Once more, his lips brushed quickly, again much too quickly, over her mouth. Kisses not of passion and yearning but of gratitude and appreciation. She could certainly tell the difference. Pulling up to a sitting position, he situated himself against her, hip to hip, shoulder to shoulder, leg against leg, all the way down to the ankle.

"For added warmth as we dry out?" She unzipped her jacket and turned her face up to the welcome warmth of the sun.

"It's working," he replied. Settling his arm around her shoulders, he used his hand to nestle her even closer against him.

"Yes," she sighed, "it is." Resting her head against his shoulder, she closed her eyes, suddenly overtaken by the sheer exhaustion of their ordeal.

****

Bird songs echoed on the balmy summer breeze

as Samantha lay in the front of a rowboat, at peace and totally relaxed, enjoying the feel of a glorious summer sun on her face. She couldn't see him, but she was sure Chase sat in the middle seat gently plying the oars atop the cool, shimmering water. She had no idea where they were headed, she knew only she was going with him where ever he chose to lead.

The warm air and hot sun followed as they drifted along, until an eruption of sea spray burst up to trickle down her cheek. She jerked at the unexpected chill. Though she couldn't open her eyes to see for sure, she suspected Chase splashed her each time he lifted the oars. She wanted to tell him to quit, but couldn't find her voice either. Another blast of sea spray hit her cheek then the bridge of her nose. She brought her hand up for protection. He was assaulting her from both sides now, first on one cheek then the other, again and again. Why wouldn't he stop? Couldn't he see she was getting drenched?

As one forceful spray hit her nose, dead-center, she opened her eyes, sat bolt upright—and remembered where she was.

Casting aside all remnants of sleep, she visored a hand across her forehead. Chase loomed above her in a futile attempt to shield her body while torrents of rain washed over them.

"What's going on?" Though he was close beside her, she had to raise her voice to compete with the constant hum of a rushing downpour.

"Summer storm!" he yelled back.

He had already taken her arm to haul her to her feet and, before she was even fully awake, she was running behind him. Having no choice in the matter as he clutched her hand to pull her along, she could only follow blindly, slipping and sliding along a fresh trail of mud. A lightning bolt speared the sky then fell to earth, hitting a spot close behind them. Its jagged edges spread like contorted talons for an instant before climbing skyward, only to be heaved back down once more.

"I think I saw..." The rest of his words were drowned out by a crashing rumble of thunder. The ground trembled in response.

Giving up any attempt at further conversation, he ducked his head. Reaching back, without looking, he grabbed her around the waist to push her in front of him, then ran with a distinct sense of purpose to she had no idea where.

Rain came at them from above, front, back, all sides. Even at times from below. A thousand tiny needles stabbed her skin. Unable to fully open her eyes, she could only keep blinking water logged lashes against the drenching assault. Seeing the blurred browns and greens of a passing landscape, still being propelled from behind, she was conscious of entering a clearing of sorts. She thought she saw the form of a small house rise up before her then figured she must still be dreaming. Though they stood on land, wave after wave blew over them as if they remained trapped in the glacier swollen river.

Still unable to make sense of her surroundings, she felt Chase pull her to an abrupt stop, the water hitting them in sheets. She heard what sounded like a door creaking at the same time as she was thrust through a small opening. Immediately, the downpour stopped, the roaring noise retreated to become more of a distant, pounding.

Hearing only the steady rat-a-tat of raindrops pelting a solid surface, she leaned against him, their bodies still heaving with the physical exertion of their run. Her hair was plastered against her head and her clothes clung just as tightly to her form. After a few seconds, she opened tentative eyes and turned her head to peer out from under damp lashes. She blinked once, twice, then over and over in quick succession until her vision slowly cleared.

Droplets of water fell onto her cheeks and down her neck. His head back against a wall as his breathing slowed, eyes closed, Chase's dark hair was pressed flat against his forehead while tiny streams trickled down his face, ears and neck. One hand came up to scrub down his face then push back his hair in an opposite motion. She reached up to squeeze the excess moisture from her own hair, and could only imagine she looked much the same.

"We sure are two proverbial drowned rats." She managed to share her immediate thought, though neither one of them was inclined to laugh.

They stood inside a small shelter of some kind. Further inspection revealed a crude, rustic cabin, one not at all like the homey cottages her parents had sometimes rented for family vacations in Northern Michigan. But it was dry, and a welcome refuge from what they had just left behind.

"It's not exactly the honeymoon suite," Chase said, pushing himself upright. "Sorry," he added at her startled look. "How about this cliché? Not bad for four hundred a night."

"Four hundred dollars?" She looked around the primitive building, eyes narrowed with disbelief. "For this?"

The look he cast her held equal parts relief and guilt. "Rustic, huh?"

She glanced his way then back at their new found accommodations. Rustic was putting it mildly.

An ancient pot bellied stove centered the place and a sink with an old, long handled, manual-style pump attached to its side sat in a back corner. She assumed additional plumbing facilities were located somewhere out in back, if they were available at all. What could be called a dining area, a round wooden table surrounded by high backed chairs, was set between the stove and sink.

Two beds, more like elaborate cots, stood side by

side along the far wall, holding thick gray mattresses which appeared to be surprisingly clean. Stacks of blankets were piled on crude shelves, and an assortment of fishing poles, nets and tackle hung from the rafters. Glass jars, on a shelf above the sink, held matches and a fistful of candles. A can of kerosene, along with a few lanterns sat beside them, and a substantial stash of neatly stacked firewood fronted the stove.

A huge couch, crafted from thick planks and heavy slats of wood, held a number of overstuffed cushions giving it an almost comfortable appearance. A stone fireplace dominated the left side wall opposite the couch.

Chase continued to stare at her with a mixture of frustration and curiosity and she couldn't blame him. When she should be grateful they had any kind of shelter, she was being critical at the lack of lavish amenities.

"Some of the locals build these cabins out here, then stock them for customers," he told her. "Those people who want to experience the wild, without having to pitch a tent or catch their own food. They get flown in here for a week or two at a time."

She looked around again. "Crude and rustic is definitely a compliment."

"It's really not bad when you consider the alternative."

He was right and she knew it. The rain continued to slam and pound at the windows with an almost life-like fury, as if angered by their escape and demanding entrance to their refuge.

"Four hundred dollars seems like a fair price," she agreed, accepting the small smile he gave her.

"If we're lucky, this one will be stocked." He moved past her to head for some cupboards above the stove, but before he did, he removed the water proof pack from around his waist and looped it over one of many nails jutting out from the wall.

She heard the scratch of the zipper being opened and looked up to see him retrieve their cell phones and flip each one open in turn.

"No signal here," he said as a matter of fact before dropping them back into the pouch. "We'll deal with that tomorrow."

Pulling her eyes from the fascination of their surroundings, she made a quick appraisal of her appearance. Her tee shirt and bra had become disturbingly transparent, making her look like the poster girl for a topless club's wet tee shirt contest. Even though they had shared the beginnings of intimacy, she was overcome by a surprising sense of modesty. With a strangled gasp, she zipped the jacket all the way up to her neck.

Chase mentioned they'd be lucky if the place was stocked. Now she was the one who needed to be lucky, hoping he hadn't noticed her wet tee shirt exhibition.

When she got up the courage to glance in his direction, dark brown eyes had taken on the deep shades of awakening passion. Without a doubt, he had seen all she had to offer.

That was when she heard his voice, thick and husky as it came to her from across the room.

"Take your clothes off. Now!"

Chapter Nine

Take your clothes off. Now!

Spoken with so little emotion, more as command than request.

As if to demonstrate, Chase freed the buttons of his shirt and shrugged it off. For a long moment, Samantha could do no more than stare at his bare chest. The sight of tight ridges on a flat stomach, ridges her fingers had traveled mere hours before, did nothing to quell her growing unease.

Unease of what? In two short weeks, she'd shared more with this man than she'd shared with any man for a very long while.

Hadn't she vowed, in the privacy of her own thoughts, and as recently as that very afternoon, to share more of herself with this man, given the chance? Here was her chance, but, please, not like this. Not while they were both riding the grateful emotions of survival and escape. When they were sensible, relaxed, and could appreciate the importance of sharing closeness and intimacy.

"Take off your clothes." This time there was the semblance of some feeling in his tone. Urgency? Or merely irritation?

Feet splayed apart, naked from the waist up, he stared back at her, his recently shed shirt crumbled in one fist at his side.

He spread the garment across a low hanging rafter next to his jacket. "Don't go coy on me now, Samantha. I'm sorry," he hastened to add at the look of daggers she shot his way. "I shouldn't have said that. I am so sorry. But, I'm talking about survival here. As in living instead of dying." His tone reeked of irritation as he bent down to loosen the laces on his boots before kicking them off. He doffed his socks just as quickly, slapping them onto the rafter beside his shirt.

"The nights come on fast around here. Fast, cold and hard." She heard the distinct click when the snap of his jeans was released. "We are both soaked to the skin. If we don't get out of our wet clothes, dried off and reasonably warm pretty damn quickly, we risk hypothermia. People die from hypothermia. And, don't even realize what's happening."

"I get the picture."

And what she got wasn't pretty. Two lifeless bodies, naked, lying side by side on the floor in that cabin. Stone cold remains left to be discovered by the next fishing party who happened along. Or maybe just their bones would survive, when the bears got finished with them. The flash of insight made her shudder.

"Then do something about it." He took a step forward, giving her the impression he might begin to remove her clothes himself.

"Okay! Okay!" She put a hand up to ward him off, but she needn't have worried. He moved no closer, just watched her.

Why did he have to stand there staring?

She reached for the zipper at her neck, but with fingers too numbed to work properly; the tiny handle of the tab kept slipping from her grasp. Frustrated and more than a little embarrassed, she dropped them to her sides.

She had yet to take off a stitch of clothes—not that she hadn't tried—while Chase, on the other hand, was now barefoot and clad only in his jeans, zipper intact. Those tight, hug his waist, legs and everything in between, fitting jeans. He took another step toward her.

"Don't worry." Conflicting emotions playing across his face indicated, for the first time, he might be aware of the reasons behind her reluctance. "Nothing is going to happen." As if to validate those words, his eyes raked briefly over her form before he turned away. "So what in hell are you waiting for?"

"The damned zipper is stuck!"

The sound hung like a whip cracked in the resulting silence as his mouth dropped open. "Oh." Face now reflecting regret, he watched her a moment more. "Can I help?"

Hands at her sides, chin lifted, she faced him straight on. "You can try."

His fingers fumbled with the zipper, as hers had with no result. He blew out a low curse as she felt his hands enter the band at her waist, became aware of the jacket being lifted off her trunk and over her breasts. He hadn't touched her with anything more than his hands, but his body remained close enough to make her aware of a raw desire radiating between them. Determined to ignore the strong but soundless call, she dutifully slipped both arms out of the sleeves. Her fingers brushed his sides as she pulled her hands downward, and a body trembled, but she had no idea which, hers—or his? He had the jacket bunched around her neck, unable to fit it over her head. With a small growl of frustration, he leaned toward her, fingers again prying at the unyielding fastener.

As he moved in closer, a drop of water slipped off his hair, landed on her forehead then trickled down her nose. From there, it dripped onto the top of his hands. Another followed the same path, then another and another. Drop after drop slithering from him to her and back to him, like some bizarre and erotic water torture. A torture which was nothing compared to the new torment she was soon to face, that of his closeness as her breasts skimmed his bare chest. Her flimsy tee shirt did nothing to cushion the contact as her nipples hardened on contact with warm flesh.

His breath washed a wordless invitation against her cheek. All she had to do was lift her arms to wrap them around his waist and press every bit of her desire starved body against him in response. It would take very little effort after that to touch her lips to his. Feel him—

She heard the zipper scratch slowly downward, one tooth at a time.

"There."

With that single remark, the Gortex parted just enough to slip over her head and she was free. His swift motion to relieve her of the covering forced her back a pace. Far enough so their bodies no longer made physical contact.

"Thanks."

"Now get out of the rest of your stuff."

She didn't move at first, looking around, seeking somewhere she could go to retain a sliver of modesty. The small cabin, having no interior walls, provided scant opportunity for privacy.

"What now?" The impatience in his voice hung so heavy between them, she could have held it in her hands.

"I'm going."

You're in a one room cabin, a little voice mocked. *And, going where?*

Turning her back, she whipped the tee shirt over her head with incredible ease, then tried not to notice the piercing scratch of another zipper being released. This one on his jeans.

Making her way across the room with renewed haste, she grabbed two blankets off a shelf as she passed by. Using one of them and a few nails set in the wall planks, she created a crude dressing room in a far corner. Tucked securely behind the makeshift shelter, she peeled off the rest of the wet, clammy layers and was soon holding up the second blanket to cover her bare form.

She had begun to fashion a sari style shift out of blanket number two, when one piece of her shelter sagged. Continuing her quest for modesty, she reached up to pull the gap closed, then peeked through it instead.

Chase had made short work of getting naked and, caught by the sight of him, she dropped her hand to stare. With the jeans and briefs piled at his feet, his position facing the opposite wall gave her an unfettered view of his well-formed and—she had to confess—appealing back side. As he moved to gather the rest of his clothes, ridges of muscle on his torso and shoulders flexed then relaxed. Beautiful in efficiency, startling in power. His skin glistened from lingering dampness. One arm reached upward to hang his jeans on a vacant nail causing his body to move in a single, flowing motion, flexing upward then back. She took in the sight of every incredibly tight muscle as it tensed then softened.

Her gaze followed the sharp, clean lines of his form, she moistened her lips, then tried to swallow to do the same to a suddenly dry throat. Every fantasy she'd ever entertained about making love with this man moved front and center in her mind, pushing out all other arguments she'd ever raised to keep a safe distance.

Eyes squeezed tight, she worked to pull out of her newest mental image then glanced through the curtain once more, and into a vast and empty room. She continued to stare at the spot he'd just vacated as if he would magically reappear when, from somewhere close by, she heard the rustle and snap of material. He walked back into her field of vision then, his body, at least from the waist down, now covered by another pair of jeans. Unlike his own, these were ill fitting and large in the seat, didn't quite make it all the way down to his ankles, and were frayed enough to reveal a good share of his right thigh.

"I'm going to build a fire." He spoke casually, as if well aware he held her full attention. "There should be some pretty good kindling around out back."

"Okay."

Moving quickly, she tightened the knot at her shoulder, leaving the rest of the crudely constructed garment to drape around her all the way down to her toes. Collecting her own clothes, she stepped from her make-shift shelter and, taking advantage of being alone, busied herself laying her jeans and tee shirt across various nails and beams about the room, scrunching her bra and panties underneath the jacket to hide them from his view.

Hearing the back door slam shut, she turned around to see Chase was already crouched in front of the fireplace stacking cross cut logs and an assortment of twigs and brush on a metal grate. She couldn't help but stare at his back, remembering again how those muscles felt beneath her hands. When he finally lifted his eyes to look at her, his gaze skimmed a cursory one-two glance up and down her blanket clad form before settling on her face.

"That's better," was all he said, then turned his attention back to the fire. "I found these pants in among some blankets in the back," he indicated the only clothes he wore. "There was nothing there that would have worked for you." He looked back at her again, his expression only a touch apologetic.

"This blanket should work." What else could she say?

Under his careful hand, one spark sputtered to flame, then blazed, with a surprising force, into many. Welcome heat began to spread through the room. Stepping closer, she breathed in the smoky rich scent of burning wood, as she let the warmth spread to her insides as well. He stood back, looking satisfied with his work, then turned her way again. "Told you I used to be a Boy Scout."

The smile and wink he gave after his comment melted her heart. Boy Scouts were known for having honor, and Chase Canfield, she now knew, was no exception.

"Yes, you did," she answered around her own smile, minus the wink. "You've certainly done your part on behalf of our survival. I'll see if I can find us something to eat for mine."

While Chase built a smaller fire in the stove, she found powdered eggs, what appeared to be beef—or some kind of meat—jerky and a canister filled with what smelled like coffee grounds. Not exactly the freshest but they would have to do. Once she got the hang of the force and motion required to work the metal pump handle, she was able to draw enough water to make a somewhat respectable meal.

The two of them must have presented quite a picture when they sat down on the couch to eat, what with tin plates in their laps, coffee cups on the floor at their feet and their clothes displayed throughout the room and fanned out to facilitate quicker drying. Starving, they ate with very little conversation. When they did talk, it was to comment on the food.

"What do you think of your first wilderness meal?" Chase asked after he'd eaten everything she put in front of him, jerky and all.

"The coffee is acceptable, the scrambled eggs passable. The jerky..." She gave that a taste, made a sour face, then put the dried meat down. Tree bark might have tasted better, but she couldn't bring herself to swallow it. "I'll save for later."

He laughed. "If you get hungry enough, believe me, you'll eat it...and like it."

"Must be I'm not hungry enough," she mumbled, watching him set her almost empty plate on top of his and carry both of them, with their cups, into the kitchen area. She heard the clinks as the dishes were deposited in the sink and, after a few moments, he returned with fresh rations of coffee, one in each hand.

They sipped at second cups alternately watching the fire and making small talk, then fell silent to contemplate the flames as they danced and leaped in ever changing patterns, each soon lost in thoughts of their own. Now that the eminent danger had passed and, with it their spiking adrenaline surges, a calm contentment was beginning to set in. In the resulting stillness, only the hiss and crackle of a growing fire competed with the whoosh and patter of an incessant rain.

"It's been quite a day."

She laughed as if he'd made an intentional joke. "That is a huge understatement. I'd call this a day to remember," she offered. "It's definitely one I'll never forget." Her tone became serious as she shifted to face him. "You enjoy being a father, don't you?"

"It shows that much?"

"It's there on your face every time you look at your daughter." The closeness she and Chase shared when it came to Lisa had finally caught up with her, until she no longer tried to deny its existence. "Having a father who never enjoyed looking at me, I guess I'm a little jealous. Your father must have been a wonderful role model."

"Not exactly." He leaned forward, elbows on his knees, then paused as if considering his next words. "I never had one."

"What?" Her response was more an expression of disbelief than an actual question.

"Biologically speaking I had one, of course. Kids don't happen any other way." He sat back and blew out a long breath. "But, I never had a father I knew." He looked at her. "I've always been reluctant about sharing that part of myself with anyone. For all of my life, it was a source of shame."

For a moment she said nothing, just drew in a quick, unexpected, breath of her own. "Never knew your father?" She repeated. "That's very sad. I'm sorry." She reached out to where his hand lay on the space between them, closed her palm over it, and squeezed.

"My mother did okay, though she sometimes wallowed in bitterness. When that happened, her sister Francine would pick up the slack with me. And my grandpa, their dad. He was great. A real father figure for me, as they say. I did all right."

"So what was it like for you? I want to know. I don't know why exactly," she was almost, but not quite, embarrassed to be prying. "But, I do."

"There is a definite sense of loss. Of something missing in your life. Being different and always knowing it's never going to change." He settled further into the cushions. "I'd forgotten how much the memory could still hurt, even as an adult. I guess that's why it's so important for me to be involved in Lisa's life. Maybe that's some of the reason why I feel I need you too."

Her heart began to flutter an answer as she felt herself open up to him. *Need you, too.* The words flowed through her mind, connecting her to him in a way she hadn't been connected to anyone before.

"Perhaps." The agreement came out on a sigh. She laced her fingers in his, trailing the fingertips of her other hand along his knuckles.

It could have been because of the afternoon they had shared—not the chaos, but the calm—the intimate cabin, the home cooked meal. Maybe all the sharing had granted them a measure of intimacy they hadn't been allowed access to before. Intimacy to help them forget who they were or where they were or what was going on in their lives. Permit them at this very moment, only to be.

Relaxing back into pillows which were, surprisingly soft and comfortable, Samantha stretched out on the couch. She had warmed up considerably, almost too much so in the heavy blanket. The coarse material was beginning to itch and scratch where it touched her bare skin which, because she had absolutely nothing on beneath it, was everywhere. Gingerly sliding one leg out, then the other, she was careful to make sure the blanket maintained a proper cover over her hips. Closing her eyes, she was unaware Chase continued to watch her.

Unaware he focused on the expanse of one shoulder down to the hand resting over his.

****

With her eyes shut, he was able to study her face. Long lashes rested on delicate cheeks, full mouth parted, she looked like a precious doll, a rare gift to be protected.

His jaw tightened at that thought. He did a piss poor job of protecting her today. He regarded her from under his own lowered lashes. And, without a second thought, she forgave him for it.

His gaze followed the inviting shape of her legs, then lingered on the top of her thigh as he tried to imagine the rest of her, those areas of her body hidden from his view. He wanted only to move his hands underneath the blanket to touch the soft skin of her thighs, her hips and beyond. He thought of his mouth seeking hers, his lips tasting her, sampling where the curve of her neck gave way to the slope of her shoulder then on to the swell of her breasts.

Now that they were safe, he could admit to the

one single idea he'd been concentrating on for most of the day. Hell, most of the month. That idea was how great it would be to make love to her. Even the near disaster in the river had only momentarily diverted those thoughts, and he felt again like some sex starved adolescent. But he wasn't anyone like that at all, he was a sane, mature capable male, one who was falling in love—or already had—big time. He'd suspected he was in love with her for awhile, and found out for certain that afternoon when he was so afraid he'd lost her.

He hadn't planned their first time as a real couple to be like this. He'd been thinking more of a real date when and where he could take things slow. Begin by properly courting her. Bring her flowers, and spoil her with a nice dinner, some form of entertainment or dancing.

Shaking his head, he lowered his gaze to the floor then back at her. But, it hadn't happened that way, it was happening like this.

He toyed with the idea of running outside and diving into the cold, glacier fed river. That would certainly help his body, his body, but not his mind. Sure as they were both alive, and alone, in this cabin, his mind would continue to be filled with thoughts of her he desperately wanted to act on.

When he cast a cautious look toward her again, she stirred, opened her eyes, gazed up at him and smiled.

Her hand still covered his, and he pulled it free to stroke up along the soft skin of her arm, stopping to play with the knot at her shoulder. She hadn't pulled away from him, which he considered a sort of victory in itself. His other hand slid beneath the blanket folds, moving lower as he massaged the sensitive skin at her side and waist. He lifted his hand slowly to reach along her rib cage until he found the swell of her breast. Cupping its softness with his palm, he rolled his thumb over her nipple in slow, alluring circles.

A small thrill of triumph became his as she released a tiny moan. He loosened the knot at her shoulder, then watched the material fall away, letting his eyes discover the same fullness his palm had just enjoyed. His hand slid behind her back and, when he pulled her closer, she complied with no hesitation, wrapping her arms around his neck and lifting herself toward him.

The heat of skin against skin, breast against chest rivaled the heat emitted by the fire. Everywhere he touched her, he felt warmth, willingness and need. His response was a scorching, molten liquid shooting through him, hitting him fast and hard, just below the waist.

His mouth moved over hers with astounding care, seeking answers to questions he couldn't even form. She tasted even sweeter than he remembered, and he wondered how that could be possible. He kissed her again just to be sure, hungrily and completely, like he was a man starving and her kiss was essential nourishment.

All sensations of time and space fell away, leaving the two of them alone with only a kiss between them. Then another and another with all the time in the world to enjoy each and every one. His lips left hers to travel in an unhurried and loving pattern over her body, touching every part of her that was open to him. She willingly granted him absolute power to explore her with his mouth, tease her with his tongue.

She moved her mouth and body against him in a way that warmed his blood and blasted it through his veins. He thought he felt her tremble, then realized the uncontrolled shudder had come from him. He was the one trembling; riding on sensations and needs he had never before experienced and didn't ever want to forget.

Lifting his lips for only a second, he drew back long enough to look at her, assure himself she was really here, and this was really happening. Her eyes were closed, her mouth was rich and full from his kiss, and her lips parted slightly as she searched again for his.

His fingers slid between her legs in a gentle assault, nudging them apart. His mouth soon followed, exploring, testing, urged on by a single purpose—to please her. Her fingers fisted then released the blanket. As his tongue slid over her skin, she arched her body on a moan of desire and longing.

"Yes, Chase, yes," she allowed softly, and he knew wave after wave of pleasure was hers, given freely by him.

Again and again, he brought her—almost—almost to the edge of sweet release and, again and again he pulled her back. She rocked in time with his guiding rhythm, her body rising then falling, like waves on the ocean. Cresting with the fury of untamed surf left to pound along the shore, then subside in retreat, to slip slowly and silently away.

One last time, he propelled her to the brink, only to carry her further until at last she crashed mindlessly over the other side as soul shattering spasms of release took her.

Afterward, she lay nestled in his arms while her body calmed and her breathing slowed. He kissed the hair back from her temple, rubbed tender hands along her shoulders before he covered her, once more, with the blanket.

A few moments passed before she looked up, smiling in total contentment, then boldly slid down into position in front of him. He didn't react as the button at the top of the jeans released under her fingers, nor when she slowly lowered the zipper—

tooth by tooth—as he had done with her jacket. His head lifted only as her hands lightly palmed him.

"I," he began, then sucked in a ragged breath as her mouth and tongue followed the movements of her hands. He reached to set her away from him. She brushed away the attempt. "There's no need...," he began again, but the breathless way the phrase gasped out of him belied each and every word.

"I think there is."

Her breath fanned the sensitive hairs on his stomach, his desire rose in response to feathery gusts that both chilled and inflamed him. The fragment of one final protest entered his mind and almost made it as far as his lips before being forever lost. Her own lips had already begun the newest and next step in the intimacy between them, and the warm sensation of her tongue rendered him helpless. His knees relaxed apart, his hands dropped to his sides, his surrender became complete.

Though his fingers gripped the edges of the cushions for support, the material proved useless as the press of her lips, the warmth of her tongue, the brush of her fingertips combined to send him spiraling upward to race along the same path he had taken her moments before. A path composed only of sensation and feeling and need.

She coaxed and teased him along, brought him to the same brink he had taken her then sat back as he slid, trembling and tumbling, down the other side. All the while he called her name, until only the residue of his voice lingered in the stillness of the deserted cabin.

She lifted her head and her loving gaze captured his, making his heart swell at the fulfillment and peace he found there.

"Me too," she replied on a sigh.

She came willingly as he lifted her up to cradle into his arms. He held her for a long time with no barriers between them. Not even words, just feelings and memories and, yes he had to admit it. Love.

The thought hit him with the impact of a spring avalanche, silent, without warning and so powerfully strong.

"So is this one of the areas where you used to work?" Her fingertips trailed lazily along his abdomen as she asked the question. The sensation alone threatened to render him incapable of all rational thought, let alone a coherent response.

"Here and elsewhere." It was a struggle to even answer her simple question. He wasn't in the mood to talk right now, he wanted only to feel. He wanted only to touch and be touched in return.

After awhile, he got his wish, but this time, he picked her up, to move their love making to the larger bed in the room. He laid her amid the soft folds of the quilt then stretched out beside her, taking her in his arms as he did so. One hand cushioned her against him, the other blazed a slow and sensuous trail along her side and down her hip. A lighter touch feathered across her stomach and along her inner thigh. Willingly parting her legs for him, she yielded to his touch, then gasped as his fingers sought, then found, her waiting warmth. Moist and warm and pliant, her body tightened to claim him as he was about to claim her.

He left her only long enough to retrieve protection from his wallet, and was conscious of her glance down, relief revealing itself on her face, as his fingers tore at the wrapper. Her breathing was coming faster now, and he cursed softly as his fingers fumbled in clumsy efforts to cover himself. Undeterred and unashamed, she reached down to help.

Not taking his eyes from hers, he rose above her then entered her with one swift and significant thrust and drove deeper as her legs wrapped securely into place around his waist. At the same time, he brought his mouth down on hers, their tongues taking up a primal rhythm matched only by the stronger rhythm of their connected bodies. To his delight but not his surprise, she matched him movement for delicious movement, thrust for passionate thrust.

He drew back slightly, not to tease her but to watch her, to gaze at her face and take satisfaction in the passion he found written there. Her eyes half closed in welcome submission, her lips barely parted as she whispered his name.

Souls and essences fused, they began to move as one, soaring ever higher, and he whispered her name as he consumed her then set them both free.

Wrapping his arms along her back, he snuggled her close. They lay together in silence for a long while, face to face, limbs entwined.

"I want to thank you for what you did for us today." She cuddled against him, the serenity of her voice reflecting contentment and peace. "Out there. When I was under the water, and so sure I was going to die." Relief and exhaustion colored her tone as her words drifted to silence.

He wanted to stop her, to assure her he would have given his own life to save hers.

"I never would have let that happen. I always protect the ones I love."

But she was already in a deep sleep beside him.

Exactly where she belonged.

Chapter Ten

Chase woke as faint rays of sunlight crept inside the cabin. He should have welcomed the all clear sight and, under any other circumstances, he might have. Sunlight meant cloudless skies, no more rain. Sunlight meant they could get out of here soon.

Too soon, as far as he was concerned.

His gaze fell to the woman who slept beside him, her face composed, her body pressed close to his. He didn't want to think about leaving here now; he wanted to concentrate only on where he was and who he was with. She snuggled nearer as she continued to dream, and every delicate curve of her tempted him until he wanted nothing more than to be inside of her again.

Head back against the cushions, he tamped down on flagrant desire, determined to let her sleep, and thought again of how close he'd come to losing her. The drastic turn of events yesterday, the danger he had put her in, was his fault, his entire fault. If he'd hurt her, if he lost her— He looked down at her again and swallowed hard, he wouldn't be able to live, wouldn't want to live, with himself. His fingertips grazed the slight indentation at her side, the permanent reminder of harm caused by the recklessness of someone else. Maybe he hadn't been around to protect her then, but he was with her now, and he'd never let anything like that happen to her again. With one single thought, he vowed to protect her as he had the day before, with all he had in him, and no regard for himself.

He marveled at how natural it felt to lie beside her now. How neither one of them had been embarrassed when, in the middle of the night, they got up and went outside, each needing to satisfy another call of nature. His arm around her tightened and she stirred at the movement, her leg sliding along his in a slow lazy motion, at once as comfortable as it was familiar and as tempting as it was erotic.

It wouldn't take much to nudge her awake. Judging from her actions last night, it would take even less to bring her passion in tune with his. Fresh desire seized him as he recalled how her passion and response had left him breathless, satisfied, and wanting much more.

As if his thoughts contained the power to bring her awake, she stirred, stretched and opened her eyes. Blinking away the last remnants of sleep, the momentary confusion in her gaze gave way to recollection and she looked up at him with a smile. "Good morning."

She barely had time to utter the greeting, and he was kissing her again, touching her, wanting her. In answer to his silent request, her fingers played lightly across his chest, then trailed teasingly down his stomach.

"Good morning," he gasped out before he caught another quick breath he released on a sigh of pleasure.

As the sensual journey she carried him on continued, her palm pressed against his growing need for her, then her fingertips dipped lower, stroking and teasing until he felt he might explode right there on the spot. Before he did that, it was time for him to take control. But then, he wondered if he would ever truly be in control of himself ever again.

Though he did manage to maintain the presence

of mind to protect them both, as he sheathed himself to prevent any unplanned events. He'd learned the hard way what could happen when he didn't.

She gave a soft laugh of triumph as he groaned and pulled her on top of him.

"I've waited for this all of my life," he growled, ready for her again.

"Really?" she teased. "I hadn't expected..."

The rest of her words were lost as he lifted her up to join his mouth to hers. Her lips were warm and reassuringly sweet and her body was soft and potent as she skimmed up the length of him. Breaking their kiss but not their connection, she opened her eyes to smile down at him as she eased him slowly and deeply inside of her.

She turned out to be the one who remained in control throughout, setting the pace as he watched her face. Her expression was first washed with pleasure then consumed with desire. She slackened her movements, courting him, teasing him with her wants and needs, until her own desire took over and her pace quickened to throw them both over to the other side of want and need, to gratification and release.

"I feel like I'm home again, being here with you," Chase said as he snuggled her beside him when gratification and release became happiness and contentment.

On a sly smile, she lifted her head to glance around their surroundings.

"Not here, here," he was quick to add. "I guess I mean home, for me, would be anywhere, as long as I had you, and Lisa, nearby."

With no shame or apology, they basked for a while longer in the sweet afterglow of what they shared, talking for a few moments in soft, intimate whispers. Then, out of necessity, their talk turned serious.

"We have to let someone know we're okay before they come looking for us."

Though Chase was the one who made the actual statement, Samantha, too, was aware of its importance. A search party would cost money, even endanger the lives of some very dedicated individuals. At the very least, initiating an unnecessary rescue could take them away from someone who might really need their help.

They had to find a location where they had a strong cell signal. Heralded at first as a way to secure their escape from this place, communication with the outside world had ceased to be a life saving tool and become instead an unwanted bridge to the equally unwanted reality and responsibility.

They dressed quickly into clothes that had long since dried, urged on by the cool air in the drafty cabin, a sharp contrast to their love warmed bed.

As they stepped outside, the air was quiet, the view spectacular. Deep blue upper ridges of the not so distant mountains, topped with the white icing of ever present snow, caught Samantha's attention; she stopped in awed admiration.

Chase came up behind to slip his arms around her waist, and she leaned willingly against him. "Beautiful, isn't it?"

"Yes," she agreed, no longer referring to the view, but feeling the length of him, warm and comforting, against her back. "It is."

They fit perfectly together, his arms around her middle, her arms over his to hold him there, fast and strong. If she had her way, she never wanted to move from this spot, never wanted to give up what they'd shared here.

"I guess it's time." It took every ounce of effort she possessed to step out of the comfort of his arms. "We need to get back."

The cell signal they sought was just a few yards

from the cabin. Chase quickly used his phone to head off any search and rescue that might have been forming, and also contacted an old friend to make arrangements for his small float plane to pick them up later that afternoon.

"I have my bearings now," he told her. "It won't be hard for me to guide us out of here. We only have to walk out a couple of miles."

Letting the fire wane to nothing in the hearth, he transferred just a bit more wood to the barrel stove so she could cook them another breakfast. She was surprised at how easily she had mastered the intricacies of the old fashion cooking method, even how she'd acquired a taste for powdered eggs. The beef jerky she'd leave to Chase.

She'd been conscious of him being outside around the cabin while she was in the kitchen. After awhile, she heard the steady crack of splitting wood as he chopped more logs to replenish the stock by the back door. What had he said? Leave the land as you found it, clean and untouched, as if you'd never been here at all.

Never been here at all. The single phrase circled in her mind.

No physical evidence of their presence would remain once they left this cabin that had become their refuge. As she folded up the blankets they used and stowed them back on the shelves, she thought how fragile their lives could be. Her hands lingered atop the bed where they had merged their souls. Then, tucking those memories safely away, she rolled up the mattress to its original position.

Never been here at all.

Only she and Chase knew the extent of what had taken place in this wilderness haven. But, given that, would it even be possible for them to pick up their own individual lives, their busy, responsibility filled, highly impersonal lives, right where they left them the day before?

There was no way to deny she had obligations to Bob, and he had even more important obligations to his daughter. Would they all be able to reconcile so many different worlds and responsibilities in a way that would allow them to be together?

"There's actually more fire wood out there now than when we got here." Chase's voice as he came through the back door scattered her thoughts. Dusting his hands, he took a seat at the table.

"I cleaned up in here. Made the bed," she told him.

As she set a cup of coffee in front of him, she couldn't help but think how, under different circumstances this was how things would be if they were an everyday domestic couple.

"I called Lisa."

She was a little disappointed he hadn't told her before, so she could have talked to Lisa too, but she let the thought pass. "How's she doing? Enjoying her self?"

His grin spread from ear to ear. "She's having a ball. She said to tell you hi."

"I'll return the greeting when I see her."

"I told her our trip took a little detour, given a combination of bad luck and bad weather, but said we'd still meet her in Anchorage on schedule."

"What else did you talk about?"

"Oh, you know. Family stuff."

She waited, expecting him to elaborate, but he said nothing more.

And why not? Of course it was his place to talk to his daughter, not hers, and certainly not theirs.

Family stuff, which doesn't concern you.

Where did she come off thinking drastic changes would occur, just because she and Chase were now together? Why had she expected she could intrude on his relationship with Lisa, something he was only, himself, tentatively a part of? She had known him for barely a month. Lisa had known him much longer, Monica too.

Thoughts and reflections spinning inside her head, she had just turned from filling their plates, and barely had time to set them on the table when he grabbed her by the waist and pulled her onto his lap. He ran one finger lightly down her cheek. "Suddenly, I'm not very hungry."

Cupping her face, he moved his thumb, slowly and tenderly, along her jaw as his gaze took on the deep brown signal of his desire. A signal which had become so familiar to her, but now she wanted more.

"Well, I am," she countered, in what she hoped to be a playful manner. Standing up she expertly dodged out of his reach. When he made another attempt at capture, she dodged that one too. "Now eat," she told him as she sat down. "We're going to need our strength for the trip out of here."

And to get our love out into the open, too. She smiled at the idea, and took the caring reflected in his eyes as proof he held the same thought.

While she washed up their dishes, he dusted the remaining ashes from the stove and the hearth, making sure no traces of embers remained. Soon, too soon, they were outside on the porch, taking in one last view of the mountains she knew she'd never tire of. The blue gray domes were becoming hidden behind the mantle of the late morning mists. Once more, he stood behind her, his arms around her waist.

"I'll never forget this." Her voice was a whisper on a tranquil background.

"It's too bad we won't be around to see the sunrise from here tomorrow." His words reflected both of their thoughts. He buried his face in her hair, kissing her temple. "But, we'll still have a tomorrow."

"Will we?"

He turned her around to face him. "Yes," he pledged, his voice thick with emotion. "Yes. We will."

Seeing his hair ruffled in the soft breeze, she reached up to smooth some stray strands back into place, only to have another gust mess up the repair the moment she took her hand away. He pulled her closer, not to kiss her, but simply to hold her.

"Lisa arrives tomorrow. We need to get back."

"I know." His arms tightened around her, his chin rested on top of her head. Then he pulled back and stood straight. "We should be able to get out quickly, barring any more adverse weather." There was no way to hide the disappointment in his voice.

Disappointment both of them felt.

The narrow and rarely traveled path that would lead them back to civilization was so overgrown with tall weeds and thick grass, walking side by side on it was next to impossible. Instead, Chase stepped in front to lead the way, holding her hand from behind him as they made their way along a rambling shoreline.

He'd been right. It didn't take them long at all to walk out. And, at the same time, to Samantha, the trip seemed to take forever. The unmistakable buzz of an approaching plane as they neared what Chase described as their *revised* pick-up point made it official. They were no longer alone, far away and removed from the rest of the world. They were very much up close and within the rest of the world. Deeply within the rest of the world.

Once their transportation arrived, things moved very fast.

Samantha wanted desperately to be alone with Chase, if only for a few hours more. He didn't need to have said the exact three words for Samantha to know he cared. He'd shown her in so many ways since the first time they met. But, he'd also made clear, both in words and deeds, his daughter meant everything to him. If Samantha were ever to become more a part of Chase's life, she'd have to become a part of Lisa's too. And that was just fine with her.

"What are you doing back here? You sure are a sight for sore eyes." The man who climbed down from the float plane after it coasted to a stop was introduced to Samantha as Jerry.

Though Chase referred to her by name only, his arm remained possessively around her shoulders even after they settled into the little four-seater. Not getting an explanation of exactly what they were doing out here, alone, didn't seem to bother their pilot.

"Jerry and I worked together up here." Chase glanced at the man. "What, ten, fifteen years ago?"

"About that."

"For the Forestry Service," Samantha added. She supposed she was trying to get in on their conversation. Or maybe she wanted Jerry to know she was a good friend of Chase's too.

"Yeah," Jerry said. "And, let me tell, you, this guy saved my butt more than once."

"If I remember correctly, you covered my back a few times," Chase responded. He was so laid back and relaxed, thoroughly enjoying himself. She'd never seen him as carefree.

Jerry kept his eyes fixed out the front window and adjusted some levers on his dashboard. "From your description, I'd say it was one of Charlie Blank's cabins you stayed in."

Chase glanced over at Samantha, and his smile couldn't have been wider as they silently shared personal, cherished, memories. "The next time you see him, tell him we owe him, big time."

As he throttled up the engine and cut the wheel to turn them around, the pilot was too busy to notice the look of sheer intimacy passing between them. In

Samantha's mind, it wouldn't have mattered if he had. She and Chase had nothing more to hide. Their love for each other could remain where it was, out in the open, where it belonged. But only after Chase had a chance to talk privately with Lisa, and she had a chance to speak one on one with Bob.

"You can thank him yourself." Jerry told them where the guy now lived, then launched into an I-remember-when story which involved the three men and a very large, very hungry bear.

Samantha smiled in pure delight at the opportunity to learn more about Chase. She had the window seat and he sat beside her. His arm around her shoulders, his cheek resting on her temple, he pointed out scenery and landmarks as they flew over them. They were like two love struck teenagers who couldn't keep their hands off each other. When Jerry asked Chase to move his *big retired butt* to the other side of the plane in order to help level their load, he did so quickly, still holding on to her hand across the aisle.

"There's a lot of talk going on around the local airwaves about you." Jerry shouted to be heard over the roar of the engine. "About CO extraordinaire Chase Canfield being lost in the Alaskan wilderness."

"Lost, hell," Chase yelled back. "We got caught in a storm. Which could happen to anyone."

"Could but didn't," Jerry replied. "Face it, man. With the career you had, anything you do in this state is big news."

"Maybe to everyone else," Chase mumbled, but his buddy was already concentrating on bringing their plane in for a landing and didn't hear.

As it turned out, Jerry's good natured observation was really an uncanny, and somber, premonition.

At first, seeing the crowd on the dock from a

distance, Samantha thought they were tourists awaiting their next adventure. It was when their plane banked to make its descent that she saw the cameras and microphones.

Chase and Jerry made the discovery the same time she did.

"I can circle around and land somewhere else," the pilot offered.

Chase shielded his eyes to take a closer look out the window before he spoke. "Thanks, but no. There aren't really that many, and they'll find me anyway if I try to avoid them. They always do. Better to face them here than at our hotel I guess."

"Face them?" Samantha asked, and tried not to notice her stomach tighten and her heart sink.

"The locals know it was Jerry's plane that came to get us and this is Jerry's slip. If we land anywhere else but here, they'll know I'm trying to avoid them." Chase took in what must have been apprehension on her face and reached out to squeeze her hand. "Hey. It'll be fine. Just follow my lead."

"Yeah." Jerry killed the engine, lowered some levers and hit some switches, then unbuckled his seat belt. "Follow his lead. He's used to this."

"Maybe he is, but I'm not," Samantha managed to get out as Jerry unlatched the door.

A small contingent of photographers and reporters made their way forward as soon as the plane had taxied nearer to the dock and coasted to a stop. Their faces carried expressions of urgent anticipation coupled with a strong sense of detached interest. She'd gotten hints of Chase's notoriety first from Bob, then from his Aunt Francine, but she hadn't thought much about how being somewhat famous could truly impact his life, and hers. She'd assumed—erroneously it seemed—the television crew of a few days before and the clerk's reaction at the kayak rental place to be no more than harmless hero worship.

"I would bet we can thank Danny and his sister for some of this," Chase noted, his tone holding more resignation than anger.

"Is thank really the right word?" She didn't yet have his sense of acceptance at the intrusions in his life, maybe she never would.

He cast her an apologetic look. "Probably not."

Though he kept hold of her hand as they negotiated the few steps across the landing plank to the pier, she expected him to let her go the moment they hit solid ground. Chase apparently, had other ideas. Quickly circling his arm around her shoulders, he held her against him and, moving as one, they made their way toward the waiting crowd.

"Is there anything special I should do?" she asked.

"Just keep smiling. Like this."

The easy grin she'd come to recognize as part of his public persona became firmly locked into place. Taking his lead, she put on an equally accepting smile of her own. Just in time for a quick succession of flash bulbs to explode in their faces.

"Officer Canfield. Can you tell us what happened out there?"

"Had you ever been lost out in the wild before?"

"Were you afraid you wouldn't survive?"

Chase raised his hand for quiet. "Hey, guys. I'm a civilian now. Remember? Just another tourist."

A spate of disbelieving laughter answered his comment.

"No really," he said again, the easy smile dipping at its edges.

Only Samantha saw the clenched jaw beneath, felt his arm stiffen as he pulled her even closer, knew every muscle of his body was rock hard tight.

"Just a simple tourist mishap," he said. "Ms. Wells and I got too close to a glacier. It calved.

Swamped our kayak and we had to swim to shore. The storm blew up and...well, you know the rest." Still holding Samantha, he attempted to take the two of them through the line of reporters which became a barrier unwilling to give way.

"Okay, guys," he tried again, his voice gripped on the brink of anger he was no longer trying to hide. "We're tired and we're hungry. Give us a break, huh? I promise you all full interviews later."

Ignoring various calls for specific times and locations, he finally broke through to a waiting cab Jerry had managed to flag down.

Even as Chase closed the car door behind them, the chance to be alone remained out of reach. For the entire hour and a half it took to drive to Anchorage, their cab driver talked non-stop.

Samantha had no idea Chase being lost for one day—and one night—would cause such a stir. Or that such news, even minor news, would travel as fast as it did. By the time they arrived at their hotel, the tape of them landing at the pier was playing on the local news which was being broadcast on a couple of televisions playing in the lobby.

First the desk clerk, then the hotel bell hop took over from where the cab driver left off, asking questions and offering advice on how they would have handled the wilderness crisis.

Finally alone, after being shown to their suite, they were able to reclaim the comfortable sense of belonging together. Chase had scant time to pull her into a swift hug before the phone began to flash and ring with the same frenzied insistence of the reporters and their cameras on the dock.

"I need a bath," she said. Once more, it took a huge amount of effort to step out of the comfort of his arms. Maybe because she couldn't shake the feeling it might be a long time until she'd be in them again. "No offense, but you do too."

"Ouch." He reached out to bring her back into his embrace. Dropping one last kiss on her forehead, he made no move to let her go. Until the telephone began to ring again, in a way that let them both know it wouldn't stop until he answered it.

"I'll meet you back out here for dinner." He indicated the common living area in the two bedroom suite then sent her a wry smile. "Unless you'd rather go down to the dining room for dinner."

"No, up here would be fine," she answered quickly as she watched him pick up the endlessly ringing telephone.

Their luggage had been delivered as planned, and was tucked with great care into one corner. Sanity amid the chaos, she thought absently, setting the cell phone Chase had returned to her on the desk.

The accommodations were plush, even opulent with thick carpets and sleek furniture. But, then she was no doubt comparing the hotel room to their shelter of the night before. The rustic cabin in the woods held a certain appeal, and she smiled at the arrival of another precious memory.

Even after the hot bath, her whole body ached from the exertion she'd put it through the past couple of days.

Both the bad and the good. The very, very good.

The last thought brought out another self-satisfied smile as she finished drying off. Then, pleasant memories fled as the telephone on her nightstand started to ring, almost as insistently as the main phone in the other room. She had just enough time to wrap into a robe and answer before the call flipped back to the front desk.

"So you guys are okay?" Bob asked the moment she opened the connection.

Bless him for asking that first.

She assured him they were.

"When I got a call saying you were missing...," He didn't need to say any more, his muffled cough revealed further thoughts for him. "Anyway. I'm glad you're safe."

"We're safe," she whispered. No sense pretending she was alone any longer.

"I saw the picture."

There was also no need to ask him what picture, or what he thought of Chase being with her on this assignment either. Though he would never come out and say it, she could tell he wasn't exactly pleased. Because she had gone and done what she'd vowed to herself, and to him, she'd never do again. She'd gotten personally involved with a client. And not at all in a subtle, low key way. This one was more of a blasting, in-your-face-for-all-to-see variety of involvement.

After a long silence, Bob spoke again. "I guess I didn't realize Chase was taking the trip, too." She knew what he was nice enough not to say. *You didn't tell me he was there, why was that?* "And where is Lisa now?"

"She was on a separate trip with the Darlings. Francine's friends. The ones she had planned to travel with all along."

She was alluding to the fact this was how everything had been planned all along, and why wasn't Bob on board with it? As if that would make this disaster more palatable. She felt like a teenager caught making out with her boyfriend while her parents were out of town and was going to be punished for her indiscretion.

"You let her go off by herself?"

"Her...Chase did." She kept her voice level, unemotional, as if she were making a daily report. Except, everything she was telling Bob wasn't exactly how the events transpired. But close enough. She went on to explain Chase's official position on the ship to further explain away the innocent reason for his presence.

"I suppose you were right to stay," Bob offered, but didn't sound entirely convinced. And bless him again for not asking how Chase happened to be along on the trip in the first place.

"I'll see you in a few days," she promised before ending the call. When she got home, he'd see how different this case was from the other.

She pulled on jeans and a turquoise tank top, no bra. *Why bother with formalities?* With a flutter of anticipation—after all, she wasn't home yet—she dried her hair. A little bit of effort with the curling iron followed, then the rumblings of her stomach reminded she hadn't eaten anything since breakfast early that morning, with Chase.

She enjoyed another pleasant memory as she dabbed tinted moisturizer under her eyes, down her nose and across her cheeks, blending the make-up together with quick, efficient movements, when again her stomach made its hunger known. This time the sensation was accompanied by, she was sure, a dinner-time aroma coming from the next room. Was she imagining it, or did she actually smell appetite inspiring food?

Opening her bedroom door a crack, she peeked out into the living room. One lamp, on in the corner, cast a warm glow on beige walls and the green and gold brocade furnishings.

A table sat to one side. Draped in white linen, it held two formal place settings complete with crystal water goblets, coffee cups on saucers and napkins in silver rings. Matching silver domes covered what were no doubt large dinner plates. A single pink rose in a delicate porcelain vase, graced the center of the table. Dinner had already been ordered, a romantic dinner for two.

Two Queen Ann chairs, much like the ones in

her office, were set on each side. Only the television, tuned to a continual cable news station and humming in the background, seemed out of place.

Chase stood up as soon as she came into the room, walked toward her, and started to pull her into his arms. She met him half-way, grabbing to hang on to him as tightly as he was holding her. His kiss was warm and potent and sweet, exactly as she remembered. And why shouldn't it be? Despite their rather public plunge—make that nosedive—back into the reality of their lives, nothing between *them* had changed. For now at least, they were able to be just the two of them, and for now at least, with no interruption from the outside world.

As if cued by Chase and Samantha once more being together, her cell phone chimed from where she'd left it. Neither moved until the chiming stopped and the call switched over to voice mail.

"I bet Bob needs you."

"We just talked. He can wait for awhile."

Smiling at that, his arms went securely around her waist and his hands settled into place just above her hips. With the lightest pressure of his fingers, he molded her to him. He lowered his face until she could feel the warmth of his breath and grew anxious for the touch of his lips.

Which was when her stomach, then his, began to growl in the most unromantic of ways.

"I thought you'd be hungry," he said, finally lifting his mouth from hers. Still, they clung to each other, keeping all other intrusions at bay. "I know I am. I ordered for both of us. Steak, salad, baked potato and broccoli."

"That was nice. Thank you."

"I took a chance. Medium rare?"

"Perfect."

"I guess I know you pretty well."

"I guess so." She paused at the truth they

uttered without thinking. He did know her better than any man had before.

Or, any man ever would again.

A flash from the television caught her attention, and she glanced over to see another round of news clips. The two of them standing arm in arm on the pier. Chase's face was set in a smile of welcome with her, sporting an equally accepting expression, firmly attached to his side. They looked like caricatures of celebrities walking the red carpet, graciously waving amiable greetings to eager fans.

"Is that how they caught us?" She nodded toward the screen, wondering why she bothered to ask. The evidence was clearly before her.

"The wire services picked that one up, too." Moving quickly, he shut the scene off, but not Samantha's regrets.

"Like I said. I just got off the phone with Bob." Suddenly very tired, she sank into the closest Queen Anne chair. "He's seen enough to be right up to speed."

"Samantha, I am so sorry." He raised his hands in emphasis then, not knowing what else to do, dropped them to his sides.

"For what? This wasn't your fault."

"It was my entire fault. I should have insisted Lisa stay with us, or something." He paused for a moment before he went on. "I got a call too." The monotone delivery signaled his call hadn't been any more pleasant than hers. "Monica. I imagine she's already collecting newspaper articles and taping sound bytes about all of this to bring to court with her. She'll use our little..." he raised one hand in a gesture of futility. "Use what happened out there against me."

The defeat in his voice tugged at her heart. For the first time she saw how shell-shocked and weary he looked.

"Now I'm the one who's sorry," she said quietly, wanting only to return to his arms, use her fingertips to smooth the worry lines from his brow, and her lips to kiss the sour expression from his mouth. "For being selfish. Any embarrassment I've suffered, being caught by Bob becoming involved with...by you being here, pales in the face of losing your daughter. I've never even met Monica," she went on, "yet I have a feeling I know what she's capable of."

"Maybe you don't." The stern delivery held a definite warning and revealed the stress and hopelessness he felt. "She is ready to do most anything to keep me away from Lisa."

When Samantha started to brush off his words, he stopped her with another raised hand. "She would have no problem at all dragging you into court and ruining your reputation along with mine. She, and that low life husband of hers, will make sure every sordid detail comes out, true or not. It could impact Bob's agency and the plans you two have for the franchises."

Samantha closed her eyes as he upped the stakes, adding one more casualty she hadn't even considered to this terrible mix. Starting to say, *but we didn't*, she stopped. *But they did.* What defense could he possibly offer in court?

"It wasn't like that."

"No it wasn't. But what's haunting us now is the way this all appears. To her, especially. That I abandoned our daughter in favor of you. *Wantonly* abandoned her, to use Monica's new catch term."

"But you didn't!"

"I know that and you know that," he said calmly. "But I also know lawyers. They confuse facts, blur the truth. It's how they earn their money."

"What is all of this going to do to Lisa?" She lifted the silver cover from her dinner. Starving as she was, the delicious aroma of the lightly spiced meat garnished with sautéed mushrooms, one of her favorites, had absolutely no effect on the appetite she'd swiftly lost. "I think that you should tell her everything that happened." She instantly regretted her choice of phrasing. "Well, certainly not everything."

"I called her as soon as we arrived here. I had to get to her quickly, so she knew what to expect, and to tell her the truth, before she saw the news reports."

Her head shot up, but she shouldn't have been surprised. That's what family members did when they've been separated. They got a hold of each other. The stab of pain at not being included in the conversation, again, countered the relief flowing through her at being spared having to make an explanation to someone who, over the course of a few short weeks, had become very important to her. Almost as important as her father.

"It's taken care of then. Good. What did you tell her?"

"As usual, the press got it wrong."

"What did she say about...everything else?"

"She couldn't see where this was such a big deal."

"That's something." *Something!* Lisa's reaction was darned near everything, at least to Samantha.

Keyed up emotions, and maybe a touch of devastation at not truly being a part of the family called Chase and Lisa got the better of her. Hard as she tried to hold them back, tears welled up and threatened to fall on her cheeks.

Chase had enough to think about. She had no right to bother him with a silly, emotional outburst.

Sweeping the back of one hand over each side of her face, she brushed them away, and could only hope he hadn't noticed her spell of weakness.

Chapter Eleven

Chase watched Samantha flick away a couple of tears, then pretended he hadn't seen a thing. Out of the respect he held for her, because he was sure she hadn't meant to let them escape? Or because he was ashamed of the pain his actions caused her?

He had no idea why, but, either way, he was still deeply entrenched in protection posture when it came to Samantha Wells. And, probably would be for the rest of his life, if he were lucky. In the span of a few short weeks, she'd become more important to him than any other woman, ever. He wouldn't allow Monica to ruin what he had with Samantha, as she had everything else he touched. A few weeks ago, his goal had been to preserve what little family he had. Now he wanted more. He wanted Samantha there as well. Maybe someday become his wife and the mother to Lisa her own mother had no desire to be.

An internal sigh of frustration was all he allowed himself at the way this evening was unfolding. His original plans—for an intimate candle lit dinner for two—took shape when he and Samantha were still out in the wild. Shortly before he spoke to Lisa. Too bad those plans were well on their way to going straight to hell. He should have trusted his instincts, and forged ahead with his original intentions regarding the woman he loved. Instead, he'd made himself wait, wanting to give her something special. A day and an evening full of memories. He glanced over and found her staring at the wonderful dinner he'd just ordered, and seeming to see nothing. He held in another sigh, this one of regret. She had those memories now—all bad—and all because of him.

Maybe he'd be better off just going to hell, too.

Samantha sat up straighter in her chair, emotions now under control, looked up at him and smiled. Trying to smile back, he knew he would do anything he could to keep her from being hurt, or embarrassed, any further by all of this mess he called his life.

"Right now, your focus has to be on Lisa," she said. And his need to protect her ratcheted up a notch or two.

"I know." *His focus, not hers.* He'd take care of Lisa, he always did, and Samantha didn't have to. Her job as Lisa's chaperone was officially over. She no longer needed to maintain watch over his daughter; she needed to concentrate on watching over herself, and preserving her reputation. Self-preservation had become the name of the game, and was the only way out of this situation. For her.

As he formed his thoughts into convincing words, she never gave him the chance to even begin. "There's no need for Lisa to be dragged through something like this. Can't we do anything to prevent that?"

He tilted his head, not sure he'd heard correctly. He'd just explained Monica wasn't above ruining her career, along with his best friend's business, to get back at him. And, she was obstinately keyed on how all of this would affect Lisa. "I can. You don't need to."

A possible solution began to take shape in the back of his mind as *he* keyed on her term, *prevent that*. "That's why I'm not going to do this to her again." He took a deep breath, and when he spoke once more, his voice was low. "Or to you. I'll talk to Lisa. Maybe if I don't contest Monica's wishes..."

"Oh, Chase! No!"

"Lisa will be an adult in a couple of years anyway," he went on as if he hadn't heard her objection. He was flying by the seat of his pants here. Verbalizing his thoughts the instant they arrived in his head. "I'll be able to see her again eventually."

For once she had no quick answer. Maybe she'd come to accept—and trust—he was determined to protect her as fiercely as he'd ever protected Lisa. And was willing to let him do that.

He watched as, with deliberate care, and calculated nonchalance, she cut a piece of warm, juicy steak and put it in her mouth, then took her time to chew and swallow before continuing their conversation. Like they were discussing some topic as banal as the weather. He had to hand it to her, she was better at the cool-under-pressure act than he was. If he tried to eat right now, he could just as well be munching on chunks of plastic and would no doubt barf everything back up.

They talked about Bob and the agency, Monica and her bastard of a husband. He didn't want to talk about the people *around* the three of them; he wanted to talk *about* the three of them. About he and her, together with Lisa, becoming a family. But how, for the love of God, would he make that family happen?

"So I'll leave the agency," she said. "I've taken myself off cases before for political or personal reasons. This time it will be for good. Bob and PSI will be fine."

She wasn't making this easy, and at the same time, she was doing exactly what he'd come to expect her to do. This very personality trait of who she was—caring and unselfish—had captured his heart from day one. She was so willing, too willing, to forego her needs for someone else's. For Lisa and for him.

She looked up with another smile he could tell was forced. "The public loves it when an organization can weed out a rogue cop, present or former, and when that cop gets their due."

"You're no where near a rogue cop. It's not that bad."

He watched an unconditional doggedness enter her eyes, and a chill colder than the inside of any glacier ran down his spine then crawled around his middle to lodge in the bottom of his stomach. Her look held the same single minded purpose he'd seen reflected there before, when she was about to defend Lisa at all costs.

"I'll do what needs to be done. Take the blame for all of it. We'll tell everyone things weren't your fault." She glanced up with an embellished femme fatale come-hither gaze that twisted his insides like so much putty. "We'll say I seduced you."

He tried to wrap his mind around the enormity of her suggestion. No one had ever—*ever* offered him such sacrifices. The day he met her, to preserve his integrity with Lisa, and now, to uphold his integrity with—what? Himself? Monica? Neither one of *them* was worth it.

"Leaving PSI wouldn't be your best career move." *But as a life move, it would be terrific. For me. It would free you up to be my wife. We'll take Lisa with us and become an honest to God family. Live on the run if we have to.* And that was where his fantasy stopped.

How was it fair of him to ask her to sacrifice so much? Especially for someone like him? He was the one who had the illegitimate child, he was the one who had to deal with someone the likes of Monica. He was the one with a life full of controversy and bullshit. Samantha deserved better than that. Better than him, and maybe Lisa did too.

Samantha had plans for her life, and a future to go back to in Detroit. Lisa had school coming up, and now Ethan. He actually liked the kid, and the way he treated his daughter. Ethan was someone who could provide something for her. Unlike what he had to offer Samantha at the moment, which was nothing but pain and struggle and ruin.

He sat down across from her. "But, Lisa's only part of it. You need to think about yourself."

"You need to think about your daughter," she countered, spearing another piece of meat.

"I am." He reached over to take the knife and fork, setting them down to capture her hands. When she wriggled those free, he grabbed her wrists and squeezed, forcing her to look at him. "And, I'm thinking about what happened out there, too."

And how he never would have changed any of it.

He had so wanted her to be a part of his world, and in the strangest way, he'd gotten his wish. She was a part of his world, the ugly public part she didn't deserve to be in. And, without batting an eye, she was accepting all of it, personal sacrifices included.

Making what he had to do, for her, suddenly very, very clear.

But, he had to be careful with his phrasing. She was one woman he knew too well, and he had to outsmart her. If he asked her to do something to help herself, he knew she'd refuse. So, God help him, he had to trick her into believing him. He had to deceive her. At the thought of deception, words like *no* and *I love you* reverberated up his throat, demanding to be spoken.

Through sheer willpower and strict training, he didn't let that happen. The willpower was built into his genes. The training occurred during one of many undercover operations when his identity as a government agent was in danger of being revealed.

He was deep in the Yukon, alone except for six men, every one of them poachers. All fully armed, who were not only willing, but downright eager, to blast the head off anyone who dared to interfere with their way of life. With conservation officers, like him, on top of the list.

Fast talk and cool action preserved his life then, and was allowing him to do what he had to now. Except, while that was bad, this was worse, far worse.

He lifted his hands away from hers spreading them open in front of him, to show he had no plans to touch her again soon. As hard as that would be. Ignoring what was between them was damn near impossible, since he'd experienced how very good they could be together.

"Quit your job over a custody hearing? That seems a little extreme."

"Why would you say that? My job is certainly not as important as Lisa and you."

Say the words, Chase, buddy. Tell the story. Weave the lies..

"There's a lot going on in all of our lives right now." He couldn't look at her as he spoke. "Neither one of us needs any added...," he lifted his hand then dropped it again. "...complication."

If the stricken look that crossed her face was any indication, he'd definitely caught her off guard, now he just needed to keep her off balance.

"Love shouldn't be a complication." Her voice was ragged, infused with raw emotion.

No! It shouldn't. Not a love strong as mine for you. He nearly doubled over with the effort to keep from expressing those thoughts. He had to remember what he was doing, and why. When he worked undercover—playing a role to achieve a definite result—any slip back into his real self could hold a distinct cost. Right here, right now was no different, except, right here and right now, he was sparing Samantha that cost.

Using gut wrenching control, he made himself look up at her in surprise. "Love? Who said anything about love?" It took everything he had to push out those words. The scoff he made himself add at the end out only added to his growing self-hate. He almost collapsed under the weight of what he had to say next, but made himself keep going. "Love! Wow!" The feigned smirk as he diverted his gaze was meant to transmit disbelief, not the real reason he dropped his eyes, because he couldn't stand to see the pain in hers. "You must have gotten the wrong idea. Sorry about that." *I am so very sorry!*

"Oh." He scarcely heard the spoken response, but her involuntary blink of disbelief spoke volumes.

His body went rigid with effort as he forced himself to keep an adequate distance between them. He knew if he got too close to her at all, he'd draw her into his arms, all the while proclaiming how much he loved her. After that, he wouldn't be able to stop.

"Okay, I guess I need to tell you the truth," he began, and his gut clenched at the suspicious look that came into her eyes. His heart pounded and his throat ached with regret at the words he was about to say. In his career, he'd faced down vigilantes holding loaded shot guns when he was unarmed, and more dangerous animals in the wild than he could even count. None of which came close to the fear ripping into him at this moment, knowing he had no choice but to give up the woman before him now. The woman he loved.

"You want to know why things happened between us back there? Here's my take on it." His voice threatened to give out, but he refused to allow such failure and pushed on. "It happens. Near death experience, life is short and all that. So why not have a little enjoyment before it ends." He wished he hadn't used the word enjoyment, too personal for his son-of-a-bitch purpose.

So many emotions flashed in her eyes, he couldn't begin to decipher what they were. Shock? Remorse? Pain? Acceptance? He didn't dare think about them now. He had to do this for her. She raised her chin and squared her shoulders much as she had the first day they'd met, when he knew she'd somehow be a part of his life forever.

Whether I ever see her again or not.

"You really believe that?"

Though he knew her well enough to know she tried to hide it, her voice was a mixture of hope and doubt. She couldn't conceal the hurt look in her eyes, and that alone tore at his heart, but he couldn't let such weakness stop him.

"Yeah. Don't you? If I remember correctly, friends only was what we decided to be." He cast her a sidelong glance, smirk intact. "And, as I also remember, the *friends only* was your call." He made no secret of making a crass and thorough inspection of her body—for theatrical effect only—while it took everything he had not to reach out to touch her for real. "And I was more than willing to go along."

He held on to the glib expression even though his heart pounded so hard, he was sure it would blast out of his chest. One more lie, one more monumental untruth and she'd be free of him forever. And, that was for the best, wasn't it? Then why did he feel as if life itself was slipping away? Why was the emptiness inside of him so intense it hurt to breathe?

Tell her, Pal. Big talker. Tell her you don't care.

"I really never thought about, you know, love, or anything close to it."

He watched a single-minded sense of purpose take over her expression, though the pain in her eyes refused to be concealed. "That's your decision, then."

"Yeah. It is," he replied coolly, even as his body shook with the effort required to let her go. Their dinner forgotten, she stood to turn away. "Oh, and Samantha?"

Looking back, she leveled a gaze on him with such a casual indifference, the tattered remains of his heart dried up and blew away. "Yes?"

"Under the circumstances, it might be better if Lisa and I fly back to Detroit alone. The way the press dogs me, we won't be on the tarmac at Metro for five minutes and they'd make things worse. Give Monica even more ammunition if we showed up there together, with Lisa. You understand."

She simply nodded. "Of course."

A stony determination permeated her body, her face, her voice, and terrified him beyond belief. But he'd done what had to be done, accomplished what he set out to do; convinced her they had no future. From the way she looked at him now, she was a firm believer Chase Canfield was the sole nominee for bastard of the year.

He could hardly believe it when she opened her mouth to say something more. "Do something for me?"

Anything! Just ask. He willed his voice not to crack. "Sure, why not? You've earned that much."

She ignored his double meaning. "Tell Lisa good-bye for me? And, tell her I had a great time getting to know her better. She's a very special person."

You are too, Samantha, my love. "I know. I'll tell her what you said."

****

The moment Chase opened his eyes the next morning he had an inescapable sense of dread and loss. There was no doubt in his mind, something horrible had happened the night before, then he

206

remembered what it was. He'd successfully given up the only woman he'd ever love.

Why couldn't he ever get it right with Samantha? The question which was his first thought this morning, had been his only thought for most of the night. Remorse was with him too, as he tried to tell himself giving up Samantha had been some very, very bad dream.

He lay still for a moment, letting his eyes gradually become accustomed to the strange hotel surroundings. Flickers of daylight entered the room from between the folds of the heavy curtains and came to rest on the rumbled bedspread he'd kicked to the floor. The final act of frustration in a long night when he only slept in fits and starts.

His arm skimmed the cold blank spot on the other side of the king sized bed he'd slept in alone. Turning his head, he spied the empty pillow and renewed frustration balled, once more, in his gut. After last night, pain pooled there too, along with irritation, anger and regret.

With regret easily overtaking everything else.

The foul taste in his mouth was a perfect match to his equally foul mood. How could waking up one morning with her be so right, and the very next morning waking up without her be so wrong?

By all rights, Samantha should have spent last night beside him. And, under him and above him and in any other positions they could have discovered together. But, more importantly, she would have been here beside him when he woke up. Where he had, for a short time anyway, convinced himself she belonged. All of that might have taken place if life were fair, but, it wasn't and she wasn't, end of story.

He scrubbed a hand down his face, uttered a low, aggravated oath, then pushed himself upright to sit on the edge of the bed. Another softer oath

207

followed. This one at himself, and the physical reaction that taunted him from beneath his stretched out pajama bottoms. He wasn't one bit surprised when similar thoughts of her stayed with him as he stood up and headed for the bathroom.

A long shower, with its final shot of ice cold spray, did little to settle his nerves or calm his frustrated body. After nicking himself twice while shaving, he dressed in jeans and a brown short sleeved Henley. Snapping his watch back on his wrist, he stepped into the living room part of their suite.

The door to her bedroom remained shut. No doubt bolted from the other side, too, he thought miserably. Striding toward it, he paused when he got there, raised his hand to knock, then thought better of it. Spying her cell phone on the desk, he shook his head. Had she been in so much of a hurry to get away from him last night to leave that behind?

The thought to disturb her under the guise of *did you know you forgot this* was discarded as soon as it came to mind. He'd said what had to be said last night. Done what he had to do to set her free. Where did he come off thinking anything could be different this morning? Only one thing wasn't different at all. He still loved her.

He thought again of being with her the day before, standing in the land he loved, with the woman he had come to love, he felt a sense of absolute contentment he hadn't experienced in a very, very long time. And might never be fortunate enough to experience ever again.

Which was just too damned bad—for him—he had a lot of damage control to do with the television and newspaper interviews. Could it be possible Samantha wasn't so off base with her dedication to the job? Maybe concentrate on work was what he needed to do today. According to some people, work was good for the soul. Right now, his soul needed a hell of a lot of work, even a major overhaul.

As he was almost at the hallway door, the very instrument he'd been ruminating about began to chirp a happy tune. He hurried to pick it up more to shut off the irritating little number than anything else.

Only after he had the thing open and to his ear, did he realize answering had been a mistake.

"Chase?" Bob's voice held a lot of shock and maybe a little embarrassment. "I...uh...was calling Samantha. I must have dialed the wrong number."

"This is her phone."

Dead air indicated his friend was taking a moment to weigh the precise scope of the information he'd just disclosed. "Oh...Well." Chase had a feeling Bob checked his watch next and was calculating the early morning hour in Alaska. "Is she there?" His voice held a definite hesitation as he asked for her.

Chase glanced at the unopened bedroom door. For him to say she was still sleeping didn't seem appropriate "Not here right now."

"Well. I just wanted to talk to her about the franchise agreement. Turns out I really need her on this."

Mouth pulled tight, Chase tried—then succeeded—in holding in yet another sigh of frustration until he thought he would explode. "She gets it, Bob, but, I'll let her know when I see her. Or, you could leave her a voice mail," he added in a tone he could only hope came off as slightly more civil.

"Maybe I'll do that. Actually, it's not that crucial that I talk with her right this second. I'll give her the details when I see her later today. When she gets home."

"Sounds good."

No it didn't. Not good at all.

"So...uh, how's the trip been?"

"Fine."

"Just fine? No elaboration?"

He was in no mood to share details. "Nope."

"You got it bad, huh, buddy?"

"Yeah." The response was more a sigh of admission. "Real bad."

"Well, hang in there. She talks a good game about being independent and unattached, but she has a soft side. You'll figure it out with her."

"We'll see."

Replacing the phone on the table, Chase wished he shared Bob's optimism. For an ill advised moment, he thought about knocking on her door to deliver an actual message, and see her one last time, too.

Then reality hit once more. Bob's message would only get him started. Then what?

Then he'd be on his own to confess he lied to her to save her from herself? That would sure make her want to trust him again real soon.

Forget it.

Taking some hotel stationery from the desk drawer, he scribbled out a couple of notes to leave her.

Just before he turned the other way to exit her life forever.

Chapter Twelve

Sunshine in downtown Detroit showed up again. As had become habit, Samantha barely noticed. Even as bright, warming rays catapulted over buildings and around street corners to settle on the ever present stream of morning pedestrians making their way to waiting jobs.

Eyes forward, mind and body locked on automatic, she blended with the flow, heading to the next assignment awaiting at PSI. Back to business as usual.

Since her return from Alaska a month before, slipping into the security routine had been easy enough to do. She didn't have the energy to accomplish much else. If she tried hard enough, she might be able to convince herself she had never really been gone at all. The fourteen days away from the job, with all the memories they contained, could have amounted to no more than a series of obscure and elaborate incidents. Ones she'd been permitted to experience as a kind of observer, but not allowed to embrace and possess as her own.

The idea of an illusion, one in which Chase Canfield had ever actually cared about her, could become accepted reality as she went on with the rest of her life. Except, while her mind insisted nothing had changed, her heart understood nothing would ever be the same. Because she would never be the same. She'd always wonder if the emptiness and desolation of losing him would remain with her forever.

She lowered her gaze as she picked up her step. Funny she would use the term losing, when he'd never been hers to lose in the first place.

Sorry you got the wrong impression.

She'd turned her back on him quickly, to keep the devastation private. Then, she walked calmly away, not wanting him to see it took a monumental effort for her to even stay upright. As she traveled along the sidewalk beside Woodward Avenue now, the agony of their last night together came back to her with such a force, unsteady knees threatened to buckle.

Her final communication with Chase had been the notes he left. She saw them on the desk as soon as she came out into the living room the next morning. For a moment the butterflies in her stomach woke up to soar toward her heart in joyful anticipation, finding only shattered pieces of her broken dreams once they got there.

The first note began by saying he was sorry because he had accidentally answered her phone and ended up talking to Bob. She could almost hear the strain in his voice as she read the no nonsense message that followed. *He says he needs you back there ASAP and will talk to you later today.*

The second page was written in short, choppy sentences explaining he was meeting with some reporters to try to deflect their focus and, *do all I can to minimize further damage.* Just before his sharply written initials was the terse phrase, *Sorry about that too.*

It took a single chord of her cell phone to sound, and she had the device open and at her ear. No need to check the caller ID before she recited her name. Right now, she'd take any diversion she could get.

"Hey, Wells. It's Franks."

Even him.

Even when he showed no mercy and started

212

right in on her. "Guess Klein called yesterday. He has another job for us, and requested you specifically."

She stopped walking. If what Franks claimed was true, she'd talk to Bob. He'd let her out of it. If he didn't, she'd insist on it. Not that she expected her boss to refuse what little business was coming their way these days, she simply wanted nothing more to do with one more genus of pond scum. Let someone else—preferably a male agent—deal with the sleaze bag.

"Did you talk to Klein?"

"Me? Not personally. Chief did. I heard him telling Jan."

She resumed her former pace. Franks had baited her for the last time. "I'll see what Bob says when I get there," she said, before disconnecting the call.

She was wrong. Franks didn't even make a decent diversion.

The mention of Harvey Klein brought her thoughts back to Chase. Client, come on, personal involvement, trouble. Funny how free association—and a traitorous subconscious—worked. Especially when she discovered herself humming an old Skeeter Davis song.

...it's the end of the world, 'cause you don't love me anymore.

As if to prevent her from sinking into the uselessness of another somber mood, the horn blast from a distant corner proved the world did, indeed, go on. And, she was right smack in the middle of it. Anyway, she had to make a correction to those lyrics. For her and Chase, it was more like, *'cause you never loved me at all.*

Devastation brought her to a standstill, first rocking her, then robbing her of the ability to put one foot in front of the other.

Reality was such a bitch.

She never planned to go into The Café and Crumbs. Pausing long enough to stuff the cell back into her purse, she found she'd happened to stop out in front of the place. Giving in to a she was there, the shop was there, so why not, kind of moment, she went inside. Making sure to avoid the self-serve line she usually used, she opted for the luxury of a table on the dining room side. Complying with the *Seat Yourself* sign at the hostess station, she chose a booth in back, then sat down facing the door. Clattering and clinked dishes punctuated the droning conversations going on in the room. What was wrong with treating herself to the little indulgence of a latte? Only, this one she didn't plan to lose in an unfortunate incident on the street as she had before. This one she'd sit down and enjoy.

A caffeine pick-me-up wouldn't hurt, since she hadn't slept well over the past month.

The occasional crying jags she allowed herself lasted well into the night. While she expected the emotional outbursts to be renewing and refreshing, they turned out to be only devastating and unproductive, doing nothing to ease the gnawing emptiness in her hollowed out insides. Not even the butterflies were knocking around in there anymore. If they'd given up on her, maybe she should take the hint and give up on herself.

She'd even gone so far as to beg off when Michelle called about getting her back on the volleyball schedule. She'd taken the coward's way out. So what? The slightest chance of running into Chase, no matter how small, was too big to take.

"What can I get you?"

The waitress stood ready for her order, looking like she had a hundred other more important things to do. Samantha hadn't even bothered to check out the menu she opened now, choosing the first item on the first page, The Continental. Then she needed to decide between orange, tomato or apple juice and a bran, blueberry or banana muffin. Those choices made, and feeling a little on a roll with her decision making ability, she requested a tall vanilla latte instead of the included black coffee. Yes, even if it was ninety-five cents extra.

When the woman left, Samantha's thoughts returned. Thoughts about how she'd been back long enough to put details of the *assignment* she'd been on out of her mind. She would think. So why did it feel a small part of her would always remain in Alaska? And, another piece of her, one she could never reclaim, was gone? Why did it feel she'd brought only remnants of herself back to Detroit? She might as well face up to facts, what she could possibly, one day put out of her mind; she could never put out of her heart.

She mumbled a curt *thank you* when her breakfast arrived, then sipped the coveted vanilla latte without tasting any of it.

"Double mocha. Save the whipped cream."

The male voice issuing the familiar order kicked her heart rate up to a pulsing rhythm. Her head jerked up in expectation as hope filled her heart.

Chase!

The name almost made it out of her before she saw the man who had spoken was thin, sandy-haired, and sitting in the next booth smiling at the woman who sat across from him. Her heartbeat slowed at the cruel reality check. If the supposed essential organ quit working overall, she wouldn't be surprised.

From what she could hear of their conversation, the couple was recently married and had plans for a bright and happy future. She couldn't help taking a few furtive looks in their direction, even though watching them and seeing the love they shared caused her throat to burn with unshed tears. Time to face facts, love and affection were items she was allowed to witness but never possess. Period.

She continued to sip her latte and half-listen to the newlyweds, until their voices changed to intimate whispers and, out of respect for their privacy, she quit eavesdropping.

Was this how it would feel for the rest of her life? Could it possibly hurt this bad forever?

Dragging herself out of the coffee shop and on to the office took more effort than she expected. By the time she walked into the PSI reception area, she was exhausted.

"Good morning." Jan's voice held its customary cheeriness.

"Morning," she replied in what she knew was a monotone response.

The receptionist looked at her strangely. Much as she had her first day back at work after her trip, when she was more a shadow of despair, than a properly refreshed vacationer. To Jan's credit then, she hadn't pushed for explanations. To her credit, she did no less now.

"Isn't it just beautiful out there today?" Jan asked. "Sunshine. Clear skies."

"Beautiful."

How could the woman be so carefree when the world had come to end? Then Bob walked by and the two exchanged a look. Jan's world—and her future—were very much intact.

She went immediately over to the message cubbyholes, finding the one above her name contained only one envelope.

"I understand Harvey Klein called." Tapping her mail on the marble counter, she made the comment in the most off-handed fashion she could produce.

"He did." Not one remnant of surprise showed on Jan's face at Samantha being privy to the information. They'd both come to understand Franks and his know-it-all-and-tell-it-all ways. "I'll let Bob tell you all about it."

Not what she was fishing for, but the last thing Samantha wanted was to appear too anxious about the topic. Before she could invent another way to ask, Jan was on to something else.

"We have the date confirmed for our presentation at the Law Enforcement Expo. The morning of the twenty-second of next month. PSI has top billing opening day, and the option to participate in a round table wrap-up session at the end. All of which should really get the franchise ball rolling for us. And, that's all in addition to the staffed information booth we'll have both days on the floor." The excitement in Jan's delivery increased in direct proportion to the importance of her news.

"That's great." Samantha wasn't surprised, only a little disappointed, when her monotone remained. Knowing how hard Jan had worked, the information deserved a little more animation on her part. Or at least comment on the presentation she planned to make. Be a real team player. Rah rah and all that.

"I was on the phone almost daily with their event coordinator to get us such prime exposure." Jan's voice reflected the pride she certainly deserved to feel, and Samantha wasn't giving her adequate credit for.

"Good work." Again, she tried to show more interest, then decided Jan carried enough enthusiasm about the project for both of them—and maybe even Bob, too.

"This came for you a few minutes ago." Joining them, Bob offered her a letter-size envelope. She wasn't sure why his tone sounded uncharacteristically apologetic. "It was delivered by courier, certified mail. I met him out by the elevators. All I looked at was the name on the return address, and thought it was something for PSI, so I signed for it."

She glanced down and did a small double take at the return address: Frederick Arnold, Esquire. One of Detroit's more high profile attorneys, Arnold was a wannabe celebrity, more flash than substance. He had a reputation for being cunning, ruthless, and able to keep one step ahead of the Judicial Tenure Commission—the state bar association's disciplinary body—for some of his legal maneuvers. She quickly flipped the envelope over to tear open the flap, too conscious of Bob and Jan watching as she pulled out some papers.

"Like I said," Bob reiterated. "I signed for it before I saw what it was."

What it was, was a subpoena for her to appear in court. She scanned the accompanying letter instructing her to attend a child custody hearing for the *purpose of determining the lawful parentage of one Lisa Catherine Canfield.*

On a laugh, she repeated the wording out loud. "Chase is the *only* parent Lisa has. Lawful or otherwise." She looked at Bob and Jan. "Do you know what this girl's mother has done?"

They remained silent, allowing her to rant. It wasn't until she saw the knowing looks they exchanged she comprehended what she had done: sung the praises of Chase Canfield's character.

"You don't have to appear if you don't want to," Bob said when she finally paused.

"It's a summons, Bob."

"Which wasn't properly served," he said. "You know the technicalities of the law as well as I do. You don't have to show up unless they actually serve you in person. They have no proof you ever saw this." He stood behind Jan's chair and put his hands on her shoulders. "We could deny giving it to you. If you want."

She shook her head. "I'm not going to take the chance of bringing the wrath of this," she extended the papers toward them, "piranha down on the two of you. You piss off this joker, things could get real ugly."

"If you're determined to go, I'll help you prepare," Bob said with quiet firmness. "How much time do we have? What's the date?"

She shuffled the letter behind the summons. "Next month, on the twenty-second." Her eyes flew up to her mentor's face. "Oh, no, that's the day of the Expo. I can't...,"

"...say no to Arnold, like you said," he replied, his tone so soft it was almost soothing. "Jan and I will handle things."

His fingers rested on Jan's neck. She nodded at Samantha, reaching up a hand to cover one of his. "Yeah. We can."

Bob glanced down at the woman he touched, true admiration and a large dose of affection reflected on his face. "She's been around PSI, and me, long enough to learn a few things." He looked back up at Samantha. "She knows what we need to accomplish. I'll brief her." His gaze took in both of them then he winked. "We have no problem working the extra hours together. For the good of PSI of course."

Jan's response was a knowing chuckle.

"Of course," Samantha replied, though, given her current situation, she had some trouble taking their intimate humor to heart.

"Bob wants the three of us to meet in the conference room sometime today to look over what you have so far," Jan said. Samantha didn't miss two pointed looks, shaded with a little worry. "Are you ready for that?"

"Sure, why not." She made herself look up and smile. "Just let me know when."

She thought she heard a chorused, *We will*, but was already on her way down the hall.

Pausing as she went, she re-read the legal documents three more times, but never did find what she was looking for. Nothing gave a hint if Arnold was legal counsel for James and Monica Wheaton, or whether he represented Chase Canfield.

Therefore, like any good investigator, she'd concentrate on what she did know to help her understand what she didn't. She knew Chase lied to her about not contesting the custody hearing. She didn't know whether that was his way to get rid of her so she wouldn't interfere and make matters worse.

And there was one thing more she knew for certain. The prospect of seeing Chase again landed a one-two punch directly in the middle of her stomach, scattering any butterflies that happened to be left, then moved up to clench a vice grip around her heart.

The pale blue office walls closed in on her the minute she stepped through the door. Her phone started to ring and blink the demands of an incoming call before she even made it to her desk. Hitting the *do not disturb* button, she shuttled the call over to voice mail as she sat down. Whoever wanted to talk to her could wait. In a small act of defiance, she swiveled in her chair so her back was to *whoever*.

Looking out on the waterfront skyline, she allowed a weary sigh to escape. She really needed to get her emotions back on track. Especially if she was about to re-enter Chase and Lisa's lives. Which she would do as gracefully as possible, then slip right out again.

After that, she could proceed with her own future. There was only one problem. Every time she viewed her future, Chase was there.

Leaning her head against the chair rest with a tiny thump, she closed her eyes.

That is not what was meant to be, so get over it!

The jarring clangor of her phone cut off further self instruction. She swung back around with such momentum; her chair almost completed another full circle before bringing her to a stop squarely in front of her desk. No sense dwelling on never gonna happens, she had work to do.

Who was she kidding? She had memories to dispose of.

She picked up the receiver. "Samantha Wells."

"Why the hell...,"

"Hi, Dad."

"It is beyond me why in the hell you never take my advice when it's offered."

Though she held the ear piece a good distance away, her father's voice came through loud and clear. The advice he referred to was given in his phone call her first day back, after he'd gotten wind of the *scandal.*

She needed to be proactive, he'd said. Sue the travel agency. He'd even gone ahead and drawn up the legal documents she needed to sign. Her sending the package back, papers unsigned, must have been what prompted this particular call.

"Other people pay dearly for the benefit of my services and expertise, and I'm offering them to you for free."

"I know, Dad." Good old Edwin practiced a shoot-from-the-hip style of law. Muddy the waters. Confuse the competition.

"Do you know who you're dealing with in this James Wheaton?"

As her father's voice grew louder, she pulled the phone back from her ear to rest against her cheek. "Yes, Dad."

As his discourse continued, he even alluded to

the fact her growing reputation had the potential to tarnish his.

"You want me to change my name? Apply for a spot in Witness Protection?" she asked, pulling the mouth piece close to her lips so he wouldn't miss any of it.

"Don't be flip with me, young lady. This Wheaton is the Midwest's answer to a Kennedy or Rockefeller. This is serious stuff."

If you only knew.

Anyone else might have wondered how Edwin Wells found out exactly whom and what Samantha was dealing with. She'd been his daughter long enough to know such inquiries were useless. He had ways of gaining information she'd rather not find out about. Though he hadn't mentioned it yet, she suspected he even knew about today's subpoena, too.

"One of the oldest and richest families in our state," she said, repeating, word for word, exactly what he had told her in their conversations before.

And a blatant idiot who doesn't recognize, or appreciate, what a wonderful young person he has living right under his nose.

"Are you mocking me? I think you're mocking me, young lady."

She brushed at a tear or two, refusing to let any hint of sorrow enter her voice. "Not at all, Dad. Just, like you, stating the facts."

"I'm telling you, we need to be proactive, not reactive. Sue their asses. Sue the guy who almost got you killed."

Even now, flares of needing to protect Lisa—and Chase—surfaced. "No, Dad."

"Hell, we'll threaten to sue the cruise line. Now there's a deep pocket if there ever was one."

"I'm not suing anyone. Go find your thirty percent somewhere else. Or is it up to fifty these days?"

Edwin would no doubt take offense at her comparing him to unscrupulous ambulance chasers who hawked themselves on local airwaves, offering help to the *little guy in trouble* while lining their own pockets. As the silence from the other end drew out, she wondered if Edwin Wells had finally given up on his only daughter.

"Forget it, Dad! I'm not suing and that's it!"

Preparing herself for another onslaught detailing what else she'd been doing wrong, she was stunned to hear his softly spoken. *Okay.* And, even more stunned at what he said next. "Who knew you had that kind of integrity? But, what kid of mine wouldn't?"

She lifted her eyes toward the ceiling at the left-handed compliment. "Thanks, Dad. Look! It's like you said somewhere back there at the beginning." At the beginning of his original call, she'd actually believed he cared about her. Giving Edwin the benefit of the doubt, she imagined his purpose in calling might even be to offer support. Silly her.

The tears were pushing their way front and center. Rather than let her father hear even the smallest indication of weakness, she pushed them back down and sat up straighter. "I got myself into this mess, and I can get myself out of it."

"It's my guess they'll use you to discredit him." She was right. He had found out about the subpoena. "You don't have to do this alone. I have connections you wouldn't believe. Find out the name of the judge. I'll make a few calls and..."

"No, Dad, you won't." She took advantage of an unexpected silence to continue. "Not everything in life has to be decided by a disinterested third party legal system. I'm going to the hearing because it's the right thing to do. This is important to me."

And hope I don't cause Lisa and Chase any more harm than I already have. Because I really don't care about your precious reputation.

"Oh, and thanks for the parental support. It means so much," she added, preparing to hang up on him.

"I'm only trying to help." She thought she detected some emotion akin to remorse in his voice, but was relatively sure her impression was wrong. But not sure enough to discontinue the call. "Something I'd think you'd recognize one of these days."

She was miserable enough, and certainly didn't need Edwin Wells, of all people, to make her feel even worse. But, then, Edwin Wells was good at giving guilt. Not this time. This time, he was going to receive some.

"Okay. You want to help? You can help."

Being careful to leave out certain self-incriminating facts about Chase, she told him nearly everything she knew about Lisa's situation. Edwin seemed to take on an uncharacteristic fatherly interest as she shared some of the child's history involving her mother.

"Poor kid," he muttered at one point.

Taking advantage of the show of sympathy, she scooted to the edge of her chair and pulled a legal pad from her top, right drawer, then lifted a pen from the cup on her desk. "Tell me everything you know about child custody hearings."

"That's family law. I'm into corporate legalities. The bigger picture."

Poor Edwin. He still didn't get what was important.

"Come on, Dad, dig deep." She issued the challenge and could picture him sitting upright and straightening the tie he always wore. "Tell me what you know."

From that point, her father became a proverbial fount of information, promising to call on his more knowledgeable colleagues to fill in where his own insight was lacking. Forty minutes later, after an appropriate expression of appreciation on her part, and the assurance to get together for dinner soon—very soon—she hung up the phone and leaned back to study her notes.

"Bob said he'll meet us in the conference room in about fifteen minutes."

Jan's voice over the intercom made her sit forward with a start. She punched the blinking button and leaned in to respond. "I'll be there."

Shaking her head as she stood up, she stepped inside the tiny bathroom connected to her office. Who knew she and Edwin could find something to cooperate on, and actually have a civil conversation while doing it?

She smoothed powder foundation along her nose and over her cheeks with practiced efficiency. The touch of lip gloss and spritz of cologne actually managed to lift her spirits, as did the equally efficient brush strokes to her hair. Then she tried out a smile at her reflection, and snapped out the light, hoping her co-workers wouldn't notice the bags under her eyes which, for the past month, refused to go away.

Bob sat at the conference table with his back to the door when she arrived for their meeting. Jan was in a chair to his right, her head angled close to his. He whispered something Samantha couldn't make out, but the tenor of his voice suggested he wasn't discussing business. Jan's responding giggle and her hand reaching up to stroke his arm confirmed that fact.

Thoughts about turning around to leave the two of them alone coincided with Bob's glance over his shoulder to discover she was there.

"Samantha. Come in." His raised arm, sweeping inward, punctuated the spoken invitation. "We are so ready for the twenty-third," he said after she'd handed each of them copies of the talking point sheets she'd prepared to compliment her formal presentation.

"Twenty-second," she and Jan corrected in unison.

A look radiating sheer horror must have crossed Samantha's face.

"Don't worry," Jan assured her, as her hand, once more patted his sleeve. "I'll make sure he gets the date right."

"That's what I have you for," Bob replied, slipping a none-too-subtle arm around her waist, and granting Samantha a wide smile.

"You already know the gist of the message we want to get across," Samantha began, standing up. "The additional information I gathered only defines the importance of good security people in today's society, and how PSI can be a player in providing some of that security." They both glanced down to study the sheets they held. "The presentation you can pretty much read like a speech, but each of you really needs to put the rest of the information into your own words, if we...if you want to be able to impress anyone who comes up to the PSI booth."

As she continued, Bob and Jan nodded in agreement with virtually everything she said. By the time she finished, they had taken about a steno pad full of notes between them.

"I can get these typed, then we can go over them again," Jan said as the two of them stood up.

"This is really going to be great for PSI, Samantha. I appreciate all of your work."

She put her palm over the hand Bob laid on her shoulder. "That's what you hired me for, right?"

"Yeah. Hired. That's a good word," he said, putting his arm around Jan's shoulders as he went on. "You know I think of you more as a partner."

Partner.

Samantha ran the term through her mind a few more times after Bob and Jan left. Partners had a harder time leaving. But, Bob probably already knew that. That he and Jan were willing to handle information distribution at the Expo so she could attend Lisa's custody hearing was one thing. She still carried the major burden of seeing to it PSI became a franchise success story.

Shoving the pile of papers toward the other side of the table, she sat back in her chair. She had an appointment with a promising applicant in half and hour, but it wouldn't hurt to enjoy a few moments of solitude before she went back to her office and donned her public persona.

Provided she had enough public persona left in her.

"Can I come in?" The derisive voice of David Franks put a hasty end to any alone time she might have snatched out of her day. She looked up and found him lounging in the conference room doorway as if he owned the place.

"What?"

"Nuthin'. Just saw you sitting there, alone, and thought about how I hadn't properly welcomed you back."

"Guess the operative word would be *alone*," she muttered.

If he heard, he ignored her. "You wanta go out for drinks later?"

She tried to keep an incredulous look off her face at yet another of his unwanted invitations, then decided she didn't care. "No thank you."

"Suit yourself."

She stood up as he walked toward the papers she'd left unattended. "Did you need something else, or was this just a social call?"

"Just came in to offer my sympathy. You know,

colleague to colleague."

Judging from the sneer he was doing a lousy job concealing, sympathy was not even on the chart of what he had come in to offer. And the colleague to colleague reference was even more of his crap.

"Really?"

"Yeah. Chief's got you staffing a booth at some job fair?"

As usual, he had the facts mucked up. Probably going on information he'd managed to pick up listening in on conversations which didn't concern him. She wasn't even going to try to set him straight. "And?"

"Just wondering what you'd want me to do. In case Klein calls while you're gone. Asking for more services." He didn't give her a chance to answer. "You gotta learn how to finesse these guys, Wells, because we both know they're gonna keep comin' on to you."

Clenching her teeth at the one-two inspection he made of her body, she said nothing. "You gotta learn how to handle yourself better."

She lowered her eyes for a moment and, when she looked back up at him, had a smirk of her own neatly in place. "Handle myself better?"

He sidled closer. "Yeah. I could help you with that. Handling stuff."

"Do say?"

He reached toward the stack of papers. "You gotta start thinking about this agency's good name." Another smug look trailed down her form. Her teeth nearly cracked from the pressure she exerted to keep them together.

"Too bad you blew it with the Canfield case." He picked up the papers, leafed through the top few sheets before she walked over, took the stack away from him, and set it back down on the table. "Must be another demotion, this *expo*?" he asked, using air quotes, and didn't seem to notice when she failed to respond. He stared over at her and smiled. "Chief's friend and all. Too bad. Canfield's daughter...Linda, was it? Nice little piece of...Hey!"

She'd had enough.

Her fingers circled his wrist, then tightened while at the same time spun him around. "Are all of you pond scum specimens interested in only one thing?"

She had his elbow bent, and his forearm shoved up between his shoulder blades before he could pull away from her. "Ow!"

"You *will not* talk that way about an innocent child," she hissed into his ear.

"What? I just..." He ran out of air when she body slammed him flat against the wall, gouging her hip into the small of his back.

"You just decided I'm right, and you will never even *think* about her in that way either."

"What way? I was makin' a joke."

"I'm not laughing." Forcing his arm higher, she kept up the pressure until she heard the joint make a satisfying little click.

"Ahh! Lighten up! You're killin' my arm."

"Better an arm than you."

His body froze, then went rigid beneath her grip. "Are you threatening me?"

"Nope. Just letting you in on the truth."

"Let me go. Please."

"I'd tell you the truth about Klein too, but you wouldn't believe me. I'll have to give you points for style, sloppy as it was. At least you offered me drinks and dinner. Klein only offered me the bed part. And, you're right," she growled. "I should've put him in his place like this." She kept a steady pressure on his arm. "Instead of trying to go the finesse route. And the agency be damned!"

"Let me go!" She ignored the pleading in his

voice. "Next time Klein calls, I'll cover for you. Promise."

"Like I need any of that from you!"

Though she could easily have inflicted more pain, she held herself back, aware this particular bout of anger was directed at Chase.

"Cut it out."

The more he squirmed, the tighter her hold. "Why? According to you, I need the practice."

"Uh, Samantha?"

She glanced up and over Franks' head to discover Bob in the doorway, shoulder resting against the jamb, arms crossed in front of him, as if he'd been standing there for some time. First, she wondered what he might be thinking. Then, she didn't much care so she released Franks with a robust shove.

Looking back at her with narrowed eyes, her *colleague* flexed his wrist and began rubbing circulation back into his shoulder before his gaze followed hers to the doorway. "Oh, hey, Chief." He looked at Bob as if expecting him to issue some form of retaliation toward her. When none was forthcoming, he kept on talking. "I was just..."

"I know what you were just." Bob straightened and looked past him toward Samantha. "I'd ask if she were okay, but I don't have to. I know she is."

"She got the drop on me. You gotta watch her."

"No," Bob responded. "It's you I've been watching. And I've decided you can get your stuff together and get out."

Franks wheeled to face him and stopped just short of stomping his feet. "You can't do that. You said you'd keep me on."

"No." Bob said. "When I bought this place, I told the former owners I'd give you a chance to prove yourself with *this* agency and *maybe* stay on. You've had more than enough time to do that, and for me to determine we don't need what you've got."

Franks' disbelieving gaze whipped around to Samantha, then back to Bob. "Well, well. You'll hear from my attorney."

"Okay," he replied without so much as a flinch in his steel hard expression. "Bring it on."

Franks turned to stare at Samantha. If he expected her to come to his defense, the guy really was delusional.

"And just for the record, she didn't blow anything with my friend." Bob retorted, before his gaze softened as it settled on Samantha. "He's the one who blew it. And, if he doesn't come to his senses soon, he's a damn fool."

"But, you see, Chief, I was..." Franks tried again.

"You were what? Leaving? Good. And, don't call me Chief. Nobody calls me that, least of all you. Oh, and," he added as Franks started to walk away. "Don't look at Jan when you pass her desk. Don't even talk to her, or I swear, I'll track you down and the results won't be pretty. Just so you know, I'm the one who taught Samantha how to *handle things*. I will be going through everything you try to carry out of here, so don't get any ideas about taking something you shouldn't."

In full retreat, Franks' answer was no more than a huffed expletive.

Samantha waited until she was sure he was out of earshot then glanced over at Bob. "You didn't have to do that."

"I think I should have done it awhile ago." He looked out the door, then back at her. "You never told me all that about Klein. You just said the guy was impossible for you to work with. I thought you meant he was treating you like, I don't know, some *girl* you know, talking down to you? Like that?" He lowered his head then met her eyes. "I even thought you might be over-reacting. Sorry about that. I should have dumped the bastard when he first called for our help."

"Start to turn down clients right after you bought PSI?" She shook her head. "Not a good business move."

"Business, no. Personal, yeah. One I should have made back then."

"But you didn't have to."

"And Franks got something else off beam, as usual. Klein called while you were on vacation. And has a few times since. He specifically requested your services. Your professional services, he said." He regarded her for a moment then smiled. "That's what's nice about working the private sector now. We can get away with telling people like him to go to hell."

"You turned down a job?"

"No, Jan must be smarter than me because she did. I just backed her up."

Samantha smiled to herself and vowed to buy Jan a special bottle of wine the next time the three of them went out to dinner.

"I was wrong, so wrong about Klein. But, I'm here to back you up, no matter what. And, I mean that." He looked at her, his face fixed in the same knowing expression she remembered the day he got her to admit to being burned out by police work. When he'd offered her the rescue of a job at PSI. "And what I said about Chase?"

She looked at him, at the nothing but truth reflected in his eyes. "Yeah?"

"I meant that, too."

A small, appreciative smile was her only answer. She didn't have the heart to tell he was wrong again.

Chapter Thirteen

The downtown court building where Samantha had testified so many times in her law enforcement career seemed so much larger and intimidating when she climbed its wide stone steps today. There was no doubt in her mind why.

Those yesterdays afforded her the professional detachment—and choice—of not having to care. Today, being a witness in Lisa's custody proceeding was personal. On this one, she had no choice. She cared too much.

Those other times, testimony consisted of facts and information she had gathered about the case. She didn't want to disclose personal information and, God help her, intimate details about the time spent with Chase. This, as both Bob and her father had taken the time to remind her again and again, was a very real possibility. Though Chase may not have taken those memories to heart, she did. They remained hers alone, to cherish.

The fifteen story structure, with its close set windows and plain cement grey exterior, blocked out every fragment of early morning sunlight as she neared one of its two revolving front doors.

As any good citizen would, she entered the lobby, walked directly to the uniforms working security behind a row of strap connected stanchions, and took her place at the back of the line. In anticipation of having to provide her expert opinion, if that was what whoever called her here was seeking, she'd worked at formalizing her thoughts into a cohesive view of Chase Canfield's merits as a father.

Caring, involved, thoughtful, protective. Supportive. She smiled at that one. The one he'd worked so hard to achieve.

"You're next, ma'am."

The smile fell away at the deputy's instruction. She set her purse on the conveyor belt which would run it through an x-ray scanner, and moved forward as directed, to pass through an x-ray beamed archway herself. As she thought more of Chase, so devoted to his daughter, his family, she had to admit, he had plenty of parental attributes, not the least of which was an unselfish and giving attitude. Slinging her purse over one shoulder as she was cleared to enter the rest of the building, Samantha continued the internal dialogue. Too bad the man's giving attitude didn't pertain to others in his life.

Like her.

"Hello, dear. How are you?"

Such serious thoughts scattered, and a smile was back on her face before she even turned toward the voice. "I'm doing fine, Francine."

Friendly eyes met hers, and the smile was returned tenfold. Chase's aunt looked stylish, as usual. A pale yellow suit with its straight skirt falling well below her knees was complimented by dyed-to-match shoes. Fluffy white lace spilled from beneath a double-breasted jacket at her throat and wrists, giving a chic and comfortable look. Standing beside her, Samantha felt a tad under-dressed in beige flats and sky-blue pantsuit with its unstructured jacket and self-sash belt.

"It's good to see you, dear." Taking her arm, they walked toward the bank of elevators at one end. "Chase told me you were called back to work on a sort of emergency when he brought Lisa home. I missed not hearing about your trip."

"Oh, it was wonderful. Simply wonderful," she enthused, hoping to make up for a homecoming reunion she regretted missing as well.

If Francine had questions about why Chase had seen fit to go along, she didn't express them. "That rascal Bob. Couldn't he even let you enjoy the full two weeks?"

"Oh, it wasn't Bob's fault," she hurried to his defense. "The franchise business is really quite demanding. Very hands on."

Francine cast over a suspicious look, but didn't challenge her excuse.

"How about you? How are you feeling?" Samantha asked.

"I'd be doing a lot better if we all weren't dealing with this," she indicated the huge old structure with a magnanimous sweep of her arm, "nonsense. I tell you, Monica just never gives poor Chasen a break. Never has. He's put up with so much."

"Lisa means the world to him."

"Lisa is his life." She had no chance to elaborate, or chose not to, as the door of the elevator they were waiting for opened.

Samantha waited for Francine to step on first. "So, your health is okay?" she asked, hoping the subject wasn't too intrusive.

Francine shook her head. "Those silly doctors decreased the dose on some of the many pills I'd been taking and I've never felt better. Even drove myself down here today. Lodge freeway traffic and all." Her good-natured reply given, her eyes narrowed and she leaned closer as others joined them in the paneled cubicle. "How are you doing, dear?"

Fine. The obvious response formed in Samantha's mind, but didn't make it out of her mouth. Concern reflected on the older woman's face left no doubt she not only expected, but deserved an honest answer. "I'm all right."

"You look tired."

Samantha knew she must have taken in the grey hollows beneath her eyes she tried to mask with carefully placed concealer, and the frown lines around her mouth the make-up couldn't hide. "Helping Bob with the franchises, I've been working a lot of hours." She tossed her head as if the action would help her divert Francine's attention from her current physical condition. "We're almost ready to launch our first one."

"Maybe you shouldn't work so many hours, dear. Take better care of yourself." Wise eyes settled evenly on hers. "I've told Chasen the same thing." She placed the back of her hand against the side of her mouth and leaned even closer. "And, he looks a lot worse than you."

The elevator doors opened before Samantha could come up with an articulate reply, even a clumsy one.

"Look at that. They even try to dress her up like one of them," Francine whispered as they arrived on the eighth floor and she immediately saw Lisa standing off to one corner. "But, that's all they can do. She'll never really *be* one of them. It's a good thing Lisa carries enough of Chasen's high-quality genes to assure *that* will never happen."

Samantha noticed Lisa, too. Her immediate reaction was to walk right up to the girl who still meant so much to her. She was stopped by the unapproachable stance of the two people who stood on either side of the girl. She assumed the rigid, stone-faced people were James and Monica Wheaton. As Francine had indicated, their clothes suggested money. *Suggested*, she decided blowing out a soft breath, was an understatement. The adults' designer outfits blared high social standing and prestige, along with uptight and buttoned down.

Lisa was in a suit which fit her okay, but she was constantly tugging at the jacket and smoothing the skirt as if she was uncomfortable.

Samantha knew her well enough to recognize she preferred her clothing loose and free flowing. Like the dress her father had helped her pick out to wear to the captain's dinner on the ship. Her thoughts continued on to remind her of the wonderful evening she had, being with Chase, and she clamped down hard on her mind to shut out the memories.

Monica appeared older than she expected. Even with the perfectly styled coiffure and expertly applied make-up, Lisa's mother held herself as if she didn't dare move for fear of jostling one hair or eyelash out of place. When Samantha tried to imagine Chase making love to her, she couldn't bring up so much as the flicker of an image.

James Wheaton's carriage was just as rigid, his hair as impeccably placed as his wife's. He seemed more than a little uneasy in the court environment. And why wouldn't he? Assuming the role of just another commoner was a position which, by his sour expression, didn't sit well. None of the three were talking. Each time Lisa started to speak, one of the adults promptly shushed her.

Samantha caught her eye and smiled in a way she hoped would convey encouragement. Seeing her, Lisa's face lit up and she smiled back. She even started to take a step forward, but her mother pulled her back and shook her head. Calling up monumental self control, Samantha kept herself from marching over to literally remove Lisa from Monica's tight-fisted grasp.

"I'm going to go greet my wonderful little niece and pay surface-respect to the puckered butts with her." Francine's descriptive comment actually made her exhale a soft laugh. "Care to join me? I'll introduce you. Although it's always a toss up whether either one of them can be bothered to say hello."

As much as she wanted to hug Lisa—so bad her arms ached—she shook her head. "That's probably not a good idea right now. Anyway, I need to stop in the restroom before court." She tried to make the smile she presented reach her eyes, even as she knew it didn't. "You never know how long we'll be in there until the judge grants a recess."

"Suit yourself. I'll see you inside. Oh, here comes Chasen."

Pretending she hadn't heard Francine's last sentence, Samantha made an abrupt turn the other way. The coward in her still alive and kicking, she fled in the opposite direction as fast as good manners would allow, willing herself to not break into a run.

Grateful no one she knew was in the hallway when she came out; Samantha saw the door to Hearing Room 6B stood open. Moving quickly, she headed for the entrance, then paused once she got there to size up the scene. With its wood and leather décor, this room contained the typical judge's bench on a raised platform up front. Facing forward, on either side, were respondents' tables, each roomy enough to accommodate four large arm chairs, also of wood and leather. Lines of straight backed benches, four deep, made up the gallery section.

With the same stealth and care she used to approach an unknown—and potentially hostile— environment out in the field, she edged her way into the room, and had to concentrate to keep from diving for cover once she got there. A seat just inside the door seemed to have her name on it. Sitting down carefully, she made herself breathe deep to calm edgy nerves and quiet the butterflies swarming around in her stomach.

From experience she knew being called to the

stand may or may not happen, and depended largely on how the hearing progressed. Good attorneys—and even the bad ones—always kept their options open and potential witnesses like her, readily available. If she were fortunate enough *not* to be called, her plan was to discreetly exit when the proceedings were over. Even if it meant not saying good-bye to Lisa. She lowered her head as she thought how painful that would be, again.

Since Lisa and the Wheatons were seated at the front table on the left, she assumed Chase and his lawyer would be located on the right, and considered the man sitting alone there now. Mark Jones was a familiar face. She and Bob had worked with the attorney a few times when they were on the force. He'd always been fully prepared and fair with his clients.

The Canfield family's fate was in good hands; she was grateful for that.

And, that Frederick Arnold was the opposition's lawyer. The other counsel was no where around. Probably off in a corner preening in preparation of making a statement to the press when this was all over. As if conjured up by the power of her thoughts, the flamboyant attorney strutted in. If she'd been subpoenaed by him with the intent of discrediting Chase, there was no telling what manner of garbage Arnold would throw at her. Some of it, she might have to throw back.

Pulling cop instincts front and center, she looked around to size up the remaining situation. She knew very little about the judge—Paul Sargeant, according to the displayed nameplate—except he was sometimes known for his rather unorthodox decisions. One could only hope he didn't buy into the *a child should stay with their mother* crap some out-dated jurists still adhered to.

The bailiff walked over to close the big double

doors, a signal the judge's arrival was imminent, even though all parties involved in the case weren't there yet. Could Chase have decided not to show?

Hearing the heavy doors swing open then shut behind her, she didn't even need to glance up to know Chase had entered the room; she sensed his presence before her mind registered any sound. As butterflies rose to flutter around her heart, she took a surreptitious peek as he passed and what she saw shocked her.

The man walking toward the front of the room was Chase Canfield all right. And though his back held the same rigid line, he was thinner and didn't stand quite as straight as before. Taking his seat, he turned to glance briefly around. Shock number two hit her right between the eyes. Clean shaven as always, his jaw held far less of its inflexible determination; his face was pinched and drawn. Plain and simple, he appeared to be worn down and exhausted.

The slow and disinterested gaze he cast around the room changed to an unmistakable glare as his eyes settled on her. Just as quickly, his demeanor went from casual observer of his surroundings to active participant as he sat forward in his chair, aiming that same glare directly into his lawyer's face. A few words and slight shrug accompanied Jones' cursory glance her way. Apparently not satisfied with that, Chase moved further into the man's space, glower intact, shaking his head.

Jones put out an arm as he gave his client a more rapid fire explanation. Then the arm came around Chase's shoulder when he said something else in conclusion, glancing Samantha's way again. Was he providing Chase with one last bit of information? Or was he trying for restraint?

"Anyone sitting here, dear?"

Her thoughts dispersed before she could settle

those questions. "No. No one." She pulled her feet back as Francine slid in front of her then settled into the empty space at her side.

"Monica had the nerve to ask if I planned to testify against Chasen," she whispered, frustration and anger still evident in her tone. "I told her exactly what I thought about her selfish antics. She may jerk Chasen around, but not me."

Samantha smiled as she imagined some probable details of the exchange. "No one would dare jerk you around."

"Don't you know it, dear," she replied. "I wanted to see Chasen too, before he came inside. I wanted to let him know I was here for him." Her eyes took on a sharp, knowing cast as if to challenge Samantha to do the same, though she said nothing more as the judge swept in from behind a door marked *Private.*

"All rise," was followed by the shuffle of bodies standing, then, at the judge's direction, sitting back down.

Judge Sargeant opened a folder he had brought in with him, read the names contained on the papers inside, and explained the purpose of the hearing. He then closed the folder and set it down before he addressed those assembled.

"At first, I considered speaking with all the parties involved in the privacy of my chambers. But, after going over the events of prior hearings in this matter, and taking into account the notoriety of those involved, I decided against it. All of the pertinent testimony will be made here." He swept his arm up. "Out in the open. In that way, nothing is left to speculation or, more likely, misinterpretation of facts by journalists in our midst."

Samantha, and every one else who had arrived there that day, knew he referred to the cache of reporters—cameras and microphones ready—who milled around in front of the building. Whether their appearance was caused by Jim Wheaton's presence, or Chase Canfield's, was a toss up. What mattered—and not in a good way—was that they were there at all.

"I'd like all of you to take a moment before we begin to understand the literal meaning of the word custody." She was conscious of Chase sitting taller in his seat as the judge continued. "It's not who can buy the nicest outfits for school, or provide the latest MP3 player. Custody is the act of guarding. Taking care of, watch over, is my interpretation." He leaned on his forearms, "and now yours.

"My decision for public access isn't precipitated only by unavoidable notoriety." He glanced to his right, then his left. "I've also spoken, privately, with young Miss Canfield at some length. I find she has the mature demeanor and poise to handle herself admirably during these proceedings, and in front of all of you. Which is why I'm calling her to the stand first."

Chase lunged forward with such force the arm of his chair hit the table with a loud bang disruptive enough to catch the judge's attention.

"A problem, counselor?" the judge asked of Mark Jones.

"No, your honor." Jones' grip on Chase's shoulder tightened. "None at all."

"Good. Miss Canfield would you please come forward?"

Samantha watched Chase as Lisa made her way to the stand. Feet flat on the floor, hands gripping the arms of his chair, he looked like he had all he could do to keep from leaping up to walk right along side of her. His parent protection meter was certainly running on high alert today.

"You can squeeze harder, dear. You're not hurting me."

Samantha started at Francine's whispered

comment, at the same time conscious she'd grabbed on to the older woman's hand she now held in a vice grip. Added to that, she was sitting so far forward, if anyone had occupied the row in front of her, she'd have been breathing down their neck.

Sliding back, she acknowledged an unavoidable truth. In her mind, she'd been the one beside Lisa, matching her step for step as she made her way to the seat indicated by the judge.

She cast Francine a sheepish smile, and gave the hand she released an apologetic pat. "Sorry."

"Don't be. I feel the same way as you and Chasen."

Samantha nodded, then stole a glance Chase's way to see if he were faring any better. The muscles in his jaw worked overtime. At one point, she was afraid he'd dislocate the joint if he didn't let up soon. His gaze never left his daughter's face. He swallowed hard, once, twice, and a third time, then coughed lightly as he shifted forward in his chair.

"Chasen has a lot of experience with courts and judges. He's served as an expert witness a number of times in his job. He'll be fine."

Again Samantha nodded. Expert witness was light years away from caring parent, but she decided not to share her disagreement. "What about Lisa?" *And me?*

"She'll be fine too." Francine patted her arm then cast her another knowing look. "You all will."

"Something to add, ladies?" The judge's voice boomed down on them.

Francine spoke up in an equally strong tone. "No! You're doing just fine."

Judge Sargeant eyed her as if she'd just sprouted a second head, but retained his composure. "Thank you."

"You're welcome."

The faint ripple of laughter following Francine's

innocent response died down quickly as soon as the judge's stern look swept over the room.

"That's my Great-Aunt Francine," Lisa told him, her voice solemn. "My dad's aunt. And his...our friend, Samantha, sitting next to her."

"Nice to meet you, judge," Francine spoke up again.

Samantha wanted only to disappear into the floor, but she couldn't help a small smile at the older woman's spunk.

Frederick Arnold looked back in exaggerated disgust before standing up. "Can we get on with this, your honor?"

"Of course, Mr. Arnold," the judge replied, though his sharp tone belied the conciliatory words. "We wouldn't want to interrupt your busy schedule."

The high-profile lawyer had the sense to reel in most of his antagonism and some of his arrogance. "I have nowhere else to be, your honor."

"Well I do!" Jim Wheaton's tersely spoken statement attracted the judge's full attention. Samantha cringed, knowing what was about to follow.

"I don't recall you being asked about your schedule, Mr. Wheaton."

Respectful silence followed the judge's strong comeback, except for Francine's poorly concealed chuckle. Samantha worked hard to hold in a smile as she clasped her seat mate's hand again, this time in support and understanding.

Jim Wheaton opened his mouth to respond, but stopped as his attorney lifted a hand in warning.

Ignoring everyone but his charge of the moment, the judge turned his attention back to Lisa. "Tell me about your parents, would you please, Miss Canfield?"

A bewildered stare took over Lisa's face and, for a long moment, she said nothing. Then she lifted her chin, narrowed her eyes and began. "My dad's always been there for me. Even though he hasn't been able to be with me in person a lot lately." Though she spoke of her father, she glanced over at her mother, and Samantha wanted to cheer out loud.

The judge shuffled through the papers before him. "Your father has paid child support for you," he checked a second sheet, "without fail." He cast an accusing frown at Mark Jones. "Why hasn't he had more liberal visitation rights?"

Jones spoke up quickly. "He has them, your honor. They just haven't always been utilized."

"You are familiar with the concept of use it or lose it, Mr. Canfield?"

"Yes, sir," Chase acknowledged, but could say no more even if he'd planned to as Lisa jumped to his defense.

"Oh, it's not his fault, your honor." She reached her hand up to place it on the judge's desk. Chase sat back, his eyes never straying from his daughter's face, a look akin to absolute awe on his features.

"And why do you say that, Miss Canfield?"

Lisa looked up at the larger than life authority figure and took a deep breath. "Because my mom always puts up obstacles for him. Hoops for him to jump through, as she calls them."

Judge Sargeant's sharp look flew over to Monica. "Really?"

Lisa looked over at Chase. "Daddy and I have talked about that. I told him sometimes it's just not worth the hassle for either one of us."

"This may seem like an unfair question," Judge Sargeant said. "But if you had to choose between living with one parent or the other, which one would you choose?"

Tears threatened as Lisa again looked toward her father. "My mother has a family. She's not alone. But, my dad is."

"Would not wanting him to be alone be the only reason you might..."

"Oh! No! No!" Lisa interrupted. "I'd want to be with my dad even if...if he were with someone else, too."

Samantha's head shot up at the passion in Lisa's voice, and she found herself staring directly into the young woman's eyes. Lisa lifted her chin even higher. "Because he could easily be with someone else...if he wanted to be." Her face took on a keen playfulness just before she broke into a grin. "I mean look at him. He's a very handsome guy!"

Another ripple of laughter swelled. The judge chuckled; even the bailiff cracked a smile. Chase closed his eyes and ducked his head as a faint blush trickled up to his hairline.

"And humble too, it would appear," the judge added, glancing at Chase over the tops of his glasses. Then he straightened and cleared his throat. "Do you and your dad have much in common? I mean what kinds of things do you talk about when you do get to see him?"

"Everything" Lisa said without hesitation. "My school, lately. In a few years, I'll be going to Michigan State University. Dad says they have one of the best veterinarian schools in the country. That's what I want to be, you know. A veterinarian."

"I'm sure you'll be a good one," the judge managed to comment before Lisa continued her explanation.

"Thanks. Dad thinks so, too."

Samantha sat back as Lisa went on to detail, for the judge and anyone else who would listen, the plan she and Chase had come up with for her future education, taking a breath only when she had to in order to keep speaking. Even Judge Sargeant had the good sense to not to interrupt her.

"Dad said he'd see to it I get whatever I need, no

matter what."

Lisa, the old self-confident let-me-tell-you-all-I-know was back. Samantha found her own spirits lifting. Without thinking, she raised her head to steal a glance in Chase's direction. Lost in the enjoyment of watching Lisa at her best, they actually exchanged friendly smiles.

"Miss Canfield. You seem to have a real grasp on what you want in a future, but I have one more question."

Lisa's hand remained on the judge's desk. She pulled it back and her eyes grew wide, as if she had just grasped a sense of the gravity about her situation. "Yes, sir?"

"What would you like to see as a result of all of this?"

Lisa bit her lip as she contemplated the latest question put to her. Then the child she still was emerged evidenced by the tears brimming her eyes, and Samantha had to literally hang on to the front of her seat to keep from standing up and taking Lisa into her arms.

"I've always been kind of a problem, you could say, for my parents. They were always fighting about where I belonged. I would really just like for my dad and mom to be happy. No matter where I end up," Lisa replied in a strong voice.

Judge Sargeant considered one then the other of her parents before bringing his regard back to their daughter. "And where would you like to end up, as you say?"

Francine let go of Samantha's hand to pull a couple of tissues out of her sleeve and dab at her eyes with one. She handed the other to Samantha who balled hers into a fist as she watched Chase close his eyes, lower his head and swallow hard at Lisa's words. If ever someone could be so devastated by what they were seeing and hearing, Chase was one such person.

Collecting herself with the poise she'd been credited with having, Lisa pulled the tears inside and set her mouth in a grim line, looking so much like her father, Samantha's breath caught.

"Where would you like to end up, Miss Canfield?" The judge prompted.

Lisa angled her body toward the judge—unyielding and determined—appearing much as she had on the ship when she asked Samantha to go to bat for her with her father.

"I don't know. Maybe with Coach."

The judge leafed through the papers before him. "Coach? I didn't see that name in here."

"Miss Wells," Lisa explained. "She referees...used to referee...some of my volleyball matches."

"That might not be an option, Miss Canfield," the judge replied. Once again, he considered first his audience, then his charge. "Despite everything going on in this family unit, someone has managed to raise a sensitive and caring young woman." He turned his full attention to Lisa. "You certainly seem to have knowledge and maturity beyond your years. For your benefit, and that of everyone else involved, I'm going to go out on a limb here and make a rather, unorthodox suggestion. But, one I've seen work well a few times before this. I have decided to forego consideration of the many options you adults are seeking for this child, and focus the energies of this office toward consideration, and approval, of what this child needs. To be emancipated from both parents, as soon as possible."

A sharp intake of air to the judge's right was the only sound in the room. Monica sat back, one hand covering her mouth. Her eyes were trained not on her daughter, or the judge, as one might expect, but on the extremely angry expression displayed on her husband's face.

Chase pulled his chair closer to the table with a small scrape, folded his arms as he sat forward, and listened to the judge's lengthy explanation—to Lisa—of just what emancipation meant.

Samantha smiled, knowing Lisa would be just fine, then stole a glance back over at Chase, wanting some reassurance he would be okay too. She wasn't prepared to discover he had sought her out as well, and when their eyes locked, then held, her smile faded. The pain on his face, so evident during Lisa's testimony, intensified when he looked at her. Enough to cause her heart to squeeze so tightly, she was sure it would become so small, it would disappear. Though she heard Judge Sargeant continue to speak to Lisa, full understanding of what he was saying eluded her. She was unable to concentrate on anything but Chase, and the way he kept looking at her. Her death grip on the bench in front of her was the only thing keeping her from standing up to fly into his arms.

Then, with a start, she saw Chase was the one standing up. Did he expect her to do just that?

Responding to the staccato rap of wood on wood, she looked over just in time to see Judge Sargeant set down his gavel as everyone else in the room stood up, too. She scrambled to her feet as the judge, looked directly at her. Then, as if satisfied she was being properly respectful at last, he turned to stride back through the door marked *Private.*

As the few people who remained began to disperse, she sat back down for a moment to collect her thoughts, and herself.

"I knew I liked that guy. The judge, I mean." Francine remained standing, looking expectantly at Samantha, waiting for her to stand up and move out of her way.

Just as she did so, and started to take her first

step into the aisle, Jim and Monica stormed toward the doors, with Lisa walking behind them, trying to keep up.

Samantha stayed where she was a moment more, forcing herself to keep from favoring the self-involved couple with some well-placed body slams.

"Your idiotic idea for me to adopt *her* was supposed to *ingratiate* potential investors, not *alienate* them once details of this fiasco hits the papers." Jim Wheaton spoke sharply, making no attempt to keep his words private. "What are they going to think about me when they find out I couldn't even manage to adopt someone as insignificant as her!"

Horror evident on her face, Monica glanced over her shoulder as if she had just recalled Lisa was behind them, and her eyes narrowed in a way that was anything but motherly love. "See if your father will give you a ride home," was the extent of her response before she hurried after her hastily exiting, and still fuming, husband. "Jim! Jim, please wait!"

Samantha didn't recall walking over to Lisa and wrapping her into a hug. She was only aware she now held the girl in her arms, and wasn't about to let her go any time soon. "Lisa. I'm so proud of you. You are so grown up." She pushed enough enthusiasm into her voice, she hoped, to counteract the insensitive behavior of the Wheatons.

"It's okay you know, what Jim just said." Lisa's face took on a knowing expression way beyond her years and she smiled. "They pretty much leave me alone when we aren't in public. And that's okay."

Samantha's arm tightened around her. *No it's not okay.* "It's their loss, sweetie, not yours."

"Anyway, look at me. I can change my name to whatever I want. Even Wells." Her face grew solemn. "Just kidding. Dad and I decided to stop fighting with mom about a month ago. Especially when his lawyer told us this judge was big into emancipation of minors." She didn't give Samantha a chance to answer. "We both agreed it's just not worth it. He's letting me take the lead on this one." Another smile flashed across her face. "He says I'm old enough now, and I guess that judge agrees."

Seeing the pride evident in Lisa's expression at being allowed to have some say in the direction of her own life, Samantha uttered a silent thank you for small favors to the powers that be. Chase did know what was right for his daughter, and the two of them would do well as the family they now were.

"I have to tell you, Coach," Lisa went on, the episode with her mother and step-father forgotten. "Being up on that stand was pretty scary, but, every time I looked over at you, I remembered our volleyball game on the ship. When I didn't think I'd be able to get the ball over the net, and you kept assuring me I would." Her face lit with a smile Samantha vowed to remember forever. "And, I did that too!"

"You sure did, sweetie. And, you did great. Just like today."

"Dad told me how you had to hurry back here. How Mr. Anderson needed you. He told me how important your job was. I was just sorry I didn't get to tell you good-bye."

Samantha's heart broke at the unquestioning acceptance of Lisa's voice. "I was too, sweetie."

"Dad said you couldn't see us back here because of work too. And, I'd just have to understand that."

Samantha swallowed the words of truth she so wanted to share swelling up in her throat. "Oh, Lisa...I..." A dry mouth kept her from answering right away. "I wanted to see you too," she began. "I just couldn't...it's complicated."

"I got the feeling it bothered my dad to talk about why we couldn't see you, so I let it go." She started to add something else, then stopped as she looked up. "Hey, Dad."

Samantha started to step back as Chase moved forward to embrace his daughter.

"Can I get in on the family hug?" She heard Francine's request at the same time as she felt herself being pushed into Chase.

He had no choice but to put one arm around her as she fell against him. After steadying herself, she waited for him to let her go, only to feel his arm tighten for an instant. She closed her eyes as she leaned into him. The scent of a familiar aftershave surrounded her, and she settled deeper into a place she never wanted to leave. It took all the effort she possessed to remind herself, this wasn't where she belonged.

For whatever reason, Chase kept one arm where it was, around Samantha's waist, as he reached out with the other to smooth back his daughter's hair. "How are you doing, sweetheart?"

Though he spoke to his daughter, the softness in his tone shot straight to Samantha's heart. If only he spoke like that to her.

"I'm doing okay, Dad." The smile on her face reflected an awareness she really was. "Except I need a ride home."

"I know." He glanced at the door Monica and Jim Wheaton had just walked out of. "I heard."

"But, not to their house," Lisa continued. "I'd like to come stay with you. If that's okay."

The day's accumulation of apprehension and sorrow washed off his face leaving his expression like fresh flowers after a summer rain. "That's fine."

Lisa grinned at her father's ready agreement. "Dad has always had a bedroom for me, wherever he's lived."

Of course he did, Samantha thought. *Your father loves you.*

Lisa glanced back toward Chase. "I could never use them all the time, until now."

"That's great, Lisa." Chase seemed surprised the moment Samantha spoke. As if he'd forgotten she remained beside him.

"Miss Wells." The voice became clipped and impersonal, the accompanying nod of acknowledgement curt. "I'm sorry you had to be dragged into this after all."

Mark Jones beckoned at the same moment as Samantha opened her mouth to respond. "Mr. Canfield. Chase. Got a minute?"

"Sure."

She had been about to tell him being there for Lisa wasn't a burden, it was privilege she'd cherish forever.

"Is he going to tell you more about this emancipation stuff?" Francine asked.

"I don't know," Chase responded, releasing his grip on Samantha.

As soon as he let her go, a sense of emptiness flooded back in.

"Well, if he does, I want to hear it," his aunt said, following him to the table where Mark Jones still stood.

"You and Dad had a fight, didn't you?" Lisa asked the moment she and Samantha were alone.

"We didn't...fight."

"Then what happened? When I asked Dad, he said I wouldn't understand. Are you going to lay that one on me too?"

Lisa was looking to her for some kind of explanation, and she struggled to come up with a suitable one. "No."

"Nothing made any sense. I mean, especially after the way he talked when he called me."

"After we got back to Anchorage?"

"No, before."

Samantha shook her head. "Before?"

"When he called to say you were safe in some guy's cabin." She could only listen as Lisa continued. "Dad and I talked a lot that day," the girl went on in typical no-breath-required fashion. "He told me the rest of it, too." The excitement in her voice grew as she took hold of Samantha's hands, eyes wide in expectation, broad smile in place as if she expected Samantha to know what came next. "He told me he loved you."

Those words swirled toward her through a fog. "He...,'"she began. Too flustered to say anything more, she swallowed hard. "He what?"

"Told me he loved you." Lisa looked puzzled at Samantha's stunned reaction. "And, that he was going to ask you to marry him." She said the words on the edge of a question. "But he wanted my permission first."

Samantha opened a mouth so dry; she thought her lips and throat would crack. "What did you tell him?" Her voice cracked instead.

A smile broke across Lisa's features. "I told him I thought the idea was great. I told him to go for it!" The smile dimmed, then went out. "Then I asked why you turned down marrying him," she went on. "And he said I wouldn't understand that either. I think I would, don't you? If you'll tell me. It wasn't because of me, was it?"

"Oh, sweetie, no! No!" Samantha replied, putting hasty arms around her again.

"Lisa, dear. You never did tell me all about Denali." Aunt Francine had reappeared at some point, though Samantha—still surrounded by the fog of disbelief—wasn't sure exactly when. "What kinds of things did you see? What did you buy?"

"You were right when you said I had to see for myself!" she heard Lisa enthuse. "The land is even better, more beautiful that dad described."

"Lovely, dear, lovely. And I want to hear just everything about the young man I understand you met."

"Oh, Aunt Francine. He is so cute." She went on to relay more details which were punctuated, as expected, with plenty of Ethan this and Ethan that. "He plans to go to college at the University of Michigan next year." She glanced down at her hands and, when she looked back up, her eyes held a glow of eager anticipation. "So we can be together."

"So you had a good time, and then some," Francine managed to get in.

"A good time. It was great! Oh, that reminds me! I promised to call him when this was over. He's been so great this past month, so..."

"Supportive?" Chase asked, joining the conversation.

Lisa's smile could have illuminated the entire block. "Yeah, Dad. Supportive. Like all of you."

Francine spoke up first. "Thank you, dear, we try. Now, if you want to call your young man, you'll have to go back to the lobby and reclaim your cell phone. I'll go with you. Then we'll stop in the cafeteria for lunch." She looked over at Chase and Samantha with a wink. "We'll see the two of you, when you're done here?"

Before either one of them could answer, Francine—with Lisa in tow—was hurrying toward an elevator with its doors beginning to close. "Going down! Wait for us, please."

With that, and with more than a little panic welling up inside, Samantha found herself facing Chase. This time all on her own. No argument to referee, no advice to give him about raising his daughter. Just the two of them alone with their feelings, and the memories they contained.

The butterflies in her stomach knew exactly what was going on. Alert and active, they fluttered back and forth until they found a new home inside her heart. She stood absolutely still for a full moment to make sure they were all safely in there, as she fought to convince herself the man beside her was no one special, just another former customer. But then he shifted his weight slightly and her body shifted an involuntary response. In her heart, she knew nothing had changed. On a purely physical level, every cell of her body was aware of him. And, after all they'd been through—together—she was attuned to him on an emotional level as well.

She put her hand up as he started to move toward her. To her surprise, he stayed where he was, watching her with such intensity, she was forced to take a step back. She couldn't think or reason with him standing so close. And, God help her, if he touched her, it would be all over.

"You have become a real influence on Lisa."

"I know, and I'm sorry. Putting ideas into her head about independence. Helping her to kind of gang up on you. I shouldn't have interfered."

"If you hadn't interfered," he continued. "I might never have realized she is a precious gift to be guided and enjoyed."

"I had no right."

"Teaching her how to become her own person. How to trust herself to make intelligent decisions about her own life? Why wouldn't you have the right to do that?"

Her troubled gaze rose up to his face. The why should be obvious, especially to him. "Because, she's not my daughter. I had no right..." She stopped speaking as his finger touched her lips.

"You had every right."

"No." She turned her head away from him.

Instead of dropping his hand, he moved to cup her cheek, pulling her eyes back to his. "Yes," he whispered. "You did. Because you care about her."

And you. At that moment, her mind became aware of what her heart had known all along. What good would life be without him? But, now it was too late, because she knew what was coming next. *Lisa and I want to thank you.* Then it would be time to say good-bye. And she hadn't even gotten the chance to tell him she loved him. Maybe now was the time, at last, to tell him the truth.

"Well, I..." Losing her nerve, she adjusted her purse strap on her shoulder, and turned in the direction of the exit. What did it matter? "Good luck to both of you."

"Don't leave. Please." The soulful plea froze her body. Even her heart stuttered and threatened to stall. "We need to talk."

Samantha looked up at him, though she had no idea what he was going to say. But, when he looked at her, the apprehension was back, and her heart tumbled to her toes.

Do I owe you another apology?

"I owe you another apology." He lowered his eyes, then looked up at her again. "I should have listened to you that night in Anchorage. I should have trusted. If I had, we might have been able to come up with a solution, for all of us. Instead, I charged ahead like some damned misguided super hero, thinking I could somehow save you both." He looked down again. "Turns out neither one of you needed me after all."

"Oh, that's where you're wrong, Chase Canfield. Dead wrong. Lisa will always need you." She lowered her voice. "And I will too," was out before she could stop it.

"If you hadn't interfered..." his voice lowered to a whisper. "And, by the way, interfere is your word not mine, I never would have fallen in love with you."

She pulled back only slightly as her eyes rose to his face. "In love..." she began.

"...with you," he finished, breathing the words into her startled mouth before his lips brushed over hers with renewed longing. "I'm in love with you," he repeated, resting forehead against forehead.

She thought of what Lisa had just told her about Chase's intentions, honorable intentions he hadn't had a chance to express. Her heart was doing cartwheels, the butterflies flying gleefully free. The need for lies and excuses fell away in favor of the truth, the full and absolute truth.

"I love you, too."

He let out a heavy breath. "Oh, thank God." His face took on a cross between apprehension and excitement and, she thought she saw him blush slightly. "In that case, I have something to ask you."

"Which is?"

"What is taking the two of you so long?" Lisa's question broke into the small space of silence between them, and they both looked up as she walked toward them from the direction of the elevators. "Aunt Francine said to leave you alone awhile longer, but I figured maybe you needed my help." She came to a stop directly beside her father. "Did you ask her yet?"

"I'm asking her now."

The girl rolled her eyes in true teenage fashion. "Finally! What's taking you so long?" she asked again, then. "No, don't answer that. Just tell me, what did she say?"

Chase looked at Samantha, and she didn't care about the tears filling her eyes as she smiled back at him. She cared deeply for Bob, and always would, but Chase and Lisa were her heart. For that reason, she wanted only at this moment to be where she was, wrapped in the comfort of Chase's arms with Lisa by her side.

Once more she could only nod.

"She said yes!" Chase smiled.

Epilogue

Though honorable intentions endure
loving intentions prevail.
For aren't they, after all, one and the same?

The hum and laughter of people having a good time floated out to the foyer where Samantha stood alone, just beyond the main ballroom of her father's country club.

Once a place she sought to avoid at all costs, today for her, the atmosphere had been transformed to one of magical enchantment and beauty.

This day when, in one precious moment, she became both a wife and a mother.

A smile enfolded in pride, maternal pride, spread warmth straight to her heart as she thought of Lisa, her new daughter, the primary architect of the magical transformation of this place.

Her smile grew into a soft chuckle as she recalled the first time the soon to be newest Canfield family, she and Chase and Lisa, met with her parents to begin planning her wedding to Chase. Lisa's unending questions about preferences and style—big ceremony or small, bold colors or pale, many attendants or a few, band or deejay—were embraced by her mother, but seemed to throw Edwin Wells for a loop.

While he made no secret he viewed his daughter's upcoming wedding as the perfect opportunity to boost his social and professional standing among his peers, said daughter, with Lisa's help, made sure the arrangements would remain focused on family and friends. Between the two of them, at least Samantha believed, Edwin just may have met his match. In fact, Lisa's preferences so reflected her own, Samantha gave her future daughter free rein—with Kathryn Wells' guidance and help—over a good share of the arrangements.

Her smile broadened in direct proportion to the love growing in her heart. The ceremony had been everything she imagined, and she was sure the reception would be equally perfect.

A reception they'd enter as husband and wife, as soon as Chase joined her. After he finished, what he jokingly called *freshening up* in the bathroom, they'd be officially introduced to their guests as Chase and Samantha Canfield, now one.

"I can't get this damned tie on right."

Smile intact, she glanced over one shoulder at her tuxedo-clad husband, formal shirt opened at the neck, and ribbon tie dangling from beneath either side of his collar.

"All I wanted to do was loosen the damned thing." Lips taut and straight, he brought his hands to his throat and picked up the uncooperative strands. "Now I can't get the damned pieces back together."

She rotated her body to face him. "Can I help?"

His fingers ceased their struggling as a slow, relaxed smile took over the grim line of his mouth, and the softness of love entered his eyes. "If you would."

Standing on tiptoe, she reached up to fasten his top button first. "Hold still!" she admonished on a whisper. Though she tried to wiggle free, his arms kept circling her waist, palms coming to rest on the swell of her hips to draw her into him. "I can't concentrate on getting you dressed if you keep that up."

"My problem is you're trying to dress me." He captured her wrists, placed her arms around his neck, then once more placed his hands around her waist to pull her against him. "I want you to undress me. Please. I can promise you a good time." He spoke the words in a husky whisper, his lips warm and inviting against her ear.

She laughed as a blush crept up her cheeks. The simple wedding dress she'd chosen had a slim, crepe skirt with no petticoat encumbrance to cushion the sudden intimate contact with her husband. She could feel, with no boundaries, no restrictions, the promise he spoke of.

"*Déjà vu* all over again?" he joked. "From the last time you helped me into a tux?"

She shyly met his eyes, much as she had that night. But this time, she didn't look away. Her furtive glance, from beneath satin lashes, combined the show of innocence with a potent come-hither promise of their own.

"Not quite," she responded, rubbing herself, just so, against him before pulling back. "As I recall, our evening back then ended with you giving me a sweet good-night peck on the cheek." She pulled the strands into a perfect bow, then ran her finger along his neck to smooth his collar. "Am I to assume your intentions for the end of *this* evening run along the same lines?"

He clasped possessive hands together at the small of her back. "Not a chance," he murmured. "Because, as I recall, that was one of the longest nights of my life."

"So you're saying the innocent kiss was just for show?"

"Yeah. To show my ability for restraint." Flexing his hands, he pulled her even closer "That's all gone now. In fact, if you're not careful, you'll end up missing the first few moments of your own wedding reception."

"You plan to take me up to our room?"

"If we get that far. How about we stop the elevator between floors?"

"Do I need to remind you that my father is in the next room with your daughter? Along with my mother, your Aunt Francine, Bob and Jan..." She stopped when he put a fingertip to her lips.

"I get the idea," he replied, following the fingertip with his mouth.

When he released her lips, she glanced down just below his waist. "That will have to wait."

Longing similar to his was evident in her tone, and he smiled. "Whatever you say, Miss Wells...Mrs. Canfield."

She poured all the love she held for him into her gaze. "Do you feel different this night than you did that?"

"Not really."

She pulled back in mock surprise. "You're saying you wanted to make love to me that night too?"

Reaching up, he covered her hands, and brought them to rest between them. His loving expression matched hers, glistening eyes and all. "Wished with all my heart, Samantha. All my heart."

"Well, Mr. Canfield. From now on you'll get your wish."

His kiss was deep and sure, honest and true, and she wrapped her arms around his neck to keep from falling.

A word about the author...

Margo has earned writing awards for her short fiction and been published in national women's magazines. Her full length romance fiction has achieved finalist status in contests sponsored by chapters of Romance Writers of America.

Work as a magazine editor, newspaper publisher, television producer and script writer helped pay the bills while she and her husband raised four children along with an assortment of dogs, cats and fish.

With the children and grandchildren near, Margo and her husband now live with two formerly stray cats and a half grown German shepherd rescue, her husband's latest contribution to the household.

Visit Margo at www.margohoornstra.com